FINAL STAND

Book Two in The Final Life Series

By Rose Garcia

FINAL STAND
Book Two in The Final Life Series

Published by Rose Garcia Books

Cover Design by Steven Novak: Novak Illustration
Cover Photo by Samuel Whitaker: The Whitaker House
Cover Model: Olivia Moriarty
Interior formatting and design by Amy Eye: The Eyes for Editing

ISBN-13: 978-1497353107
ISBN-10: 1497353106

Other books by Rose Garcia

THE FINAL LIFE SERIES

Final Life, Book One
Final Stand, Book Two
Final Death, Book Three
First Life, Book Four

ACKNOWLEDGMENTS

To my amazing husband and kids—who also happen to be my biggest fans—thank you for everything! For believing in me, encouraging me, and loving me! I love you all immensely!

To my family—the Garcia side, the Moriarty side, the cousins, the in-laws, and the out-laws—thank you for your encouragement as I chase my dreams full steam ahead! You guys have always believed in me!

To my critique partners: Heather Elliot—I'm so lucky to have landed you as a critique partner! I love working with you. You've taught me so much about the craft of writing and I am forever grateful. Amber Troyer—you read my MS speedy quick and sent me some awesome notes, not to mention the most hilarious texts. Can't wait to Happy Hour with you! Shannon Duffy—I love your amazing insight, and your shoe closet! lol And last, but not least, to my eagle eye brother, Arnold Garcia. Thanks for catching all the tiny errors that flew under my radar. You're the best!

To the folks in my writing community that have lifted me, educated me, and have been there for me when I needed you! The InDivas—especially Mary Ting for introducing me to the group and Jennifer Miller and Angela Corbett for inviting me to join the ranks. I'm truly honored! Rachel Harris—I love that I can text you or message you with the dumbest question and you always have a brilliant answer. To my local Houston YA/MG writing group—you guys always fill my cup when I go to the meetings! Plus, you're a lot of fun!!

To the industry professionals in my life: Damaris Cardinali—the most amazing publicist EVER. Laura Hidalgo—the cover designer for *Final Life*. Steven Novak—the cover designer for *Final Stand*. Amy Eye—book formatter extraordinaire. For my book swag designers—Lisa of Rock Wat Designs and Jolinda of Swagalicious.

To the people who have read my books and written reviews at various media outlets and review sites, THANK YOU SO MUCH! I appreciate you more than you know! To stay in touch regarding my appearances and future releases, please subscribe to my newsletter at:

www.rosegarciabooks.com/download-finallife.

You'll also be able to access some deleted scenes from *Final Life* when you sign up! And for those active on social media, you can find all my social media links at the bottom of each page of my website www.rosegarciabooks.com. I'd love to stay in touch!

For Wade
The most amazing man any girl could ask for.

And also for Olivia and Jake
The coolest kids on the planet.

Chapter One

Cold seeped into my tired and achy bones as we drove away from our Houston home for the last time. Rain drizzled against the car windows. Thick, gray clouds filled the sky. The humming of the car lulled my mind until it became lost in the memory of the last two months.

My parents were Transhumans, or energy beings known as Pures, part of a race of humans that existed before mankind. Tavion, an evil Transhuman and leader of the Tainted, had marked me for death. He had even killed me in each of my past lives, but in this life, my final life, I had defeated him. And even though I had won, I didn't feel like the winner. Instead, I felt empty. Lost. Like I wasn't me anymore. Because I wasn't. Too much had happened. Too many had died—because of me.

"You okay?" Farrell whispered.

I studied his perfectly angular features and sympathetic green eyes before shifting away and staring out the backseat window. According to Farrell, in each of my eight lives he'd fallen in love with me, and I had loved him back. But I didn't remember any of it. Even though flashes of memories of him would come to me now and again, and strong emotions for him had bubbled to the surface, they didn't belong to me. Instead, they belonged to another version of me. Someone who didn't exist anymore.

"I'm fine," I muttered. I ran my fingertips over the rough bandages that covered my hand, my dry skin catching on the fabric. The only me that existed was the one who had sliced open her hand, covered her dagger with her blood, and plunged it into Tavion's chest and killed him; the one who had shared a passionate kiss with Trent Avila—a normal guy I'd never see again. I closed my eyes for a moment and pictured his face in my mind. Tan skin, brown hair with long bangs that hung into his deep blue eyes. His grandmother had given me the bloodstone cross that hung around my neck, and without it, I wouldn't have been able to defeat Tavion. Sadly, Trent would never know because Farrell had erased his memory.

Memory erased... That was it! A sliver of hope sprang in me. I'd ask Farrell to do that to me—wipe my mind. After all, he was my protector, and if erasing my life and starting over would help me, he'd have to do it. I snuck a glance his way. He rubbed his hands on his jeans and grabbed his knees. Emotional pain etched across his face. If only he didn't remember our past lives, our lost love, things would be easier for him. But he remembered everything, they all did. I was the only one who didn't. And that's when it hit me. He needed his memory erased, too. Like the *Men in Black* movies. Flash a bright light in our eyes, insert a new memory, and live happily ever after.

If only…

With a heavy sigh, I wrapped myself in my soft blue blanket. Happily ever after didn't exist. But I did win, and Tavion was dead. Yet here we were, leaving Texas and going back to Michigan and somewhere along the way faking our deaths in order to cut off ties with everyone we had ever known. I knew Mom and Dad wanted to be cautious, but taking off like this didn't seem like something a "safe" person would do. I couldn't help but wonder if they were keeping something from me. Again.

The busy highway flanked by restaurants, bars, and car dealerships finally evolved into the open road. Cows and horses dotted the flat fields for miles and miles. Dad drove while Mom eyed the map, plotting our course home to Michigan. "We'll cross Arkansas and go into Tennessee, stopping just outside Memphis. We'll stay there for the night." She folded the map on her lap and looked over her shoulder. "You may as well get some rest, Dominique. We've got a long day of driving ahead of us."

Rest? How could I? Doubts about my future turned my stomach upside down. Mixed emotions about Farrell and Trent plagued me. And then there was Infiniti—my one true friend who'd soon think I had died in a car crash. I wrapped my arms around my waist and told myself it was better for her to think I was dead. I just hoped she'd be okay.

Even though fatigue had settled deep in me, I had crossed over into that place where your brain can't shut down no matter how hard you try. And so my thoughts stretched out like an eternity while I watched the world creep past. Cows, fields, cows, fields, over and over. The peaceful solitude of the landscape entranced me. The repetitious thud of the windshield wipers swiping back and forth created the perfect background noise for slumber. After a while, my breathing deepened. My heart rate slowed. Finally, I drifted to sleep.

"Dominique, can you hear me?"

My body slept. Yet the voice calling out to me rang so clear in my head I could've sworn I was awake. A dream, it had to be a dream.

"Dominique, I'm here," the hoarse voice said again, this time urgent and prodding.

My heavy eyelids refused to open, as if weighted down by bricks and glued shut. Even the muscles in my body ignored my commands to move, get up, and find the voice calling me.

"You know who I am," the scratchy voice said again, louder this time.

My sleeping body tensed from a zap of fear. Yes, I knew. The voice belonged to Tavion. I'd recognize it anywhere. And it came from within me.

An army of goose bumps dashed across my body. *Wake up,* I screamed to myself. *Now!*

"Waking won't help you, Marked One."

Panic rushed through me. My body jerked. My eyes flew open. Farrell sat close, his hands on my arm. "Hey, you alright?"

Mom studied me from over her shoulder. Dad peered at me through the rear-view mirror. I rubbed my eyes. "Yeah, I'm fine. I was just… having the weirdest dream."

"You sure, Dominique?" Dad's eyes shifted from the road back to me. His brow creased with deep worry lines. He had spent his whole life worrying about me, hiding me from the Tainted, and protecting me from the truth that an evil Transhuman wanted me dead—the same evil Transhuman I had killed and who had just now invaded my dreams.

I cleared my throat. "I'm fine, Dad. Seriously. But I could use a bathroom break."

Mom kept a suspicious eye on me, not really believing my excuse. "We should be coming up on a rest stop in a few minutes. Can you wait?"

It was well past noon, and I had already held my bladder for a few hours. A few more minutes couldn't hurt. "Yeah, that's fine." I peeled off my blanket and combed my hair back with my stiff and achy hands when my stomach growled. "Guess I need some food, too."

Farrell kept his eyes on the road. I followed his line of sight out the window, at the fields we were passing. Was he worried about something? Did he know about my dream? I swallowed hard. Maybe I was still in danger and they weren't telling me.

"There we go," Mom said.

A gas station up ahead sprang into view. It sparkled white and blue with a flashing sign that promised clean bathrooms and juicy burgers. Peering at the neon signs, I realized the cloud and rain from the morning had disappeared. I placed my fingertips on the window. Still cold even though the sun shone bright. Dad parked in front of a grassy area with picnic tables. He thrummed his fingers against the steering wheel before turning off the ignition, then turned and looked at Farrell. "Stay close to Dominique."

My body tensed. "What? Why does—"

"Dominique," Mom placed her hand on Dad's knee, as if to silence him. "Some habits are just hard to break."

Her words were meant to make me feel better, but fell far short. A nervous laugh escaped my lips. "If I were in danger, you guys would tell me, right? I mean, Tavion is dead. We did win." Another laugh rushed out of me. "Right?"

Farrell reached out to me. "Yes. Tavion is dead."

Dead yet violating my mind, I thought to myself, not wanting to tell them I had just heard his voice. It would only worry them more than they already were. They didn't need that. Plus, I didn't want them hovering over me.

Dad rubbed his stubbled face and sighed. "I'm sorry Dominique. Your mom is right. Old habits." He opened his car door. "Come on, stretching our legs and getting a bite will do us good."

The cool crisp air filled my lungs, replacing the stuffy air from the car. Even the grassy, earthy scents from the nearby fields smelled good. As we got closer to the entrance of the gas station, we passed a silver car parked at the pump. A golden retriever stretched his head out the back window, nose sniffing the air, tongue hanging out. When he spotted us, his eyes locked on me. His ears lay back. He bared his teeth and growled. I froze, afraid he'd jump out the window and attack.

"Rexie, down!" a woman called out from inside the car.

Farrell stepped in between me and the dog and wrapped his arm around my waist. He pointed at the dog. "It's okay, boy." A spark flickered from his fingertip, right at the dog. The retriever let out a whine and sat back.

The woman praised the dog for calming down. And me? Well, I started to panic. Farrell swiftly ushered me inside.

"What happened?" Mom asked, peering over my shoulder at the car we had just passed.

"That dog freaked when he saw me." I didn't realize how fast my heart was beating until Farrell squeezed my hand. A warm peaceful feeling rushed over me like it always did when he touched me—followed by a deep yearning for him.

"Some canines are like that," Farrell explained. "He probably sensed your recent conflict with Tavion." Another squeeze calmed me even more. "I wouldn't worry about it, Dominique."

My breathing steadied. My heart rate slowed. Butterflies fluttered in my stomach. Farrell held onto my fingertips for a second before letting my hand fall. I almost reached back out for him, but didn't. "Thanks, Farrell."

Mom's worried face relaxed. "Come on, let's go to the restroom." She walked to the back of the gas station as if everything was okay. As if I was just her daughter and she was just my mother. As if I hadn't killed an evil energy being the night before.

My thoughts filled with memories of Tavion as I went to the restroom and washed my hands. As I lathered the soap, mom joined me. I looked up at the mirror, catching our reflection. I was almost her exact replica. Long brown hair, tall and slender. Her eyes sparkled true green while mine were dark olive, sometimes gray. My gaze lingered on hers. True green eyes—the mark of a Pure.

"Why are my eyes different?" I shook the water off my hands and grabbed a paper towel. "I mean, they should be like yours and Dad's and Farrell's, right?"

She tugged out some paper towel, too. "Yes, as a descendant of Pures you should have eyes like ours, but you don't. You never have." She tossed the paper in the trash. "It's something we've never been able to... understand."

"I've never had eyes like you and Dad? Not in any of

my…" I whispered, even though I knew we were alone, "past lives?"

"No," Mom answered. She turned me to her and held my face. "You've always had beautiful olive-colored eyes."

Tavion's thin, pale, wrinkled face popped into my mind. His eyes were dark as night. I thought of Fleet, Farrell's brother, originally a Pure who had turned and joined Tavion's ranks and who had been killed during our final confrontation. What color were his eyes? I couldn't remember. "And the Tainted have black eyes?"

"Yes, they do. But sweetheart, it doesn't matter." She stroked my hair and tucked a strand behind my ear. "All that matters is this is over. We made it. And we're all okay."

Something inside me said not to believe her, but I ignored it. I needed something to hold onto. "I hope you're right."

"Of course, I am." She smiled. "Now come on, let's get some food."

We met up with Dad and Farrell at the burger counter and placed our order. While we waited, people rushed in and out of the station, and each time, Dad and Farrell went on alert. Dad caught my worried glance right away. "Sorry, Dominique. Remember—old habits."

Yeah, right, I thought. My gaze wandered over to the girl getting our food together. She looked to be around seventeen, like me. She wore tons of make-up and smacked her gum like she didn't have a care in the world. How lucky to have a simple life.

"Here's your order," she said. Farrell took the bags and thanked her, causing a sigh to escape her lips while her cheeks turned red. Farrell smiled and when he did a sharp pang of jealousy jabbed inside me. I turned away from him, embarrassed and confused about my feelings. I mean, could I really blame her for having that reaction around Farrell? He was drop dead gorgeous. And that's when I realized I had feelings for him—true emotions of my own and not connected to anything that might've been between us. So why was I resisting him?

He positioned himself in front of me and tilted his head. "You feeling okay?"

I grabbed one of the bags, suddenly feeling exposed and vulnerable. "Yep," I huffed, with a hint of irritation in my voice.

Before he could say anything else, I led the way out of the station and to the picnic tables. The cars that had stopped for gas or food had traveled on. It was just us. Alone. Surrounded by a cool breeze and bright sun. And yet, the weight of everything we had been through back in Houston kept me cold and dark inside. I wondered if they felt it, too.

We laid out our things and ate in silence. I thought of their plan to fake our deaths. How would we pull something like that off? The cheeseburger I nibbled at tasted worse with each bite. The stale bun and bland meat turned my stomach. I washed it down with a gulp of flat lemonade and pushed my food aside. "So, how exactly are we going to fake our deaths?"

Dad wiped his mouth. "The plan is for Colleen to meet up with us tomorrow morning. We'll ignite our car in such a way that it'll look like a mechanical explosion. The fire will be so intense there will be no human remains."

Shivers cascaded up and down my body. Farrell sat closer, his leg touching mine. I almost inched away, but decided I wanted him near, and not just for his calming effect. "And everyone will think it's us?" My gaze met Mom's and Dad's before resting on Farrell. "Is that really going to work?"

Silence hung in the air. I pictured Infiniti and Trent learning about the crash. I knew Infiniti would be devastated. Trent, too. I threw my half-eaten food in the nearby trashcan. "Have we tried this in any other life?"

Farrell angled his body to me. "No, but I'm pretty confident it'll work. If everything goes as planned."

Any ounce of hope I had quickly vanished. "Whoa, wait a second. *If* everything goes as planned? That doesn't sound very reassuring."

Dad cleared off the rest of the table. "Well, right now we have no idea where Colleen is."

Colleen—a Pure who had disguised herself as my teacher. She had a wise air about her, an authority that surpassed that of my mom and dad. Even Farrell. "So what's up with her? What's her story? And where is she?"

"She's the oldest of the Pure and has a lot of power," Dad said. "And unfortunately we haven't been able to make contact with her all day." He rubbed his temples. "If she's missing, or something has happened to her, it can only mean something bad."

I shivered. "Something worse than Tavion?"

"For lifetimes we've never survived past your confrontation with Tavion," Farrell explained. "So whatever happens from here on out is completely new." He touched my fingers. "But nothing can be worse than what we've already been through, okay?"

"We're just all flying blind," Mom said. "And we're not used to it."

"Join the club," I muttered.

Nobody spoke as we drove the rest of the day and into the night. We were all on equal footing now, and no one knew what our future would hold. But I had to believe Farrell when he said that whatever might happen next couldn't be bad. After all, what could be worse than being hunted and killed for lifetimes?

Chapter Two

I nuzzled my head into that perfect space between Farrell's chin and collarbone and inhaled the sweet and spicy smell of him. I had always loved falling asleep in his arms. Not just because his scent was intoxicating, but because here, so close to him, I always felt safe. Like nothing bad could ever happen to me.

Wait! Those weren't my memories! How could I have let myself fall asleep on him? I jerked away from Farrell so fast my head knocked his chin and his teeth clanked. "Ouch," he said with a laugh.

"Farrell, I'm, uh, sorry." I rubbed my head while I caught my bearings. "I didn't realize I had fallen asleep on you." The sky had turned dark and we had parked outside a two story yellow motel. Mom and Dad stood inside the double glass doors, no doubt getting us a room.

"No, I'm the one who's sorry. I should've woken you up sooner. But you were sleeping hard and I figured you needed the rest."

Crusty drool had dried at the corner of my mouth. I turned to the side and wiped it away. "Please don't tell me I was snoring."

He laughed. "Well, maybe a little."

I had never really seen him laugh, and instantly it warmed me. Like he could be a regular guy and I could be a regular girl. And maybe, just maybe, I could let him into my heart.

Mom and Dad hurried back to the car and jumped in. A blast of cool air rushed in after them. I scooted away from Farrell before they could notice how close we were. When I did, a smile flashed across Farrell's face.

"Our room is in the back," Dad said. "And I don't know about you guys, but I'm exhausted."

When we drove around to the back of the motel, my eyes drifted over the mostly vacant parking lot. Flanked by fields on either side, only two eighteen-wheelers were parked nearby.

Mom unbuckled her seatbelt. "It's not the best, but it'll do."

Dad handed her a bronze key attached to a big plastic orange circle imprinted with 18. "You and Dominique go on ahead to the room. Farrell and I will get the bags."

Our beige on beige room had two beds, a couch, a small TV, and a small wood table with one chair. The chill in the room felt almost as cold as the outside air. Mom set her things on the bed closest to the door and made her way to the thermostat. "Your father and I will sleep here. You can take the bed by the bathroom. Farrell can camp on the couch."

I flopped on my designated bed. The springs creaked under my weight and the bedspread crackled like crusty old vinyl. I was eyeing the couch, thinking it looked more comfortable than the bed, when Dad and Farrell came in.

Too tired even to complain about our accommodations, the four of us got ready for bed as the smell of burnt gas from the heater filtered into the air. After a little while, the odor evaporated. Only the whistling winds outside, the musty scent of the room, and our tired and worn out bodies remained.

Nestling myself under the rough sheets, I imagined they offered me some sort of protection from my fears. The coarse material could be like my own little shield. I tugged the fabric all the way over my head, satisfied that I could safely cave to my exhaustion.

"You are not alone, Marked One."

I didn't have waking dreams very often, but here I was, caught in another nightmare of Tavion's voice calling out to me. Just like in the car, I tried to wake, but couldn't. And so I decided to speak to him.

"Go away!"

My words echoed in my mind before silence took over. For a second I thought he was gone, but then he responded.

"I can't. I'm here with you. Forever."

My body snapped awake and I flung the covers off the bed with a scream. Farrell dashed over, grabbed me, and held me tight. "What?" he asked, rubbing my back. "What is it?"

Back in Houston, Tavion had invaded my mind through waking visions. Each time he visited me, the birthmark at the nape of neck exploded in pain. The sensation transported me to a red desert—the place where I had been killed in each of my past lives. But this was different—there was no pain, no red desert, just the voice within me.

"Dominique, please don't shut me out," Farrell pleaded.

I shimmied around him and flicked on the lamp. I was about to tell him about hearing Tavion's voice when I noticed my parents were gone. A look of sheer terror must've darted across my face. "It's okay," he said. "They're outside, using the pay phone."

As planned, none of us had used our cell phones since leaving Houston. Even when I wanted to take a sneak peek and see if Trent or Infiniti had tried to contact me, I didn't. What was the point? We were all about to be branded as dead anyway. So why did my parents need to use the phone? Farrell turned the lamp off. Bits of light from the outside filtered into the room. "I'll show you."

We crept to the window and pulled back the thick drapes. Mom and Dad stood together at the far end of the parking lot at a pay phone underneath a flickering light post. Pale yellow light illuminated them. Dancing moths scattered overhead. "Who are they calling?" I asked in a whisper, the dark room forcing me to a hush.

"I think they're trying to find Colleen. Make sure she's on track to meet us later."

Dad held the phone while Mom circled around him. "Pacing is not a good sign," I muttered.

"No, it's not," Farrell agreed.

After another minute or so, Dad hung up. Mom stood in front of him. He cupped her face in his hands, stared into her eyes for a moment, and kissed her for a long time. I wanted to turn away, but couldn't. I had never seen them kiss like that. When they separated, they stared at each other for a moment before Mom rested her head on his chest and Dad wrapped her in his arms.

I dropped the curtain and stepped away from the

window, my heart beating out of control. I twisted a long strand of hair around my index finger. My vision had adjusted enough to the darkness that I could see a questioning and confused look on Farrell's face—the same look I'm sure must've been on mine after seeing my parents like that. I dropped my hand. "That was not a normal kiss." My voice raised mid-sentence and continued to get higher. "There is something up. I know it!"

Farrell remained cool and calm on the outside, but the look in his eyes told me his thoughts were a million miles away. "If there's something we need to know, they'll tell us," he offered.

I could tell by his tone he wasn't sure of his own words. I snapped and threw my hands up in frustration. "Seriously? You think they'll tell us?" As my protector, he was used to following orders. Me? I'd had enough. I flicked the light on. "The three of you have kept me in the dark for months, but not anymore." I crossed my arms. "Got it?"

Farrell came close, his body just inches away from mine. He rested his hands on my shoulders. A memory of him standing before me like this filled my mind. A flood of emotions surged inside me. Suddenly I wanted him closer, my body screaming for his.

"You're right, Dominique."

He moved his fingers in a circular motion, my body melting under his touch. I moved in, closing the gap between us, suddenly knowing I belonged with him. His strong hands travelled up my neck and cupped my face. His eyes searched mine. "What are you thinking?"

It took me a few seconds to find my voice. "I'm thinking that I'm tired of fighting my feelings for you."

"Then don't," he said, the heat coming from his stare sent my head in the clouds.

I moved in even closer and pressed my body up against his.

He looked down on me and studied my lips. "Dominique, I—"

The door swung open. Cool air from outside swept through the room. Farrell backed away from me while the drop in temperature sent shivers down my arms. Or did I shiver from the excitement from being so close to Farrell? I couldn't tell.

I wrapped my arms around my body and focused on my parents. "So who were you talking to?" Mom paused for a second and eyed Dad. "And no more secrets," I added. "Okay?"

Dad rubbed his hands together and blew into them. "The days of secrets are long gone." He double-checked the lock on the door. "I promise."

"We didn't want to wake you, Dominique," Mom explained. "That's all. Your father and I were going to tell you about the call in the morning. But seeing as we're all up," she sat on the couch, "we may as well do it now."

Everyone took a seat. Dad next to mom, Farrell by the table, and me on the edge of the bed. Mom pinched the bridge of her nose and a sick feeling overcame because I knew their phone call outside could only mean something bad. "We still can't locate Colleen," Mom said.

Farrell ran his fingers through his messy blonde hair, something he always did when he was worried. "Did you try all the usual channels?" he asked.

"Yes," Dad said.

My mind worked overtime processing Mom's news. At first, confusion filled me, but my puzzlement quickly made way for a blast of fear. "We need her for tomorrow, for our big car accident explosion, right?"

"Ideally, yes," Mom said. She placed her hand on Dad's bouncing knee. "If she doesn't show, we'll just have to make do on our own."

On our own… Those three words repeated in my head while Mom and Dad explained how we'd pull off the explosion. Mom, Dad and Colleen had already selected a remote town with a small gas station. They'd ignite the fuel pump while the car filled with gas. The explosion would be massive. No one would know we weren't even in the car. And if Colleen did her part, we'd drive away with her in a second vehicle without being spotted. Without her, the only thing we had to worry about was securing a second car.

"It shouldn't be that hard," Dad assured.

Doubt over our plan invaded me like a virus and stayed with me as I tried to sleep. It even saturated my thoughts while I got ready in the morning. Suddenly I felt isolated, separated from the rest of the world, helpless even. And then I thought of Tavion. My parents had promised me no more secrets, yet I still hadn't told them about hearing Tavion's voice. They needed to know, but not now. First, we had to get back to Michigan.

We continued with our drive early in the morning. "Closer to home," I whispered. My gaze fixed on the gray sky. The sun struggled to peak through the thick blanket of clouds, but couldn't quite make it. I wondered if it ever would. After a few minutes, my focus turned to Mom. She drove while Dad's eyes stayed on the near-empty road. What was he looking for? Without even realizing it, I had shifted closer to Farrell, and he closer to me.

"There," Dad said.

I stretched my neck. A gravel farm road twisted to the right. Mom turned down the empty two-lane road. Farmland stretched out for miles. I watched the rolling fields pass by when Farrell's body stiffened. His jaw clenched.

"Stop!" he yelled.

Fear gripped my chest. A bright light exploded from the sky. Smokey wisps appeared on the horizon. The vapor cleared quickly, revealing three black cloaked figures. Dad hollered a warning. Mom slammed on the brakes. Farrell twisted toward me, smashing one arm across my chest like a shield and tucking my head down with the other. The car spun out of control until it struck the embankment at the side of the road, hurtled up in the air, and flipped. Trapped by our seatbelts, we rolled over and over and over. The crunching of metal and breaking of glass exploded in my ears. After only a few seconds, but what seemed like an eternity, the car rocked to an abrupt stop.

My vision blurred. My body shook. A high-pitched hum filled my ears. My hair hung down, my arms and legs dangled. Shards of glass glittered like little diamonds on the roof of the car. We were upside down, and I couldn't move.

"Farrell!" Dad called out. "Get her out of here!"

The cross around my neck swung back and forth before my eyes. Thick liquid dripped from my hair. I reached out and caught a splatter on my fingers. I brought my hand to my face. Dark red blood—my blood. But there was no pain. A creaking door shattered the silence. It was Mom, falling out of the car. She scrambled to her feet and rushed over to Dad. She flung his door open.

"Stone!" She pressed her fist to her mouth. "Your legs."

"Never mind me," he grunted. "They're coming."

My gaze flicked about nervously, trying to see through the cracked windshield, and there they were. The three figures that caused our crash. They closed in on us, moving effortlessly, as if gliding our way in slow motion. Mom made eye contact with me for a split second. Fear and alarm etched on her face. She erased it quick and offered me a nod of encouragement before turning to face them.

I started to call out to her, when another crashing noise filled my ears right beside me. I strained to see Farrell had blasted his door away. He dropped to the roof while dad and I hung upside down by our seatbelts.

"Get... her out…" Dad moaned.

Farrell maneuvered his body around, stretching out right under me. Cuts laced across his face and neck. "I'm going to unbuckle you, okay?"

"Okay," I whispered, while a hard knot formed in my gut.

He reached over me just as blasts of light burst from the road. "Mom," I managed to get out as I dropped into Farrell's arms.

"I know," he said.

He carried me out of the car and placed me on the grass. Then he went back for Dad. Ringing continued to fill my ears. Blood seeped out of a cut on my head and trickled down my face. Farrell returned with Dad and laid him next to me. Bones protruded through ripped and mangled flesh at his knees. I gasped, my stomach wrenching so hard I almost vomited.

Dad jerked his chin at Farrell. "Go to Caris! Now!"

Tears flooded my eyes as Farrell squeezed my hand before dashing for Mom. "It's going to be okay," Dad groaned through gritted teeth. But I knew there was no way. "Stay. Close," he panted. "I'm going to shield us." He moaned for a second until his silver light, his energy source, radiated from his body. Usually bright and bold, this time it barely filled the air.

Sweat beads formed along his face while his body shook. I scooted close to him, praying he had enough strength to protect us. A metallic taste filled my mouth as drops of my own blood slipped between my lips. I wiped away the trail of blood tracking across my face and spit. For a second, I reached for my injury, but stopped short. I didn't want to know how bad off I was. Instead, I wrapped my fingers around Dad's, hoping to give him strength.

"What's happening with your mother?" Dad managed to ask. "I can't see." Another pang of fear stabbed at me as I realized his eyes were clouding over. I had no idea what that meant, but I was pretty sure it had to do with his energy source fading out of him.

Trying not to sound completely horrified, I said, "I'll look."

A twinge of pain zapped my forehead as I positioned myself for a better view. Mom and Farrell stood before the three cloaked Tainted. Like wax figures caught in a face-off, nobody moved. I strained my ears, trying to make out their conversation, but couldn't hear anything. Before I could tell

Dad what was happening, Mom hurled a blast of energy at the figures. A barrage of smoky explosions filled the air.

"Dominique," Dad urged. "Tell me!"

"Mom just attacked them," I said. "And there's a lot of smoke."

I didn't know how long Mom and Farrell could fend off the three attackers, when suddenly the figures disappeared. I caught my breath and looked around frantically because I knew they were coming for me.

"Dad," I warned, "They're—"

They reappeared—right at my feet and just on the other side of the energized shield my dad had created.

I gasped. "Here."

With a grunt, Dad gripped my hand. He tried to pull me closer, but his hold was weak and shaky.

The two bulky figures towered over me while the petite one knelt down. She drew back her black hood. Short-cropped brown hair fell around her pale face. I was shocked to see she couldn't have been much older than twelve. She leaned in and stared at me, and I caught my breath. Her eyes… they were a dark green, just like mine. My mind reeled.

Who is she?

She opened her hand and ran her fingers across my dad's thin energy shield, pulling it back like a spider web. "Come out, come out, wherever you are," she said with a smile. I flinched, pressing my body back against the grass. Farrell and Mom called out for me in the distance, and I thought I saw them racing to me, but the girl leaned in and blocked them from view. She shot a purple colored mist from her palms, forming her own energy bubble around herself, her two Tainted companions, Dad, and me.

"No!" Farrell slammed his fists against the dome. His hands sizzled as he clawed at her thick barrier.

"Come," she said, reaching her slender hand out to me. "You belong with us."

Dad grasped at my arm. "Fight," he whispered, his eyes completely clouded over now, his grip so weak he could barely hold on to me.

Everything inside me said not to listen to the girl, to fight like my dad had urged, when Tavion's imposing voice rasped in my ears. *"Go with her."*

Tavion's command worked its way through me like a slow-moving whisper that magnified until it almost tore through my very soul. I bit down on my lip, fighting to resist him, when I felt my will starting to bend.

Why am I listening to Tavion? He's the enemy. He's killed me eight times. I hate him.

Right?

"Come, Marked One," the girl urged. "Don't be afraid."

I knew I shouldn't go with her, I knew I shouldn't leave my dad, but a little piece of me itched to be with her. My body trembled, my arms stretched out on their own. My fingertips almost met hers when a shudder shook the earth.

"Stop!" Farrell called out. A burst of golden light flooded my sight. Heat sprayed across my face. My skin burned as if a fire ball had rolled over me. And everything faded to black.

Chapter Three

When my eyes fluttered open, I found myself lying on a blue couch. The familiar smell of vanilla hung in the air. Antique furnishing surrounded me. Jan's house—I was at my neighbor Jan's house back in Houston. But she was dead. So if I was here, I had to be dead, too! The crash! It killed me! My hands shot up to my head, searching for my injury, yet didn't find one. I threaded my fingers through my hair—still nothing. My hand inched its way to my chest. The steady thrumming of my heart against my palm told me I was alive, but what was I doing here? And where were Mom, Dad, and Farrell?

"They aren't here," Jan's voice called out from behind me.

I sat up with a start to find Jan in the kitchen, pouring steaming water into two cups. She set them on the kitchen table. Bewildered, I searched the room for Abigail, the young Pure who had traded her life for mine and was last seen with Jan. But I didn't see her. "I thought you could use some tea, dear." Jan slid into the pantry and came out with tea bags and a box of crackers. "Come, join me. And don't worry about him."

Him? I scanned the sitting room. There in an oversized corner chair sat Tavion. His dark eyes were glued on me. His pale, thin face set in a grimace.

I bolted over to Jan and crouched down behind the kitchen counter.

She chuckled. "Dear, you are in the space between and for some reason he's following you around." She patted my shoulder. "I assure you he's harmless and you're safe."

"Because he's dead, right?" I asked with a shaky voice.

She held out her thick hand and helped me to my feet. "That's right. He's dead."

My heartbeat slowed. I peered at Tavion. Like a realistic wax figure, he sat perfectly still. "I'm in the space between? Like last time back in the red desert? I'm dying, but not all the way dead?" I hesitated before taking a seat at the kitchen table. As usual, interesting objects hung from the glass chandelier—pieces of metal, glass beads, silverware. I shifted in my seat a little, searching for the white feather Farrell had left in my memory. It had transported me to my safe place—Elk Rapids beach. It was a symbol of hope. I had seen it here the last time I had tea with Jan.

Jan dunked her tea bag. I reached for one and did the same, overcome with sadness that I didn't see the feather. Somehow, I believed it could make everything better. "Your accident was quite serious," she explained.

My head throbbed where my injury should've been. I almost reached out for it again. "Yes, it was," I answered automatically, not completely understanding what was going on.

"Dear, let me explain what's happening before you have to go."

"I'll have to go?" I asked, terrified at the thought of returning to the crash and the Tainted girl.

"Eventually," Jan replied.

Tavion remained motionless in his chair. Jan watched me patiently in her replica kitchen. And somewhere in the real world I was dying. I placed my tea bag on the edge of the saucer under my cup. "Okay. Explain."

Jan sipped her tea. "The Tainted attacked your car. With great effort, Farrell managed to ward them off. He transported you and your mother to the cabin at the Boardman River. He even managed to explode the car so that everyone would think you all had died. Miraculously, with your grave injuries, you survived the transport. Your mother, too. You've been in a coma, on the brink of passing over, your body slowly recovering."

Relief washed over me. So I wouldn't have to go to the scene after all. I wrapped my hands around the warm cup when another thought sent a new jab of panic through me. "You said Farrell transported me and my mother. What about my dad? Is he okay?"

The walls of the kitchen started to distort. The chandelier swayed. Jan eyed the space around us. "Seems you're starting to wake."

Tavion now sat next to me, rigid and stiff. The sitting room had vanished. I needed answers before Jan disappeared, too. "Why is Tavion following me? And how did the Tainted even find us? If we killed their leader, shouldn't the Tainted leave us alone?"

Jan's kitchen started to fade. "That's why I brought you here. The Tainted will never give up. As for finding you, they knew where you'd be." She leaned forward. "Understand?"

"They knew?" I whispered. The kitchen blurred out fast. Even Jan herself barely remained, her body turning into a cloud of smoke. I reached out for her, my fingertips whisking the dense vapor. "Stop! Jan! What do you mean, they knew? And what about my dad?"

Thick, warm fog descended on me. I waved the air from my face, trying to catch a glimpse of Jan, when Farrell appeared. "Hey," he said, brushing a strand of hair from my eyes.

I strained to sit up, suddenly realizing that I was lying down. Farrell handed me a glass of water, but my weakened hands couldn't grip it.

"I've got it," he said. He held the glass to my lips. Small sips slid down my sore throat as I surveyed my surroundings. The wood beams of the room reminded me of a log cabin. I remembered Jan's words that Farrell had taken Mom and me from the wreck and brought us to the cabin on the Boardman River, the cabin of my mom and dad's friends who were also Pures.

My legs tingled, like they were starting to fall asleep. I wanted to get up, stretch them out, and check on Mom and Dad. "Help me up."

Instead of giving me a hand, Farrell gently eased me back down. "You should stay in bed. You've been out for a while and you're really weak."

Alarm filled me. "A while? How long?" My voice sounded funny, like I hadn't used it in days. Farrell ran his fingers through his hair. I sat up and said again, "How long?"

Farrell got up and paced the room, rubbing the back of his neck. "One month."

My mouth hung open. My body shook. I searched the room to make sure I was really here. "Where's Mom?"

"She's in the room right next to this one."

I glanced at the window. Sheer curtains revealed darkness outside. "It's three in the morning," he continued.

My mind quickly processed my reality. One month. I had survived a car crash caused by the Tainted. I had missed my eighteenth birthday while hovering in a coma. I had even visited Jan in her kitchen. She had said the Tainted knew where we'd be. She explained that Farrell had saved me and Mom. Yet she never mentioned Dad. I yanked the covers off my body, swung my legs over, and placed my feet on the cold wood floor. I tried to stand, but dizziness overtook me.

Farrell swooped in before my knees buckled. "Whoa. Slow down."

He guided me back to the bed. "I need to see my dad," I whispered. A massive lump formed in my throat. My chest tightened. "My dad," I repeated. "I want to see him."

Farrell stood in front of me and took my face in his hands. His eyes watered over. "I'm so sorry, Dominique." He drew in a deep breath. "He didn't make it."

A high pitch ringing in my ears filled my head until it drowned out all other sounds—no breathing, no heart beating, nothing. Even my vision narrowed until a deep and dark despair wrapped tight around me.

"We did everything we could," Farrell whispered. He looked at his feet, then at the headboard of my bed, before meeting my gaze. His hands still cupped my face. A trickle of calmness from his energy and power filtered into me, but didn't stay.

I jerked my head away from his grasp and pushed him away from me. "You're lying," I said through gritted teeth. I hopped to my feet, but quickly found myself on the floor. Farrell came to my aid, but I batted his hands away. "I know he's here," I spat out. "He has to be."

Farrell sat beside me and held me tight. "I'm so sorry."

My mind flooded with visions of Dad next to me with crushed legs. I could see his clouded over eyes; could feel his weakened grasp on my arm. The horrifying truth of Farrell's words started to sink in.

"He's… dead?"

Farrell tightened his hold around me. "Yes."

I buried my face into the crook of his neck and let a sea of tears spill out of me. He rocked me gently and rubbed my back while I broke down. After I let out every last drop of sorrow, Farrell pulled away. "There's something else I need to tell you."

Even though he sat close, I didn't even see him. My thoughts had dashed to our ambush. To the Tainted girl that had tried to take me away. Farrell moved my chin, forcing me to look him in the eye. He wiped my face. "Hey, stay with me."

I snapped back to reality, my gaze connecting with his. Before he could say anything, I thought of what Jan had told me in the space between. I echoed her words. "They knew where we'd be."

Farrell remained close. A questioning look crossed his face. "Yes, how did you know?"

"Jan told me." He tilted his head, trying to understand my words. "I visited her while I slept."

He moved closer to me. "There is a traitor among us. Only your mother and I, and now you, know this. The others don't."

A howling wind sounded outside. The walls creaked. I stared into his tired and sad eyes. The cuts that had littered his face after the crash had disappeared and I knew he must've healed himself. "Others?" I asked.

He studied my face for a moment. "Richard and Sue who live here."

I grabbed his arm. "What about Colleen? Is she here?"

"No, we can't find her." He paused. "But there is someone else here."

A wave of fear flowed through me. Tingles shot up my back. "Who?"

"Fleet."

My heart raced out of control. The pumping of blood roared through my ears. Fleet was Farrell's brother, a Pure who had switched sides and joined Tavion's ranks as a Tracker. He's the one who had found me back in Houston. "No, no, no," I whispered. "He died back at the beach. How could he—"

"He says he joined Tavion in order to help us and that he's been filtering information to Colleen all this time," Farrell said. "He also says he faked his death back on the shore so Tavion would think him dead."

Anger blasted through me, propelling me to my feet. "It's not possible," I said between clenched teeth, hatred for Fleet erupting inside me like a volcano. "He's one of them—I know it." The image of Dad lying dead on the grass popped to mind. "And he's responsible for my dad's death."

Farrell shook his head. "I thought the same thing, but his story sounds pretty convincing."

He tried to usher me back to the bed. "Farrell, you

don't believe him, do you? After everything he's done to us?" I dug my fingers into his arm while I steadied my wobbly legs on the hard floor.

After a long pause, he said, "I just don't know. Neither does your mother. The only thing we can do is watch our backs."

A soft knock sounded on the door before it creaked open. I snapped my head to meet Mom's troubled gaze. Tangled hair cascaded around her pale, thin, face. Dark circles underlined her eyes. Any shred of strength inside me crumbled when I saw her. She rushed over and scooped me into her arms while fresh tears poured out of me.

Dad was dead. A traitor lingered in our midst. And the Tainted still hunted me.

Chapter Four

Sometime in the night, between crying and talking with Mom and Farrell, I had fallen into a troubled and restless sleep. When I awoke in the morning, my body ached worse than ever. Farrell couldn't have fared much better. He slept in the chair by my side, guarding me. His long legs stretched out. His arms crossed. I watched the steady rise and fall of his chest.

After a minute, my gaze left him and travelled the small, cold, room. The bed, desk, and even the nightstand were hand carved wood, like someone had chopped down some big trees and whittled away for hours. My fingers traced the top of the smooth headboard. I thought of the armoire Dad had built and stained with his own hands. It took him days to finish it. For the first time I wondered what had happened to our stuff back in Houston, especially since we were all "dead" now. The thought of not having something Dad had created with his own hands depressed me. I needed something of his to hold on to, something to remind me of him. But I had nothing. Just my pain.

A small round clock, sporting different fish at each fifteen-minute increment, chimed—seven o'clock. Eventually I'd have to get up and leave this room. May as well get it over with.

I tried to slip out of bed and not wake Farrell, but he shifted the moment my feet hit the floor. "Hey," he said.

"Hey," I said back.

He got up to help me. "You ready to face the day?"

Ready? No, not at all. But I couldn't stay locked away in this room forever. And even though Mom had explained how she had cared for me while I was out, including giving me sponge baths and washing my hair, I longed for a hot shower. "What I'm ready for is a shower." I examined my clothes. I wore white boxer shorts, a long sleeved white cotton shirt, and thick socks. "And a change of clothes."

I took my time under the hot stream, washing every inch of my stiff bones. I even inspected myself for cuts and bruises—none. They must've all gone away while I slept. Or maybe Farrell had used his healing powers. Either way, I was glad.

The water washed away most of my headache, but not the budding anxiety of meeting Richard and Sue for the first time, and standing face to face with Fleet. Mom, Farrell, and I had agreed to act as if we believed Fleet's story that he was one of us until we could find any evidence to the contrary. Except I didn't know if I could do it. To me, Fleet was guilty of murder and no one could convince me otherwise.

A knock sounded on the door just as I stepped out of the shower. I wrapped myself in a towel. "Yes?"

"It's me, Dominique," Mom said. "I've got some fresh clothes for you."

I let her in and she placed my things on the bathroom counter. "Thanks, Mom."

She studied my face and rubbed my arm. "We'll be downstairs when you're ready."

Every move I made upstairs as I got ready echoed around me. Each footstep creaked on the smooth wood-planked floor. Even the voices from down below drifted up and through the house. I made a mental note to be careful when talking to Farrell and Mom since noise travelled easily through the house.

After putting on my jeans, a black long sleeved shirt, and my favorite brown boots, I peered out the window. Trees surrounded the house. The ones that had lost their covering looked stiff and naked. The others, the pines with their thick green needles, stood tall and comfortable. I shuddered. I was like the naked ones. Out of place. Paralyzed by my circumstances. And I didn't like it.

On the ground, remnants of snowfall clumped on the brown grass. I placed my hand on the glass and allowed the cold air to travel through my skin. For a minute, I missed the mild Houston winter. But Michigan was my home. I belonged here, even if I still didn't have my life back.

After stalling as long as I could, I made my way down the wooden spiral staircase. Each step moaned louder than the first. Talk about a grand entrance.

"There she is," a male voice called out.

When I got downstairs, I found myself in a wide-open space filled with mounted antlers and fish. There was a den, a breakfast area, and a kitchen. Tall windows lined the back wall and all the wood furnishings were hand carved, just like the bedroom. The name BROCK was proudly displayed over the huge stone fireplace and heat radiated from the roaring fire within. I instantly loved the place.

I recognized Richard and Sue right away from the

picture back home and figured they were the Brocks. Tall and slender with a long, pointy nose, Richard smiled wide, as if he were greeting an old friend. Sue, petite with short red hair and freckles, covered her mouth with her hand. A look of joy and surprise covered her face. But I didn't care about them, my gaze landing squarely on Fleet.

Dressed in black jeans and a dark shirt, just like the last time I had seen him, he narrowed his eyes at me. A scowl covered his face. Hatred shot from his stare, like a laser beam, and I was the target. Apparently, he didn't like me any more than I liked him.

Perfect.

I was making my way over to them when a strange out-of-body feeling struck me. I stopped mid-stride. *"Kill him,"* Tavion's voice whispered.

The room faded. Everyone seemed to disappear. Only Fleet remained, and a searing hatred for him boiled inside me. I marched to the kitchen island, unsheathed a large knife from the butcher block, and pressed the blade against Fleet's neck before anyone could even blink.

"Dominique! Stop!" Mom called out.

"You killed my dad," I said.

Fleet's dark eyes stayed on mine. He raised his hands, as if to surrender. "No, I didn't."

"Dominique," Farrell said from somewhere beside me. "Put the knife down."

My gaze flicked over to him and then back to Fleet. "His eyes are black. That's the sign of the Tainted." I pressed the tip of the knife harder until it broke Fleet's skin. He didn't even flinch as a drop of blood tracked down his neck. "He's one of them."

Farrell came closer and stood next to Fleet. He broke my line of site. "His eyes are like that because he's been one of them for so long, that's all. It's an energy adjustment. Like a sunburn. Now that he's with us, they'll eventually turn green. Okay?" He reached his hand out to mine. "I'm going to take the knife." His fingertips made contact with my skin. He kept them there for a second before wrapping his hand all the way around my wrist. "Let's lower the knife together. Nice and slow."

"Kill him," Tavion said again.

My hand shook while the tip of the knife scraped across Fleet's skin. I wanted to slice his neck. Wanted to see his blood spray the room, but that wasn't me. It couldn't be me. "No," I whispered, dropping the weapon. It clanked on the floor.

Fleet grabbed a nearby kitchen towel and held it to his neck. "Well, nice to fucking meet you, too," Fleet said.

Farrell shoved Fleet's chest. "Watch it."

Fleet tossed the towel into the sink. "She tried to kill me, man!"

"Just like you killed my dad and almost killed us!" I shot back.

Mom jumped in the middle of the fray. "Hey! We're on the same team here. Let's not forget that."

The same team? Like hell. I made my way to the glass sliding door behind the kitchen table and stormed outside. Farrell came after me as I followed a small trail into the woods.

"Wait up," he said, catching up to me. "What happened back there? I thought we had planned to go along with Fleet's story?"

The small path led to an open pit with wood and ash inside. Around the pit were benches and logs. The cool chill in the air filled my lungs and steadied my temper, making way for confusion. Why did I keep hearing Tavion's voice, and why did I listen? Back at the car accident, Tavion told me to reach out to the Tainted girl, and I almost did—to a girl with the same colored eyes as mine. And now, Tavion had told me to kill Fleet. I needed to tell Farrell everything. Like Dad had said back at the hotel, the days of secrets were long gone.

My boots crunched on pockets of snow as I walked past the fire pit and continued along the path to the Boardman River. I stopped to watch the stream push its way through fallen logs and clumps of ice. Farrell stood beside me, patient as ever. He shoved his hands in his pockets. "Well?"

"Let's sit," I said.

We walked back to the pit and perched on one of the logs. I angled my body towards him. I started to reach for my hair, but instead patted my shirt to make sure my cross still hung around my neck. A young Pure named Abigail had died and stored her energy in it. It had brought me back to life so I could kill Tavion. If it could save me back then, maybe it could save me again. I dropped my hand. "I've been hearing Tavion's voice."

Farrell's jaw clenched. His usually peaceful and tranquil eyes stormed over. "I knew something was up. Why didn't you say anything?"

I wrapped my arms around my body as a chill settled in my bones. "The first time I heard him was in the car on our way to Tennessee. I swear I was going to say something..."

My voice trailed off because I couldn't bring myself to talk about Dad's death. Farrell scooted close. "I'm sorry," he whispered. "We don't have to talk about it."

Our eyes locked. Like magnets, our bodies leaned in. Even though I had felt a connection with Trent in Houston, my mind always took me back to Farrell. But I kept resisting him because he represented a part of me I didn't know—a part of me that didn't exist anymore.

My body trembled. Even though I wanted to be with him, I wasn't sure if I could trust my emotions. "Farrell, I don't know if the feelings I have for you are really mine. Or if they're glimpses of another version of me."

He traced the side of my face with his warm fingertips. "It's you, Dominique. Here. Now. And nobody else. I promise."

Desire coursed through my veins, and I knew, without a doubt, he was right. I wanted him. I needed him. In this life. Right now. And I was tired of fighting it. "Farrell," I whispered.

He brought his face within inches of mine and stared deep into my eyes before brushing his warm, soft lips against my mouth. Tingles erupted all over my skin. Warmth spread throughout my cold body. He wrapped his strong arms around me and brought me closer. Our kiss was slow and deep. His breath and his taste drew me in, and I wished I could melt into him.

He moved his mouth down to my neck, sprinkling kisses all over my me. "I've waited so long for this," he whispered.

I ran my fingers through his thick hair and moaned with delight. "Oh, Farrell."

Footsteps crunched in the distance, killing the moment. We separated fast, pretending like nothing had happened even though everything had happened.

I was his, and he was mine.

"There you are," Mom said. She sat on the other side of the pit and rubbed her hands together. "Farrell, can you light that?"

With a flick of his fingertips, the logs inside roared with fire. Heat filled the wintry air.

"What happened back there?" Mom asked me.

This was it, my chance to come clean. And so I told her about Tavion speaking to me. I even mentioned seeing Tavion at Jan's when I was in the space between. But I didn't tell them that I had wanted to reach out to the creepy Tainted girl at the car crash. An overwhelming surge of guilt flooded me for wanting to take her hand.

Mom took it all in with a hard and serious look on her face. "No one can know of this," she ordered. "Understood?"

Nervousness began mounting inside me. "Fine, we don't tell anybody. But Mom, how do we stop it? The Tainted still coming after me and the fact that I can hear Tavion's voice in my head must be connected, right?"

"Probably," Mom said.

Farrell got up and poked the fire with a long stick. The flames popped and grew bigger just as a gust of frosty wind swept through.

Abandoning familiarity, Mom asked Farrell, "Walker, what do you suggest?"

Suddenly he wasn't just the guy I had kissed. He was my protector, chosen to walk with me through each of my lifetimes. He had to have an answer. "We need someone with the gift to take us back and search the past. It's the only thing I can think of."

My body shuddered. "The gift?"

Farrell explained. "Like I told you, Transhumans have the ability to control the energy in and around us. Some of us, however, have specialized talents. I'm a Walker, or a protector, and along with that comes the power to heal. Your parents are Shielders. Fleet is a Tracker. Richard and Sue, and even Colleen, are Seers. They have the ability to see into the past. Since it is so specialized and rare, we simply call it the gift."

Mom stared into the fire. "They can even show it to others."

"Are you talking about time travel?" I asked.

"Not exactly," Farrell said. "We call it time jumping. We can only see. We can't interact."

Excitement and fear filled me. I was the only one who didn't remember any of our past lives. Now I could go back and see what the others knew. I could even see what Farrell and I were like together. Even better, maybe going back could help me get rid of Tavion for the last time.

At least, that's what I hoped.

Chapter Five

Before going back to the house, Mom, Farrell and I agreed on our strategy. Continue faking we believed Fleet, no matter how hard that might be, and tell no one I was hearing Tavion's voice.

Sounded simple enough.

Back in the house, Richard and Sue were busy cooking. I casually scanned the room for Fleet, but he was gone. Sue gave me a sympathetic smile. I didn't want or need pity. It made me uncomfortable. And so I deflected her attention from me. "Your house is amazing."

"Really?" Richard piped in, excited I had taken interest in the cabin. "Well, wait until you see this." He ducked into a room just off the kitchen and came out with a photo album. He handed it to me. "We built this place by hand. Your mom and dad helped. Colleen, too."

Black and white photos filled the pages, all snapshots of the house in different stages as it was being built. One was just the slab. Another, the beams, followed by a photo of the sheetrock. Finally, the completed cabin. But where were the people?

Richard must've sensed my thoughts. "We don't like to take pictures of ourselves. With our changing lifetimes and different clothes, it's not like most people would understand." He let out a laugh. His green eyes twinkled. "However, I did snap a few."

Sue swatted his backside with a dishtowel. "He can never help himself."

"Who, me?" He laughed while he flipped to the back of the album. He held it up for me. He took the last photo out of its clear sheath. Just behind were more photos. He handed them to me one by one. "That's me with your dad, mom, Aunt Sue, and three of our friends who helped us build the house."

I eyed the picture. "Aunt Sue?"

"Yeah, Aunt Sue," Richard said. "You used to call us Aunt Sue and Uncle Richard." He gazed up at Mom with a look of sadness before focusing on me again. "You really don't remember?"

I waited for a moment, hoping for a flash of recognition, but none came. I shook my head. "No, I don't."

My attention returned to the black and white group photo. Dad, Richard, and the other men wore white sleeveless undershirts, suspenders, pants, and thick belts. Mom, Sue and Colleen wore white ruffled shirts and dark skirts that went down to their ankles.

"What year is this?" I asked.

"Oh," Richard looked up, calculating the time in his head. "The late 1800's."

Dumbfounded, I continued on to the next picture. Two young teens, around thirteen or so, stood knee deep in the Boardman River. The girl wore a white dress pulled up and knotted at her side. Long white bloomers came past her knees. The boy held a long stick. His dark pants rolled up mid-calf. When I got to their faces, I froze. My breathing stilled.

"That's us," Farrell said.

It took me a few seconds to find my voice. "Us?"

Mom looked over my shoulder. "Yes."

Seeing the evidence of our past lives struck me hard. Same hair, same features—just a little younger, and lifetimes ago. "What… life is this?"

"Hmmm," Richard said, "that would be—"

"Life number five," Farrell answered.

"Number five?" I placed the pictures on the table, suddenly afraid to see more.

Mom picked up the small pile and started going through them. She stopped on a picture, brought it close, and then put it down right away. She left the room without making eye contact and went upstairs to her bedroom.

I picked up the picture. It was Mom and Dad, sitting on the porch. Hands clasped, faces smiling. Tears sprang to my eyes. Farrell took the photo and handed it back to Richard.

"Oh heck, I'm sorry," Richard said. He gathered up the pictures and took them back to the study. He changed the subject fast. "So, uh, how was the weather back in Houston?"

Farrell took my hand and led me to the couch while he engaged in small talk with Richard. As for me, I sat in silence and stared at the crackling fire. I didn't realize how hard it would be to see my past life. Suddenly our plan to visit those other times didn't seem that great.

The front door opened and jarred me back to reality. "Is it safe in here?" Fleet asked, glaring at me. He took off his jacket and hung it on a hook in the foyer.

"Come on in," Sue said.

Fleet steered clear of everyone in the house and sat alone at the far end of the kitchen. An awkward tension settled in the room. Farrell fidgeted while I tried to suppress my anger toward Fleet. Then I thought of a quote from a movie I'd seen. *Keep your friends close and your enemies closer.*

Fleet was the enemy. No doubt about it. And even though I wanted nothing to do with him, I needed him to think we were allies. I squeezed Farrell's knee, a sign for him to trust me, and walked over to Fleet. I stuck my hand out for a shake. "Hey, I'm really sorry for—"

"Almost killing me?" He looked so much like Farrell, except with dark hair instead of blonde. He stared at my hand for a minute before taking it. "It's fine, just don't do it again."

A laugh came out of me that sounded faker than I'd hoped. "I won't."

Mom came back into the room, her puffy eyes evidence of a hard cry. After our quick meal, we cleaned the kitchen and gathered around the island. I stayed close to Farrell and Mom. Richard and Sue stood together. Fleet positioned himself on the other side of the island—away from us.

"We should get our plan together," Sue said.

Mom straightened her back. "Our objective here is two-fold: find out why the Tainted are still after Dominique and find out who ambushed our car and killed Stone." Her voice caught when she said Dad's name, and nobody spoke. She drew in a deep breath and raised her chin. "I think we should visit the past in hopes of finding clues. I don't see any other course of action."

Her words lingered in the room, each of us no doubt thinking about the implications of seeing our old selves. Anxiety crept through me. Did I really want to see the me who'd been murdered several times over? The me who loved Farrell? Would I even like the old me?

"Yeah, that's a good idea," Richard said. "But Sue and I had a thought." He placed his attention on me, his eyes wide. "I've been thinking about everything that happened to you in Houston. Especially with that boy, Trent."

I took a breath so fast that a trickle of my own saliva caught in my windpipe. I started hacking uncontrollably.

Fleet looked from Farrell back to me. He raised his eyebrow. If he didn't know how I felt about Trent, he knew now. Sue handed me a glass of water. After a few small sips, my coughing stopped.

"You okay?" Mom asked.

I cleared my throat. "Yes, I'm fine." I gave the glass back to Sue. "What do you mean?"

"Well," Sue said. "Let's look at the big picture of everything that's happened over these lifetimes. Your parents, Farrell, Fleet, Richard, Colleen, and I are linked to each of your lives. In each prior life, you die in the red desert at the hands of Tavion."

Richard rubbed his hands together, excitement growing in his eyes. "Enter the new soul, this Trent kid who's on life number one, and suddenly you've survived past a point you've never reached before. Heck, you even killed Tavion, the leader of the Tainted!"

Farrell crossed his arms and considered the logic. "You're right, Richard. Adding him to the equation changed things. It's something I've thought long and hard about."

I bit the inside of my lip, hoping they wouldn't say what I knew was coming.

"We need to talk to him," Richard said.

"No!" I shot out. I pictured Trent clearly in my mind, including our kiss goodbye in the rain. "He almost died because of me. Twice!" I turned to Mom. "We need to leave him alone and let him live his life. Please."

Mom took my hand. "We must explore every lead." She gave me a squeeze. "It's what your father would've wanted."

Really? She had to do that? Play the dead dad card? My heart sank. How could I argue with that? "Fine. We ask a few questions, wipe his mind, and then leave him alone. Forever. Deal?"

Mom nodded once. "Deal," she answered.

"I'll check the flights," Sue said.

"Flights?" I thought of the times Farrell had used his energy to transport me.

"Yes, flights," she answered.

"We only use our energy to transport when absolutely necessary," Farrell added. "It's too draining. And not all of us are going. It's too dangerous."

Fleet leaned forward and joined the conversation, suddenly interested in what we were saying. "So who's going?"

"Just me and Dominique," Farrell answered.

Keep your enemies closer, I thought. "And Fleet," I blurted out. "He should go, too."

Farrell studied me. His brow creased. Confusion swept across his face.

"She's right," Fleet agreed. "After Farrell, I'm the next

strongest Transhuman here. You might even need my tracking abilities."

Farrell remained steady while Mom considered his words. Fleet crossed his arms, his stance wide, while doubt invaded my mind. Did I do the right thing by suggesting Fleet join Farrell and me? Did I really want my enemy *that* close?

Mom broke the silence. "Fine, Fleet goes."

Sue booked three round trip tickets for the next day. We'd arrive in Houston in the morning and return at night. No packing necessary. After all, a quick conversation with Trent wouldn't take long. After we finalized our plans, Mom wanted me and Farrell to visit the past right away.

"Whoa," I said. "Why the rush?" My tired body wanted a break. Plus, I wasn't ready to see my past. Not yet anyway. It all seemed so sudden.

Mom would have nothing of it. "We need to push on, Dominique. Idleness lets the mind wander into places better left uninhabited."

Instantly, I thought of all the places in my mind I didn't want to visit, like the red desert where I had been killed eight times. I shuddered and considered backing out, until I thought of Dad. I couldn't let him down.

As if sensing the conflict within me, Farrell took my hand. A bit of calm eased my nerves. "Let me explain what it means to use the gift." He zeroed his attention on me, and suddenly I felt like we were the only people in the room. "You and I will join hands with the Seer, in this case either Richard or Sue. Flashes of our past lives will appear before us, almost like watching a movie. When we want them to stop, we call out with our minds, and step into the moment."

I pictured watching a movie, pausing it, and stepping into the screen. "And they can't see us?"

"No, they can't."

Mom's face relaxed. "I know you're worried, Dominique, but you'll be fine. Farrell will be right there with you."

"And if you get scared, just shout out with your mind and we can bring you back in a flash." Richard snapped his fingers. "Just like that."

The room stilled. No one spoke. Only the crackling of the fireplace filled the air. I rubbed the back of my neck, right at my birthmark. According to Mom and Dad, the mark branded me as Tavion's target, and each time he had threatened me, it blazed with pain. But I had killed him. Now it was just a mark. Nothing more. I started to pull my hand away when my fingers brushed the cool silver metal chain at the back of my neck. I traced the necklace with my fingertips across my neck until I found the cross that hung underneath my shirt. I let out a breath. "Okay, I'm ready."

Farrell and I followed Sue and Richard to the round wooden kitchen table. Sue pulled out two seats. "You and Farrell sit here." She pulled out a seat just opposite. "The Seer will sit here. Now who would you like that to be?"

Aunt Sue and Uncle Richard. If I had called them that, they had to be trustworthy. Like family. "I'm fine with whomever," I said.

"Okay," Sue said. She glanced at Richard. "I'll do it then."

Farrell and I sat in the two chairs she had pulled out for us. Sue positioned herself on the other side. Richard and Mom stayed near. Fleet hung back by the kitchen island, his sinister eyes glued on me.

Sue stretched out her petite, freckled hands. "Take my hand and join hands yourselves."

I wiped my sweaty palms on my jeans before reaching out and taking hers. Small and slender, it reminded me of Infiniti's hand. For a second I thought of her and wondered if she was all right, especially since by now everyone in Houston thought us dead in a horrible car crash.

"You okay?" Farrell asked. He had already taken Sue's hand, his other outstretched and waiting for mine.

"Yeah, I'm fine." I took his hand, and threaded my fingers through his. He squeezed and the feeling of calm that often followed trickled through me, but didn't stay. Instead, mounting fear drowned it out.

"Close your eyes," Sue said. "Relax. Breath deep while I focus on our previous life, life number eight."

With my eyes shut, my other senses kicked into overdrive. The fire in the fireplace popped. The wind from outside whistled as it travelled around the house and brushed against the tall windows. The woodsy and outdoorsy smell of the house intensified, and a chill crept up my spine. *Relax*, I told myself. It'll be just like the movies. That's all. A movie I've seen, but don't remember.

My shoulders tightened as I continued to squeeze my eyes shut. I thought of Fleet. My body shuddered. No matter what anybody said, he couldn't be trusted.

"Here we go," Sue muttered.

Chapter Six

The temperature around me changed from cool to warm and breezy, as if I had stepped from one climate into another.

Farrell squeezed my hand. "You can look now."

When I opened my eyes, I saw images darting before me, blurring across a cloudless sky. And I knew exactly where we were. Still blue water lay before me. My boots had sunk down into soft sand. We were standing on the shore of Elk Rapids beach. A wave of relief washed over me because I knew nothing bad could happen to me here.

"Watch," Farrell whispered. The sky filled with scenes of what must've been my past. They whirled by so fast I started to get dizzy.

"Ease up, Sue," Farrell said. "You're going too fast."

The flashes slowed. "Sorry, it's been a while since I've done this," Sue said from inside my head, as if I were wearing headphones and she was talking into my ears.

The images now passed by at a crawl—houses, trees, random people I didn't recognize. All of a sudden I saw myself, my parents, and even Farrell. My mouth hung open as one image caught my attention. Farrell and I were in a room. From the looks of it, my bedroom. I recognized the familiar color scheme of different hued blues that I loved so much.

"My favorite colors," I whispered.

"Stop here," Farrell called out. Like a camera zooming into focus, the picture of me and Farrell steadied and sharpened. Farrell squeezed my hand. "Yes, those are the colors for your room in just about every life."

I examined the setting. The décor in life number eight looked a lot like my life now—white headboard, side table, and dresser. Then I studied our clothes and hair. We both wore high-waisted jeans. Farrell's blonde hair was styled exactly the same—short and messy. But mine, good lord, was teased and puffy on top.

"The eighties?" I asked.

Farrell let out a chuckle. "How could you tell?"

The ridiculousness of my fashion quickly gave way to the scene before me. Farrell and I sat on the bed, facing each other. Tears trickled down my face and he wiped them away tenderly.

My mind raced. Why was I crying? What was happening to us in life number eight?

Farrell rested a hand on my lower back. "Do you want to go into the moment?"

The knot in my stomach intensified, but my desire to know more outweighed my fear. "Yes," I uttered, completely caught up in seeing another me with another Farrell.

He squeezed my hand and together we started walking to the water. After a few steps, we were in the bedroom, standing by the door. I never bothered with perfume, but a familiar floral scent lingered in the air. It had to have been a scent I used to wear. I breathed in deep and the comforting aroma settled my nerves.

"We're completely screwed, Farrell, aren't we? My dad is barely holding on. All I've got right now is Mom. If something happens to her, I'll be exposed," I whispered. "And then he'll find me and take me and kill me… again."

Shivers raced through me. What had happened to my dad in life number eight? And what did I mean when I had said I'll be exposed? Farrell scooted closer and wrapped his arm around my waist. "You okay?"

"Yes," I murmured, riveted by our other selves. I watched as the other Farrell edged closer to the other me.

"I love you, Dominique. With everything that I am, I love you completely. I promise – we'll figure something out."

Dominique leaned in and stared into his eyes. "I love you, Farrell. So much. Please, whatever happens, don't let me forget that. Not again."

Farrell hung his head low. Dominique grabbed his face in desperation. "I'm serious. Don't let me forget."

I could feel the love between them—from the way they sat together to the way they touched each other, even the tone of their voices. Their love filled the room. I moved forward, wanting to be closer to them, when my leg bumped into the dresser. Something from up top crashed to the ground. Panic raced through me. How did I do that? I backed into Farrell as the other Farrell and the other me jumped to their feet and stared in our direction.

"Who's there?" Farrell asked.

"Sue, take us out!" Farrell yelled from inside my head.

Like being ripped from a page, we were back at the kitchen table. My stomach lurched. My head spun. I grabbed on to the edge of the table and steadied myself. "Holy crap," I panted. "What just happened?"

Mom stood behind Sue, her panicked eyes glued on me. "Something happened?"

"We bumped into a dresser," Farrell said. "And something fell."

Mom covered her mouth. Richard and Sue's eyes widened. Even Fleet approached.

Needles of panic pricked my body. "You guys told me it would be like watching a movie! And they wouldn't see us!"

Richard rubbed his head. "Maybe we went too fast. Maybe we should've explained things more."

"Ya think?"

"Just wait a minute, everyone. Let's all calm down," Sue said. "Nothing happened, so everything is okay. And yes, Dominique, it is like a movie because you watch and they can't see you. But while you are in a different time and space, you still emit energy. A force, if you will. And touching that dresser produced a result."

My nerves settled some. Even though Sue had explained how I made the furniture move, I had a ton of questions about what I had seen. But the question that really burned in me was about my dad.

Fleet crossed his arms, his face perfectly calm and devoid of emotion. "So? What did you see?"

Yeah right, as if I'd tell him anything. "Nothing useful. Just me and Farrell in my room talking about stupid stuff." I avoided eye contact, squeezing Farrell's knee under the table. I didn't want anyone to know about the conversation we had seen, least of all Fleet.

Fleet's eyes narrowed. Confusion and disbelief crossed Sue and Richard's faces. They didn't buy it.

"Enough," Mom said, coming to my rescue. "Dominique needs to rest before the flight tomorrow."

The remainder of the day passed without incident. I kept my distance from Fleet, and he kept his from me. Finally, when we went to bed for the night, Mom and Farrell paid me a visit.

Mom and I sat on the bed. Farrell leaned against the wall. "I know seeing the past was hard on you," Mom said. "But you must tell me everything."

I clasped my hands together and replayed the scene in my head. "Well, Farrell and I were in my bedroom. We were talking about—" I stopped and glanced his way, remembering how the old me had begged him to help me remember my love for him should I forget.

"Her shield and Stone's injuries," Farrell said.

I snapped back to reality. "My shield? That's what I meant when I had said I'd be exposed if something happened to Mom?"

"Yes," Farrell said, coming closer to the bed. "Your mother and father shield you in every life."

I could tell Mom wanted to cry. She explained. "So far one thing has always been the same in each life—the attack on your father." She rubbed her temples. "But he's always survived." She turned her head down. "Until now." I took her hand and held it tight. "Now that he's gone, it's just me shielding you, Dominique."

My lip quivered. "That can't be good."

"Shielding is like throwing a blanket over a lamp. No one can see the light if it's covered."

"Unless the blanket is removed," I whispered.

Mom shifted and the bed creaked. I held my breath at

the sound, slowly exhaling when thick silence returned to the room.

"Yes," Mom said. "If the shield is removed, your energy source will be exposed."

I pictured Mom and Dad covering me with a blanket. With him gone, it was up to Mom to keep the blanket in place. With both of them gone... I was screwed, just like I had said back in life number eight. And then Trent popped into my mind. He had the power to see people's auras, except he couldn't see mine. Now I understood why. "So that's why Trent couldn't see my aura."

Mom's face paled. "Trent can see auras?" She looked at Farrell. "Did you know?"

"No, I didn't."

My chest tightened. A fresh wave of fear washed over me. "What does that mean? To see auras?"

Mom's eyes looked a million miles away. "It means he could be one of us. A Transhuman."

Chapter Seven

Farrell and Fleet sat on either side of me as our flight took off to Houston. Because we had purchased our tickets last minute, we got stuck with the last seats available—the very back. I hated flying in the rear of the plane. The seats rattled, the engine roared, and the plane jerked. For a second, I even thought we might crash. That would be a great ending to the battle over my life. Killed mid-flight, and the rest of the world lived unhappily ever after.

My mind turned from visions of crashing and burning to everything I had learned the night before from Mom and Farrell about Transhumans... and Trent. Transhumans existed before modern man and had special powers related to the ability to use the energy in and around them. Of course, I already knew this. What I didn't know was that some Transhumans had integrated into mainstream society. These people didn't even know who they were even though they retained a connection to the power of energy in one way or another. Some could communicate with the dead, even predict the future. A few, like Trent, could "see" people's energy. These Transhumans who still maintained a connection to their abilities were usually visionaries, religious leaders, even heads of state. Others were insane.

But our purpose for flying to Houston was only to gather information, not to tell Trent what he could be.

The rattle of the snack cart as the flight attendant came by with our drinks snapped me alert. When she handed Fleet his water, we both reached for it. His outstretched hand brushed against mine.

"You must kill him," Tavion said. *"Before he kills you."*

My arm jerked. Fleet's drink flew into the air and came crashing down in a watery splash. I jumped to my feet and started climbing over Farrell. The poor flight attendant stared at me like I was some kind of lunatic, barely dodging out of my way.

"Dominique, what are you doing?" Farrell asked, looking as alarmed as the flight attendant.

"Bathroom," I muttered. "Emergency."

Luckily, since we were in the back, I made it to the bathroom within a matter of seconds. I splashed water on my face before stumbling back onto the toilet. When I was little and Mom had wanted to take my mind off pain, whether it was a shot at the doctor's office or a bump and a bruise after a tumble, she used to apply pressure on my hand between my thumb and my forefinger. *"This will transfer your attention and keep your mind off the pain,"* she used to say.

With my right hand, I found the spot on my left and squeezed, hoping it would drive Tavion out of my mind.

A knock rapped at the door. "Dominique, it's me. You okay?"

My nails dug into my skin. "Yeah. I'm fine, Farrell." A long pause told me he didn't believe me. "Really, I'm fine. I'll be out in a few minutes."

Another long pause. "Okay," he said.

My shaking body stilled. Tavion's voice had vanished.

The only ache that remained throbbed in my hand. Mom's trick still worked. After pulling myself together, I started to make my way back to my seat, but stopped short. There was no way I could sit by Fleet. I scanned the nearby rows for an empty seat, but found none.

I was stuck.

Farrell slid out into the aisle. He studied me for a second. "I'll take the middle," he offered, obviously sensing my hesitation about sitting next to Fleet. "You take the aisle. You know, in case you have another emergency."

"Thanks, Farrell."

My body remained tense for the remainder of the flight. My legs fidgeted, my pulse raced. I wasn't even sure what had me more on edge—hearing Tavion's voice, being close to Fleet, or knowing I'd be seeing Trent in a few hours.

Either way, it all sucked.

We landed without anything else happening and rented a car. Since school hadn't let out yet, we decided to follow Trent home from there. My stomach knotted as we parked across the street from the high school and waited. After just over an hour, the bell rang. The parking lot filled with bodies and cars making their way out of the school. Finally, Trent came into view. Dressed in faded jeans and a t-shirt, he slung his backpack over his shoulder and made his way to his old black Camaro. My gaze became glued to him. My body shivered. What would he say when he saw me?

"Here we go," Farrell said as he turned the car ignition. We stayed two cars away from Trent and followed him to his house. He went inside and came back out with his grandmother. We followed him to his church where he dropped her off, and then we tailed him right back home. We parked across the street and one house away.

The last time I had been at Trent's, his perfectly manicured house sparkled with Christmas decorations. Now, weeds sprouted on the lawn and fallen pine needles had clumped beneath the bushes and trees. The once proud and clean house had transformed to downtrodden and neglected. Guilt shot through me because I knew it had something to do with me.

Farrell tapped his fingers on his leg. He cleared his throat. "Fleet and I are going in. You'll need to stay here, Dominique."

"What?" My nervousness over seeing Trent vanished, anger taking its place. How could Farrell make that decision for me? "I don't think so."

"Your mom thinks it would be best." Farrell kept his gaze on the house, avoiding mine. He ran his palm across the steering wheel. "She thinks it'll be easier on you."

Heat crept up my cheeks because I knew he was talking about my feelings for Trent. Even though they still lingered, my heart had filled with Farrell. Trent could never compare. And after seeing my old self with Farrell, I knew he never could. As much as I wanted to tell him so, I couldn't with Fleet in the car. And that's when I realized Mom had agreed on Fleet coming with us to keep me and Farrell on task. Clever.

I sat back and crossed my arms. "Fine. Whatever."

Farrell and Fleet got out of the car and walked side by side to the house. Both tall and lean, they shoved their hands in their pockets at almost the same time. I wondered if they even knew how alike they were, except for the traitor thing. No matter what Fleet said, everything inside me said not to trust him, that he had tipped off the Tainted and told them where to ambush our car. I know Mom and Farrell wanted me to pretend to believe him, but the longer I was around him, the harder it was.

I chewed my bottom lip and wrapped a strand of hair around my finger as Farrell and Fleet reached the door. With a flick of Farrell's hand, a small burst of white light ignited at the doorknob. The door swung open. I held my breath. Farrell glanced over his shoulder at me for just a second before he and Fleet slipped in and closed the door behind them.

My heart raced. My stomach twisted. I shifted in my seat while my gaze darted over the house. What were they going to do to Trent? My fingers traced the leather door handle of our rental car. If anything happened to Trent, I'd never be able to forgive myself. I gripped the handle and was thinking of going against my mother's wishes, when a petite figure jogged by. Long purple socks that came up to the knees, navy gym shorts, a tight white shirt with a tie-dye peace sign on the back, wild black hair pulled up in a high ponytail—Infiniti. She stopped her run in front of Trent's house, placed her hands on her hips, and took short and labored breaths. Exercise was not her thing.

I crouched down in my seat. *Please, keep running,* I thought to myself. *Don't stop. Not now.*

Infiniti wiped her forehead. She smoothed out her shirt and started for Trent's front door. Without giving it a second thought, I flung open the car door and ran toward her. Just as she got to the porch, I yelled, "Don't go in there!"

Infiniti froze in place while my voice echoed through the barely cold Texas air. I slapped my hand over my mouth. *Crap.* Inch by inch, she turned to face me. Her big brown eyes almost popped out of her head, her mouth hung open, and a scream shot out of her. I instantly regretted getting out of the car and stopping her.

"Oh! My! God! Dominique!"

Before anyone could come out of their house and see me in the flesh, a girl who'd supposedly died in a car crash, I rushed her and slammed my hands over her mouth. "Shhhh."

Her muffled cries left my palms wet and slimy. "I'm going to let go," I said. "After you calm down. Okay?"

She nodded as I quickly led her to Trent's front door. Farrell was not going to be happy. I peeled my hand from her mouth and rubbed my palm on my jeans.

She stared at me, her eyes still huge. "You're, you're, you're… dead."

"I know. I mean, I'm not." I banged on the door. "Let's just get inside."

The door opened with a jerk. It was Fleet. He took one look at Infiniti and said, "Shit."

I grabbed Infiniti's arm and led her past Fleet, as if he wasn't even there. And what I saw in the normally cozy and comforting den shocked me. Trent hunched over in a small brown leather chair. His head hung low, his arms dangling at his sides. Farrell loomed over him. A beam of light shot out of his hand and pierced Trent's head like a laser.

"What the hell is going on?" Infiniti yelled.

I wanted to echo her words, but couldn't. Stunned surprise had silenced me.

Farrell lowered his hand. The energy stream faded. "I was searching his mind, that's all," Farrell replied to her question while keeping his gaze locked on me.

Infiniti grabbed the sides of her head, like she was going crazy. She looked from me, to Farrell, to Fleet, to Trent, and back to me again. "Somebody better explain why you're not dead!" She pointed at Fleet. "And who the hell that is!" Lastly, her gaze settled on Trent. "And what the hell you're doing to Trent!"

Trent moaned and lifted his head. His muted blue eyes settled on me. "Dominique?" He squinted. "Is that you?"

"Man, just wipe the girl and get her the hell out of here," Fleet said to Farrell.

Trent glanced around the room, blinking his eyes into focus, confused about what was going on. Infiniti's mouth hung open. And even though I hated Fleet, he was right. For Infiniti's sake, Farrell needed to erase us out of her mind and get her back home.

"Do it," I said to Farrell.

Farrell approached Infiniti. Step by step, she backed away from him until she bumped into the wall.

"It's okay," he said while he towered over her. "I'm not going to hurt you. I just want to show you something."

I had seen him wipe Trent's mind twice. Each time he had placed his fingers on Trent's head and sent his energy source in and around Trent's body. Not only did Trent not remember anything, but Farrell had also transported him away. I held my breath and waited for him to do the same to Infiniti.

A spark shot out from Farrell's hand. "Whoa," Infiniti whispered. Her stare fixed on him while the energy at his fingertips grew into a white misty strand that wrapped around his hand.

She reached out to touch it. "What's that?"

Farrell got closer. "It's energy," he said. "And when I touch your forehead, it'll explain everything that's going on."

He placed his hand on her temple and closed his eyes. The light intensified. Infiniti's eyes grew bigger. I waited for her to vanish. Instead, she swatted his hand away. "You're freaking me out!"

Farrell gaped at Infiniti and tilted his head. He backed away from her, looking from her to his hand. "It didn't work," he muttered.

She put her hand on her hip and stuck out her right foot. "What didn't work?" She widened her eyes for a second before narrowing them in suspicion. "You better start talking right the hell now, or I'm calling the cops!"

I knew I had to explain things. And if anyone could understand, it'd be her. I sidled in front of Infiniti and blocked her view from everyone else. "An evil energy being tried to kill me. Before it could, I killed it instead. For my safety, and everyone else's, we had to leave Houston and fake our deaths. The only reason we're back is to get information from Trent because my life is still at risk."

Her lips parted. Her hands shook. "I knew it," she whispered.

"What?" I asked, taken aback.

"Jan—she visited me in my dreams. She said you'd come back for me and that I needed to listen to you. I thought I was going nuts. That I was losing it because I had lost another friend."

Relief washed over me. Jan had prepared Infiniti for our visit. But that still didn't explain why Farrell's energy had no effect on her.

"Someone better tell me what the hell is going on!" Trent yelled. He swayed from side to side on his feet, leaning against the chair for support.

"Great," Fleet said. "Now him, too." Fleet glowered at Farrell and pointed at Trent. "Transport him and yourself to the cabin. I'll fly back with Dominique and Tiny."

"Hey! My name is Infiniti!"

"I don't see another way," Fleet added, ignoring Infiniti.

Trent took a few steps, stumbled, and almost fell back on the chair. "What's going on?"

Frustration mounted on Farrell's face. He flicked his wrist at Trent and a blast of energy pushed him on the seat and wrapped him in silence. Trent jerked his body back and forth wildly, trying to get up again, but he couldn't.

My head spun. My stomach plummeted. I scrambled to gather my thoughts and figure a way out of this mess so no one got hurt. "Nobody move," I said, yanking Farrell into the kitchen and away from the others.

In the spice-laden room, the crosses lining the walls seemed to mock me. Even the large portrait of Jesus eyed me disapprovingly. "Is there any other way?" I whispered to Farrell.

He ran his fingers through his hair and circled the room. "We need more time with him. But now that Infiniti's involved and can't be wiped, I just don't know."

My heart beat wildly, like an out of control drum. "So we take them?"

Farrell came to a standstill. "As much as I don't want to agree with Fleet, his suggestion appears to be the only viable one for us right now."

I hated agreeing with a traitor like Fleet, but Farrell was right. Fleet's plan made sense. That, plus I immediately thought Infiniti and Trent would be safer with us back in Michigan than alone here in Texas.

"Are you okay with that?" Farrell asked.

Hell, no. I wasn't okay with it, but it had to be done. "Yeah. Let's do it."

Back in the den, Farrell got in Fleet's face and rammed his finger into his chest. "You get Dominique safely back to Michigan tonight, or I'll be after you."

Before Fleet could respond, Farrell turned to me. He pressed his forehead to mine and kissed me on the lips. "You'll be fine. I promise." He tromped to Trent and placed his hand on his shoulder. Bright white vapor laced out of his fingers and covered both of them. "I'll see you tonight," Farrell said to me, just before they vanished.

The house creaked. The lights flickered. Despair settled deep within me. Infiniti came close to me and whispered, "Holy shit, this is all for real, isn't it?"

Even though my mouth had dried over, I managed to squeak out a yes.

Fleet paced the room, his mind obviously racing.

"Uh, now what?" Infiniti asked.

My gaze swept the room before it landed on Fleet. I hated the idea of being stuck with him, but we needed to move. "We get out of here," I said. "Fast. Before someone else comes."

Surprisingly, working with Fleet on what to do next

was easy. We decided to leave a message on the answering machine for Trent's grandmother. Fleet replicated Trent's voice with ease and said he'd be gone a few days to sort things out. He even called the church and arranged for her to be brought home and checked on for the next few days. Infiniti assured us his grandmother would buy it since Trent hadn't been the same since my death. As if I didn't feel bad enough, hearing that made me sick. Then we packed a few of his things and left.

After that, we went to Infiniti's and got some of her things, too. As usual, her mom wasn't home. Infiniti left a note saying she'd be gone for a few days and not to worry. Nothing more. She claimed her mom wouldn't even care. Sadly enough, I knew she was right. Infiniti's mom let her do whatever she wanted. In this case, that was a good thing.

We had done everything so quickly, I didn't have time to second-guess our plan, or linger in Trent's room, or study my old street, or feel any guilt or remorse... until we drove to the airport. That's when reality descended on me.

We had just taken Trent against his will. Infiniti and I were going to get on a plane with a traitor. And for the first time in months, maybe even lifetimes, I was without my protector.

Things couldn't have been worse.

Chapter Eight

Infiniti frantically chewed her cinnamon gum all the way to the airport, her eyes practically bulging out of their sockets. She studied Fleet who focused on the road, then whipped her stare on me beside her in the back of the car.

She inched up to the edge of her seat. "So… you're Farrell's brother."

At first, Fleet answered her questions, but he soon stopped because she kept asking the same ones over and over.

She gave up on him, sat back, and angled her body to me. "And you're hunted. And that's why you guys had to fake your deaths."

I hadn't told her yet about my dad being dead for real. I couldn't talk about it, not yet anyway. "Yes, Infiniti," I said. "We're being hunted and we had to fake our deaths. Now please, let's get to the airport. We can talk all you want once we're on the plane." I rubbed my head. "Right now I need to think."

She wrapped her arm around mine, scooted closer to me, and rested her head on my shoulder. "I'm just glad you're alive," she whispered.

I squeezed her arm, suddenly feeling like a jerk. "Me, too."

We got to the airport in plenty of time only to find our

flight delayed. Great. That meant I'd have to endure a few more hours with Fleet. My enemy. The person I hated most in the world. Maybe even more than Tavion himself.

Infiniti and I got some coffee and found a couple of seats away from the crowds, yet close enough to the gate to hear the announcement for our flight. Fleet sat two rows behind us. I didn't even have to look over my shoulder to know his eyes remained locked on us. I could almost feel a glaring heat coming from his direction. Even my skin prickled with unease. I prayed Farrell was right and we'd make it back to Michigan okay, because so far nothing had gone as planned.

I spent the next hour or so telling Infiniti everything—from Transhumanism to my past lives, and finally to the car accident that had taken my dad's life. She oohed and ahhed, shed some tears, and when I had finished she said the strangest thing.

"Hey, remember when I told you how Jan came to me in my dream and told me you'd come back for me? And for me to listen?"

The serious tone in her voice worried me. "Yeah, I remember."

Infiniti fidgeted in her seat. "Well, she said something else." She chewed her nails, seeming afraid to go on.

I pulled her hand from her face, forcing her to continue. "What?"

"She said you were changing."

Her words echoed in my head a few seconds. "Changing?"

"Yeah, changing." A nervous laugh came out of her. "Weird, huh?"

My stomach tightened. Changing… I had no idea what that meant, but it couldn't be good.

"You must kill Infiniti, too."

I jumped to my feet, as if someone had poked me with a hot stick. Tavion had invaded my mind again. This time he wanted me to kill my best friend. I squeezed my left hand with my right, digging my fingernails deep into my skin.

"Hey, dude, you okay?" Infiniti stood in front of me with worry-filled eyes.

"Yes, I'm, uh…" I backed away from her. "Tired. That's all." I faked a smile. "I think I need to stretch my legs a little." I backpedaled, holding up my hands before she could follow me. "Alone. I'll be right back."

My legs couldn't take me away from Infiniti fast enough, my breathing increasingly rapid and shallow with each step. How could I hurt, let alone kill, my best friend? There was no way.

Thudding boots sounded behind me. Was it Tavion? Coming for me somehow? Back from the dead? I spun around, sick and tired of his stupid tricks, when Fleet almost crashed into me. He grabbed my wrist and jerked me to an empty corridor.

"What are you doing?" I yanked my arm away. "Are you crazy?"

He slammed both of his hands on either side of me, trapping me against the wall. If we were dating, this would be the perfect place and position for a kiss. But we weren't dating. We were enemies.

"I know who you are, Dominique."

His words stunned me. He knew who *I* was? Well, I

knew who the hell he was, and he needed to know. Even though Mom and Farrell had said to pretend we believed he was one of us, I couldn't do it anymore. "Oh yeah?" I slammed my hands into his chest and pushed him away. "Well, I know who *you* are."

He stepped forward and brought his face within inches of mine. He cocked his head. "Really? Well, let's hear it, sweetheart."

Anger seethed inside me. "You're a traitor, Fleet. I know it. My mom knows it. Even Farrell knows."

He smirked and shook his head from side to side. "I knew you guys thought that. Truth is…" He came close, so close his lips almost touched mine. I jerked back and hit my head against the wall. He brought his mouth up against my ear. "You're the traitor. And you don't even know it."

I pulled in a sharp breath, my body now fully pressed against the cool wall. He backed away, his heated glare locked on me. I wanted him to get away from me and leave me alone. Instead, he went on. "You were chosen, *not* to die at Tavion's hand, but to kill him. And now that he's dead, you're the new leader of the Tainted. Congratulations."

Immediately I thought of the young girl who had reached out to me back at our car accident. She was one of the Tainted, and had eyes like mine. She had even said I belonged with them. I could see here pale face, her olive-colored eyes, the purple mist that trickled out from her hand. Tavion had told me to go with her, and I almost did.

But I'm not one of them!

I wanted to run, get away from Fleet, but my body froze. Me? The new leader of the Tainted? Infiniti's words from earlier rang through me. She'd said that had Jan told her I was changing. A cold realization dawned on me. Is that what Jan had meant? That I was transforming into some evil being and leader of the Tainted?

My body shook. *No, it can't be!*

Fleet's jaw clenched. "It's always been your destiny to take over, Dominique. That's what you're really chosen for. Only the Tainted know this, and now me since I had infiltrated them for so long. But I'm not one of them, or, I guess I should say, not one of you. I'm a Pure." He paused. "You're the only one here who's a traitor. And when you reveal yourself," he moved closer to me, "I'm going to kill you."

Panic and fear ripped up and down my tense body. I had no idea how he could come up with something so evil, so wicked.

"You're lying," I whispered.

"Hey! Guys!" Infiniti showed up right on time. "They called our—" She stopped, eyed us together, and threw our bags on the floor. "Seriously?"

Fleet lowered his arms. I stomped past him and joined her, snatching up my stuff. "It's not like that."

"You always get the hot ones," Infiniti muttered under her breath.

By the time we got on the plane, it was almost ten. The day had long gone, and so had my energy. We ended up sitting in the back, again. This time there were a few extra seats. I nabbed two for Infiniti and me and left Fleet to sit alone. I had to process my thoughts and try to figure things out.

How could I be the new leader of the Tainted?

"So I thought you said you and Farrell were an item now?" Infiniti whispered to me.

"We are." I glanced over my shoulder and saw Fleet giving me the death stare. "That back there at the airport with Fleet was him being an idiot jerk, that's all."

"Oooh, so he's available?" She smiled wide and wiggled her eyebrows up and down. She turned to get a better look at him, when I slammed my hand on her wrist and squeezed.

"No! He's a total jerk!" The one thing I didn't tell her back at the airport was our suspicion that Fleet was a traitor. I mean, why would I? It would only freak her the hell out, and right now I needed her to remain calm. "Besides, aren't you with Billy anyway?"

She shrugged her shoulders. "Nah, I got tired of him."

Great—here we were flying cross-country with a guy I knew in my heart of hearts was a traitor but somehow thought *I* was the traitor, and all Infiniti could do was salivate over him.

"Can you just focus, please?"

Infiniti smoothed her wild hair back and put on a serious face. "You're absolutely right. Your life's in danger. I haven't forgotten." She got up and retrieved two blue blankets from the overhead bin. She dropped one on my lap and wrapped herself tight with the other. "I'm going to think about all this while I get some sleep." She tapped her forehead. "I get my best ideas when I'm sleeping because that's where I can," she let out a big yawn, "connect with the spirits."

She angled her body away from me, pulled down the window cover, and leaned against it. "You know," she yawned again. "They say you can't change destiny."

Fear prickled at my skin, her words echoing in my mind. Since I had died in all my other lives, why would this life be different? Maybe she was right. Maybe I couldn't change destiny. And if that was the case, what was this all about? What the hell was I fighting for?

I started to say something to Infiniti but saw her mouth open, drool dripping. I reached for the cross around my neck and held it tight. The carved rock warmed in my hand. A tiny vibration sent courage through me, telling me I had to follow this through. No matter what. If not for me, then for everyone connected to me, especially Trent and Infiniti. I needed to fight like hell to change my future. Destiny be damned.

Please, I prayed to whoever might be listening. *Let Fleet be wrong. Help me change my life path. Help me… live.*

Chapter Nine

The deafening roar of silence filled my ears as I lowered my seat and cuddled up with my blue blanket. The plane seemed a safe enough place to rest, but I couldn't fall asleep. Instead, my mind worked overtime. I thought of what Fleet had said about me being a traitor and the new leader of the Tainted. His crazy talk had to be a way to deflect attention from himself—it just had to. Then my thoughts roamed to Infiniti. Nothing had happened when Farrell tried to wipe her mind and transport her away from Trent's house. Trent… I shivered, wondering what was happening to him back at the cabin. If only I could communicate with someone over there.

Wait a minute—I *could* reach someone over there! I sat up and shoved my hair behind my ears. Every time I used my mind to call out for Farrell, he would come. It was like we had a permanent link. But I hadn't done that in a while. Would it still work? And if so, how would it work in a flying airplane? I didn't know and I didn't care. I had to try.

I scanned the seats across the aisle and to my left. A businessman sat with his laptop on the tray table. With ear buds on, his fingers flew over his keyboard. In front of him a mom and her baby were fast asleep. I folded my blanket in my lap and snuck a peak behind me and over my shoulder at Fleet. My gaze travelled up his long outstretched legs, over his crossed arms, to his narrowed stare.

Crap! I averted my eyes and fiddled with my hair, pretending I didn't see him even though our gaze had locked for a split second. So much for being subtle.

Infiniti shifted beside me and a trace of cinnamon filled the musty, recycled air. I had to call out for Farrell before she woke up because the last thing I needed was to play twenty questions with her. Again.

Calling Farrell had always come naturally to me. Most of the time, I didn't even know I was doing it. Now, I had no idea where to even start. I wrapped my hands around the soft blanket and steadied my breathing.

Farrell? Are you there?

Nothing happened—no swooshing of air, no crackling of lightning. The only sounds were the click-clack tapping of the keyboard across the aisle and soft snoring from Infiniti. I stretched my neck side to side, forcing my tense body to relax.

Farrell. It's me. Dominique. Please, I need you.

Still nothing. Defeated, I leaned my head back, slouched down in my seat, and squeezed my eyes shut. What happened? Why didn't it work? Why couldn't he hear me? The creaking of the beverage cart sounded from behind me as the flight attendant made her way up the aisle.

A hand dropped on my shoulder. I startled, annoyed at the flight attendant's interruption. Weren't they trained to leave sleeping people alone? Irritated, I opened my eyes.

There stood the young girl from the car crash—the

Tainted who had eyes like mine. I barely contained my gasp while my body jerked upright, my legs crashing into the seat before me.

"Hello, Dominique," she said in a soft whisper.

I covered my mouth, shocked. Then I looked around, wondering if anyone else could see her. The typing man glanced at me with a raised eyebrow before resuming his work. Even Infiniti peeled one eye open before turning away from me. How could they not see her? I peered at Fleet. He tilted his head slightly. He may not have been able to see her, but he definitely sensed something.

I leaned away from the aisle and closer to Infiniti, trying to put distance between the girl and me. She laughed. "I'm not going to hurt you, Marked One."

Like hell, I thought. Anger exploded inside me. She and her Tainted friends had appeared in front of our car and caused our crash. My dad had died because of them. She was a murderer.

"Come," she said. She wrapped her warm petite hand around my wrist. I flinched, waiting for some sort of shock or zap or something. "I need to talk to you," she whispered in haste. "Now."

The beverage cart rattled in my ears as the flight attendant continued to the front of the plane. I had started to pull my arm away from the girl, when a shiver shot down my spine, followed by Tavion's echoing voice in my head. *Go with her,* his raspy voice instructed.

The pale-faced Tainted girl captivated me with her olive eyes. In an instant, it was like I knew her and she knew me—better than anybody. Suddenly what she had done to my dad didn't matter anymore. But it didn't make sense! And deep down I knew it was wrong! I rose to my feet, unable to ignore her call. My body quivering as I trailed behind her.

Fleet moved his legs out of the aisle so I could pass and watched me with a puzzled look. I followed the girl just beyond the bathrooms to the back of the plane. She pressed her back against the metal wall, folded her arms, and scanned the empty area before focusing on me. I started to twist around, hoping to catch Fleet's attention, when she zipped forward and jerked me around to face her.

"He's not coming." Her small hands gripped my arms and held me in place. "Now stand here with your back to him and listen. We don't have a lot of time." She studied my face for a moment. "Tavion survives within you."

Icy fear shot though my veins. What the hell was she talking about? Tavion was in me? The last time I had seen Tavion was at Jan's, in the space between, while my body slept in a coma. Jan had said he was following me. Nothing more. But she had also confirmed he was dead.

The girl inched closer. I wanted to back away, but my legs were planted in place. "He's part of you."

I had visions of him back in Houston. Now his voice penetrated my mind. But I had no idea what she meant by him being a part of me. Was she crazy? "I-I-I don't know what you're talking about."

Her olive eyes darted back and forth while she examined my face. "When you killed Tavion back at the red desert your blood mixed with his." She took my hand and traced my palm with her warm fingertips. "You sliced your hand right here." She licked her tiny lips. "And you covered your dagger with your blood and plunged it into Tavion. When you did that, his blood joined with yours. Now he is in you and will take you over completely." She released my hand. "He planned it all along. Soon, you won't even hear his voice anymore. It'll be just you. The new Tainted leader."

My stomach tightened. Everything that had happened at the red desert flashed before me. I could almost feel the desert heat burning my lungs, could almost feel the slash of metal across my throbbing hand. Worse? Deep inside, I wondered if she was telling the truth. Her claim matched what Fleet had said back at the airport. Even Infiniti herself had said that Jan warned of me changing. "No," I muttered, dazed, as if convincing myself to believe otherwise. "You're lying."

Hatred sparked inside me, a deep loathing I had never known before. It was directed at no one and everyone all at the same time. But it wasn't right! It wasn't me! It couldn't be me! My thoughts frantically shifted to Farrell. Maybe if I concentrated on him hard enough, he'd appear. He had to! I pictured his angular features, his green eyes, his messy blonde hair, the way I felt when he touched me.

Nothing!

I even thought of our safe place at Elk Rapids beach—the refuge where he and I went in our past lives. That's where I had found the white feather. I had called it a sign of hope. But thinking of the beach didn't help. Instead, revulsion continued building inside me until any trace of salvation vanished.

"You must accept your fate," the girl said.

The plane quaked. My heart raced. I twisted my hands together and dug my fingers into my skin, praying she'd disappear. "I'll never want to join you."

"I knew you'd say that." She flicked her fingers with a smirk. A crackling electrical current blasted from her hand, twirling into a purple haze. The plane swayed. I stumbled, barely catching my footing. "If you refuse your new role, I will bring down the plane. You, Infiniti, Fleet, and all the other souls on this plane will die." She kept her hand raised. "It's your choice."

Her threat didn't make sense. Why would she kill me if she wanted me to be the new leader of the Tainted? I decided to call her bluff. "Fine. Crash it."

The plane shook—a violent tremble this time. A smattering of gasps rang out from the passengers. The seatbelt sign blinked on, followed by a flight attendant's warning to sit down. The girl's eyes narrowed as a loud creaking sounded all around me.

"As you wish," the girl said calmly, as if I had just given her permission to do something ordinary and mundane.

She dissolved into a hazy mist and blasted straight through me, knocking the wind right out of my lungs. Warmth engulfed me, like a flash fire, then quickly disappeared. I gulped, gasping for air, suddenly terrified and waiting for the plane to burst into flames. A strong hand clutched my arm and yanked me around.

"What the hell are you doing back here?" Fleet asked.

The plane took a sharp dip, flinging me into Fleet's arms. High pitched screams filled the air. I stared up into Fleet's startled eyes, and I noticed something. Instead of dark black, they now looked brownish. Maybe he was a Pure after all. Maybe he wasn't a traitor. Maybe I could… trust him.

A flight attendant called out from the intercom, ordering us to sit down. I ignored her, and kept my attention locked on Fleet. "The plane is going to crash," I blurted.

The plane dipped again. This time it didn't stop. Fleet and I tumbled to the floor, my knees stinging as they made impact. Overhead bins flew open. Luggage hurtled out. Oxygen masks dropped. Gravity pinned me down as the plane nose-dived, plummeting faster by the second. I wrapped my arm around the base of the closest seat and held on. With my free arm I grabbed Fleet's shirt and pulled. "You have to stop it!"

Shock, fear, and then determination flashed across his face. He focused on me a second before he closed his eyes. I recognized that look—I had seen it on Farrell many times. A soft gray mist trickled from his hands until it covered his body. He rolled to his feet and crouched low to the ground. He placed his palms flat on the floor of the plane. A spark blasted from him and drilled down into the floorboard. The plane swooped like a runaway roller coaster struggling to find its tracks, yet Fleet remained steady.

Fleet gritted his teeth. "There's an energy disturbance in the front of the plane."

It was the girl. I knew it. "Can you get rid of it?"

Passengers continued screaming. The plane continued falling. Fleet's gray energy source grew thicker and darker, pulsing from his hands and seeping into the body of the plane. His arms started shaking. "It's strong," he groaned.

This was it. We were all going to die. I craned my neck, trying to get a glimpse of Infiniti two rows ahead of me, but I couldn't see her. And then I thought of Farrell. I closed my eyes and pictured him in my mind. I loved him, really and truly loved him, and I instantly regretted not telling him how I felt.

A moaning creak pierced the air, like rending steel. A rippling shudder raced through the plane. As quickly as it had plunged, the plane leveled out with a jerk, wrenching my arm away from the base of the seat and flinging me backward. I sat up with a groan and studied Fleet. Beads of sweat trickled down his forehead. He stared straight ahead, eyes glazed over. I crawled over to him, and put a hand on his shoulder. He snapped to and shrugged my hand away. "Don't touch me," he warned.

"Oh my God!" Infiniti called out, rushing over to me. She grabbed my arm and helped me to my feet. Mascara streaks stained her ghost white face. Her lip quivered. "We almost died." She hugged me tight, sobbing into my shoulder.

She was right. We had almost died. All because of me.

The flight attendants ushered Infiniti, Fleet, and me to our seats. They checked our seatbelts with a tug before checking everyone else's. Infiniti wrapped her arm around mine and huddled against me while I sat motionless and in a state of shock. Slow moving despair traveled through me. It clogged my throat and wrestled my gut. I had no idea what else was in store for me. Had no idea how much more I could take.

Jan had warned of Tavion following me. Later she appeared to Infiniti in a dream, warning her of my change.

Fleet insisted I was a traitor. And now the Tainted girl that killed my dad had said that Tavion was within me. She even attempted to crash my plane to make her point. But why did she want me to go with her? And where did she want to take me?

Tension and fear mounted in me as we continued on to the Traverse City airport. Infiniti's pale face never regained its color. The people all around me sat stiff and upright, their fingers gripping the arms of their seats. Even Fleet stayed on the edge of his chair. And me? I couldn't wait to see Farrell and tell him everything. If the young Tainted girl was right, Farrell would know what to do. At least, that's what I hoped.

Frigid air hugged the nearly empty terminal as we made our way to passenger pick-up. Infiniti wrapped her arms around herself and her flimsy purple jacket. "I need a bigger coat," she complained. Fleet ignored her, quickening his pace.

Outside, the cold wind pierced through me. I searched through the blustery snow flurries until I spotted Richard parked nearby. Farrell leaned against the car, popping up as soon as he saw us. He rushed over, walked past me, and slammed his fist against Fleet's face. Fleet stumbled back, barely able to stay on his feet.

"Hey!" Richard ran over and grabbed Farrell from behind.

Farrell curled his lip. "You blocked her from me!" he yelled at Fleet.

Normally calm and cool, Farrell stunned me with his outburst. And his words struck a chord. He had tried to connect with me? Fleet rubbed his cheek and steadied himself. I dashed over to Farrell and placed my hands on his chest. "Stop! Please!" With everything that had happened on the plane, I had begun to doubt Fleet was the traitor.

A police officer approached. "What's the problem over here?"

Infiniti walked over to him. "Um, we're just having a—"she raised her hands and made quotation marks with her fingers, "—special reunion."

Richard pulled Farrell toward the car, and the rest of us followed. "Sorry, Officer," he said. "No problems here. We were just leaving."

Fleet jumped in front with Richard while Farrell, Infiniti, and I climbed in the back. Once we were clear of the airport, Richard peered at Farrell in the rear view mirror. "What was that all about?"

Farrell clutched his knees. He jerked his chin toward Fleet. "He knows."

"Man, you don't know what you're talking about," Fleet said.

"I'm the one who doesn't know what anyone is talking about!" Infiniti said.

Infiniti was right. No one really knew everything that was going on, especially her. Only I did, and I had to tell them. "Let's just get back to the cabin and I can explain everything," I said.

Farrell laced his fingers through mine, relief flashing across his perfect face for a moment before his usual look of worry set in. "I'm glad you're okay," he whispered.

Okay? I didn't really think I was okay, but at least I was alive. And still me.

For now.

Chapter Ten

The heater blasted through Richard's dusty jeep as we made our way to the cabin. The warm air filtering through the car suffocated me, and suddenly I dreaded being back in Michigan; regretted killing Tavion back at the red desert. I even wondered what would've happened if I had died and not come back to life to finish Tavion off. Mom and Dad had said my death would doom the Transhuman race and change the world forever, but how?

Infiniti chattered a million words a minute, filling in Richard and Farrell on everything that had happened on the plane. While she spilled information, my hand wandered to my neck, feeling for the cross just beneath my shirt. I patted around, but couldn't find it. My body tensed.

"What is it?" Farrell asked.

I continued searching for the bloodstone cross that Trent's grandmother had given me, my fingers clawing for its touch. "My cross." A sick aching filled my gut. "It's gone." That cross had saved my life, and now I'd gone and lost it. I sat back while a flood of tears tightened my throat.

"I'm sorry," Farrell whispered, slipping his arm around my shoulder.

I was the sorry one. Especially since now I'd have to face Trent without the necklace. I already knew he'd hate me for taking him from his home and being with Farrell.

He was bound to hate me even more for losing a family heirloom.

We turned off the main highway and onto a winding dirt road surrounded by tall trees. The car jostled as it labored over patches of snow-covered dirt. The tall pines blended into the thick darkness; the bright headlights barely cutting through the steady snowfall. Richard leaned forward a bit. "This is our first winter storm of the season." His hands gripped the steering wheel. "If it continues like this, we'll be stuck at the cabin for a few days."

"Stuck at the cabin?" Infiniti gulped. "That doesn't sound very good. Unless you have an endless supply of hot Cheetos and root beer, then I might be okay."

Richard laughed. "No Cheetos or pop, though I'm sure we can find you something. But don't let this weather scare you. It happens every year. Some years are worse than others." He peered out the windshield. "This isn't so bad."

Richard slowed until the two-story log cabin loomed into view. The brakes squeaked as we rolled to a stop by the front porch. Everyone started to pile out, except me. I needed a minute to think in silence. We had taken Trent against his will and now I was about to come face to face with him. Infiniti dashed to the front door with Richard and Fleet not far behind. Farrell waited for me by the porch, but came back to the car when he realized I wasn't getting out. He hopped back in and sat next to me.

Frigid air started creeping through the car, the warmth from the heater now long gone. My body shivered. "What does he know?" I couldn't even bring myself to say Trent's name, but I knew Farrell would know who I meant.

"Everything," Farrell said, rubbing my knee. "Your mom thought it best we come clean. You know, tell him exactly who we are and what we're up against. He also knows I've mind-wiped him."

My body twitched from the penetrating cold and the nervous feeling growing in the pit of my stomach. "How'd he take it?"

Farrell ran his fingers through his hair. "He said he wasn't going to talk to anyone until he could see you."

Great. Now I really felt like shit. Trent had to hate me. I knew it. And I couldn't blame him. Even I would hate me. Farrell inched closer. "Dominique, please tell me having Trent around won't change things between us."

Trent's presence definitely complicated things, but Farrell was the one for me. I had known it all along somewhere deep inside me. It just took my brain a little longer to catch up. My near ice-cold hands took Farrell's warm ones and held them tight. "When the plane was about to crash, you know what I thought of?"

He lifted a curious brow. "What?"

"You." I scooted closer to him. "And how much I love you, and how sorry I was that I had fought my feelings for you for so long, and how I regretted never telling you."

He cupped my face and stared into my eyes before bringing his lips close. He brushed them over mine. "I love you, you know."

My body shuddered while warmth spread inside me, the touch of his lips on mine sending me to another reality where nothing else existed but us. A reality I didn't want to leave.

"I love you, Farrell. More than I even know."

I leaned toward him and pressed up against his hard body, my deep desire for him taking me over completely. Our mouths became one. Our bodies pulsed in perfect rhythm. If we were alone, there'd be no stopping us.

With a groan, he slowly pulled away but kept his forehead pressed against mine. The car windows had steamed over. He caught his breath, and brushed the hair away from my face. "We better ease up before someone comes out here."

I didn't want the moment to end because I didn't know if we would ever have it again. But Farrell was right. Someone was bound to come out here and check on us. The sooner we went in, the better.

The cabin filled with the warm glow from a roaring fire. Infiniti sat on the hearth, palms up to the flames. Fleet hung back by the kitchen island with Richard and Sue. Mom rushed over and took me in her arms. "Oh, Dominique. I was so worried."

I hugged her back, holding her tight. "Me, too," I whispered. I craned my neck, searching for Trent, when he walked into the great room from another room just off the kitchen. Flashes of our last kiss in the rain filled my mind, making my stomach drop. Mom released me and studied my face. "I could sense something happening to you on the plane." Her face grew serious. "You need to tell me everything."

My gaze stayed glued on Trent. "I know. And I will, Mom. I just need to talk to Trent first. Okay?"

From the corner of my eye I could see Farrell turn his body away from me and stare out the back window.

Mom rubbed my shoulders. "Sure."

Trent crossed his arms while I made my way over to him. "Let's go back here," I said, leading the way back to the room he had just emerged from.

I sat on a small orange couch while Trent took the wooden rocking chair in the corner. Even though the room was closed in, freezing air oozed through the window panes

Trent locked his hands in a death grip. My mind raced while I tried to figure out what to say. "Trent," I said, my voice cracking. "I'm really sorry I've gotten you messed up in all this." I paused for a second, searching for the right words to say. "It's the last thing I wanted, believe me—"

"Bullshit!"

His reaction slapped me in the face, leaving me stunned and speechless.

"If you didn't want me mixed up in your shit, you would've left me the hell alone back in Houston!" He jumped to his feet. "But you didn't! Now I'm here—kidnapped!" He pointed at the window. "And my grandmother is back in Texas, all by herself!" He turned away from me and pounded his hands against the thick glass. "You had no right to do this to me."

My fingers scraped at my jeans. "Trent, I'm really—"

"Stop!" He spun around and narrowed his deep blue eyes at me. "I'm not interested in your excuses, got it?" He clenched his jaw. "And if you ever gave a damn about me, you'll help me get back home. You owe me that much."

I wanted to reach out to him, explain things my mother couldn't, but his hate-filled stare made it clear he had no intention of listening to anything I had to say. I swallowed hard, trying to steady my emotions. "I'll do what I can. I promise." He turned away from me and directed his attention to the falling snow outside. My hand went to my neck. "Oh, and one more thing. I, uh, lost your grandmother's cross on the plane. I'm really sorry."

His shoulders tightened. He kicked the basket on the floor. "Stay the hell away from me," he muttered.

With nothing else to say, I made my way back to the warmth of the den. Mom and Sue hovered over Infiniti, drilling her for info. When Infiniti saw me, she exhaled a sigh of relief. "It's been like *Criminal Minds* in here and I'm the freaking star witness," she said. "Even though I don't know what happened on that plane—other than we almost died!" Her hands shook. She brought them up and studied them. "I could really use a drink right about now. Or a smoke. Hell, I'd even settle for a bag of hot Cheetos."

Fleet kept his probing eyes on me while Farrell continued looking out the window. Seems every guy in the room had an issue with me, except for Richard. I took a seat near him and across from Infiniti, perching myself on the edge of the cushion, every sense on high alert. "I saw a Tainted on the plane."

"What?" Mom asked with eyes wide in alarm.

"No you didn't!" Fleet spat out.

"Hey!" Infiniti interjected. "If she says she saw a whatever it is, then she saw it! Okay?"

"There's no way," Fleet barked back. "My eyes were on her the whole time. If a Tainted was on that plane, I would've seen it." He crossed his arms. "She's lying."

A wave of confusion descended on me while everyone started arguing. I *had* seen her! Her olive eyes and pale face were clear in my mind. A whisper shot through my head. *"Nobody can see me. I'm a part of you."* The voice sounded like the young girl on the plane. I closed my eyes, straining to hear her again, wanting to be completely sure it was her. *"I'm going to kill you all. Every last one of you,"* she whispered.

Wind whistled through the fireplace. A chill crawled down my spine. That's when I noticed the silence. I opened my eyes to find myself on my feet, in the middle of the room. Infiniti's big brown eyes brimmed over with tears. Mom covered her mouth and stared at me. Fleet's eyes were narrowed with hostility. Sue and Richard held each other's arms.

I looked back at the chair where I had just been sitting, then down at my legs. How did I get from there to here? "What just happened?"

Fleet glared at me while Farrell approached and took my hand. Trent stayed back by the kitchen. I could see worry and confusion splashed across his face.

Richard spoke up. "You just said you were going to kill us."

"See? She's the traitor!" Fleet yelled. "I would've told you guys earlier, but I knew you wouldn't believe me!"

Mom jumped to my defense and even more arguing broke out. My head began to spin. My knees started to buckle. Farrell tightened his grip on my hand and helped me to the couch. "I've got you."

Did I really just threaten to kill them? I buried my hands in my face, desperate to hold back the sea of tears churning inside me. There was no way! I'd never hurt them, ever! But Mom would never lie—or Farrell. My mind buzzed with panic. Tingling sensations shot up and down my body. Farrell knelt before me and rubbed my knees. "We'll figure this out," he whispered. "I promise."

How could we figure something out we didn't understand?

I uncovered my face just as Trent joined Farrell on the floor before me. "I want to help," he said, offering an apologetic smile. "That's what friends do."

Infiniti crawled over too, leaving Mom and the others to their fighting. "I'm in," she winked, trying to make me feel better. "The faithful sidekick."

Farrell—my protector who had walked beside me for lifetimes; Infiniti and Trent—on their first life and now merged with my messed up existence—their offer made tears spring to my eyes—and something else spring up in my heart. Hope. Something inside me said that together we could do anything.

The hollering in the room stopped. Mom studied me with my friends gathered around. She came closer to us. "There is a traitor here, make no mistake. Otherwise, our car wouldn't have been ambushed."

"Exactly," Fleet chimed in.

"But we don't know who it is," Mom cautioned. "That much is certain." She paused, letting her words sink in. "All we can do is stick together and follow the plan."

"And what exactly is the plan?" Trent asked.

Mom straightened her shoulders. "The plan is to find out why the Tainted are still after Dominique and who attacked us back on that road. We had started searching the past for clues, and I think we should continue that course of action." She shot a glance at Fleet. "I also think we should be careful with our trust since someone in this room is against us."

Her words echoed in the room and hovered around us like an unwanted visitor. "We also need to find out what role, if any, these two first lifers have in all this. They may hold valuable information and not even know it."

"Whoa, what?" Infiniti asked.

"Us?" Trent added.

Before Mom could answer, the front door flew open and crashed against the wall. A gust of frigid air blasted through the house. Everyone rushed to the door. There on the porch stood Colleen. Her long black hair whipped across her face. She clutched her walking stick in her left hand. In the other, she gripped a tattered and worn book. I recognized it right away. It was the journal of Julian Huxley, the first professor of Biology at Rice University. We had moved to Houston to study his writings. When we found the book, we had hoped it held answers, but water damage had made it mostly illegible. The only thing we learned from it was how Huxley had studied and accidentally killed the young Pure named Abigail. We didn't find out until later that she had wanted him to kill her so that her energy source could later save me.

"Colleen?" Mom asked, shock evident on her face.

Colleen's eyes glazed over, like she didn't even see us. Farrell waved his hand back and forth in front of her face. She flinched, dropped the book, and said, "Trust no one."

Colleen's statuesque frame started to sway. Her eyes rolled back in her head.

"She's going down!" Infiniti called out.

Fleet and Farrell grabbed her arms just as she went limp. Richard collected the book and her staff. "Bring her in," he ordered. "Quick."

"I've got it," Farrell said. Everyone backed away from the door as Farrell scooped her up.

"Back here, in the study," Richard said, leading them through the house while the rest of us followed. He threw a stack of papers off the couch. Farrell set Colleen down gently. Mom went to her side and checked her wrist for a pulse. "She's alive, barely."

I thought of the time Farrell had healed Trent back in Houston. He had placed his hands on Trent while his aura oozed into Trent's body. Maybe he could do the same for Colleen. "Farrell, you need to help her," I said.

Mom brushed Colleen's hair away from her face. "It's too dangerous."

"What?" Richard asked. "Colleen is our friend and our elder."

"He's right," Sue added. "We have to do something." She frantically searched our faces, as if probing us to support her. But if Mom said no, there had to be a reason.

"Come on!" Richard pleaded. "The Walker has to heal her! He's the only one powerful enough!"

"No!" Mom hollered. She whipped her glare around to Richard. "The Walker is here to protect Dominique. He cannot compromise himself."

Colleen's face had paled over. Her chest barely showed signs of breathing. If Farrell had super healing powers, why couldn't he try to help her? "Mom," I whispered. "I don't get it. Why can't Farrell try?"

"Maybe Caris is a traitor, too. Like her daughter," Fleet sneered.

Mom's eyes widened. "That's absurd!"

Fleet pointed to Colleen, but kept his glare on Mom.

"She said it herself. Trust no one. Even you said one of us might be a traitor. That includes you, Caris."

"And you!" I snapped at Fleet.

If I had had a weapon, I would have killed Fleet without hesitation. I thought of the daggers I had used against Tavion in the red desert. Farrell had trained me to use them. I needed them now more than ever, but had no idea what had happened to them. Suddenly, I felt weak and vulnerable, and I didn't like it.

"Mom," I said. "We need to do something for Colleen. She needs—"

"Enough," Mom said. "I'm now the elder here, and what I say goes." She shot a warning glare at each of us. "Right now my concern is for Dominique—the Marked One. Even Colleen would agree if she could." She gently touched Colleen's shoulder before continuing. "Colleen stays in this room where we'll monitor her progress. The Walker will not assist her. And we stick with the plan."

And trust no one, I thought.

Chapter Eleven

Sleep—I desperately needed a good night's sleep. And by the looks of the dark circles around Infiniti's and Trent's eyes, they did, too. But where would we crash? With the growing suspicion in the house, nobody wanted to take their eyes off anyone else. Eventually we agreed that Richard and Sue would stay in the master bedroom like normal, Infiniti and I would take one of the rooms upstairs, and Trent would take the other. Mom said she'd be fine on the couch, and Farrell told everyone not to worry about him.

As for Fleet, he had grabbed a blanket off the couch and plopped down on a chair by the window.

When Infiniti and I crawled into bed, I expected a ton of questions. Instead, she lay eerily quiet.

"You okay?" I studied the splash of light from an outdoor floodlight that cut through the room.

She pulled the covers to her chin. "Dude, I'm freaking."

The supernatural never used to spook Infiniti. She played the Ouija board, had magical tarot-like cards, and smoked to "connect" with nature. If she was freaked, things had to be bad. I brought my covers up to my chin, too. "I know. Me, too. And I'm so sorry you're here with me and caught up in all this."

She turned to her side to face me. "No, it's not like that! I mean, crap, I thought you were dead! I'm just so confused about everything." She pushed her long wavy hair away from her tiny face. "Like I get most of it—these bad Transhumans called the Tainted want to kill you—but how do I fit in? You know, since I'm a first lifer like your mom said. And Trent, too. And then there's that energy thing Farrell tried to do to my mind that didn't work—what was that all about?" She scooted away from me. "And why did you, you know, say that back in the den?"

Yeah, what kind of friend would threaten to kill another? I brought the covers even closer to my chin and gripped the fabric tight. I sighed, seeing the fear in her eyes. "I could never hurt you, Infiniti. Never. I don't even remember saying that back there—or even getting up from my seat."

I sucked, big time, and didn't deserve Infiniti's friendship, or Trent's. Yet they were still willing to stand by me. And even though I regretted putting them in danger, I was relieved to have them on my side.

Infiniti gulped. "Really?"

"Really."

"Shit," she whispered.

"Total shit," I whispered back.

A blustery wind howled outside. The windows rattled. Richard and Sue had turned on the furnace, but it wasn't enough to drive out the cold air filling every crack and crevice in the house. Infiniti huddled into a ball. "And that mind thing with Farrell?"

"He can use his energy to wipe out memories. I've seen him do it before. It's safe and painless."

"Why didn't it work on me?"

It was a good question, and one I'd thought about off and on since leaving Trent's house back in Houston. "I don't know. We'll need to ask my mom in the morning."

Infiniti flung off her covers. "I'm freezing my ass off." She flicked the light switch, opened her duffle bag, and rummaged through her things. We had already borrowed sweatpants and sweatshirts from Sue, but given Infiniti's tiny frame, I could see how she'd still be cold. She pulled out some socks. She placed one pair on her feet and the other on her hands. She turned off the light and hopped back into bed.

"Better?" I asked.

"A little."

Another blanket of silence descended on the room. "So," Infiniti said, "what's up with you and Farrell?"

I had been waiting for her to ask me about him, especially since she loved talking about guys. "Well, apparently we've been in love in each lifetime."

"Whoa," she whispered. "You have?"

"Yeah."

"Oh my God, that's insane." She buried her hands under her pillow and propped her head up a little. "And totally cool. Do you remember any of it?"

I sat up, grabbed a lock of hair, and twisted it tight around my finger. Moments of familiarity with Farrell would come to me now and again, but hadn't in a while. And back on the plane, I had tried to call out to him but couldn't get through. Was our connection severed somehow? And if so, what did it mean?

"Well? Do you?" she pressed.

"I used to have flashes of memories with him, but they've stopped." I lay back down, my mind deciphering the possible reasons why glimpses of the past with Farrell had suddenly stopped.

"But you've chosen him, right? Over Trent? He's the one?"

Deep emotions for Farrell had rooted in me. Whether they were really mine or a mixture of memories of the past didn't matter anymore. He was in me. In my heart. In my soul. In my everything. And even though Trent was amazing, he couldn't compare. Nobody could. "Farrell has always been the one."

She sighed and draped her sock-covered hand over her forehead. "That's so romantic."

"Well, romance aside, nothing matters right now except staying alive."

Her mouth stretched into a huge yawn. "You're right. So, we ask your mom about why the mind thing didn't work on me," she whispered, her voice trailing off a bit. "And do the whatever it is your mom said about visiting the past."

"Yeah."

"Maybe I can call home. You know, just to check in."

Mom had taken Trent's and Infiniti's phones as soon as they had arrived at the cabin. She even confiscated mine back in Houston before we left. I didn't think she'd let Infiniti use hers, but didn't want to say so. "Sure," I whispered.

She yawned again. "And you and Farrell are together."

My lips tingled at the thought of his kiss. "Yes."

She nestled her head into her pillow. "Hey, does Trent know?"

Even though I hadn't said anything to him, and for sure no one else had either, it seemed like Trent knew how I felt about Farrell. Or maybe he was just pissed about being taken from Houston and his anger had nothing to do with me and Farrell. I sighed. "I don't know if he knows. I mean, I think so. Maybe I should tell him. Or maybe I'm just being stupid and he really doesn't care. What do you think?"

Infiniti didn't answer. "Hey, you listening?"

A light nasally snore that sounded like humming came from her. I turned to my side and faced the wall. I had no idea what to do about Trent, or anything else for that matter. And even though I wanted to pick apart the events of the last two days, I couldn't. Exhaustion overwhelmed me. I closed my eyes with one last thought—something I knew for sure. I needed to prepare myself for a final stand with the Tainted.

No matter what.

***

Bright sunlight filled the room, I could tell from the red glow inside my eyelids. Instead of getting up right away, I lay still, too tired to move. As much as I wished it wasn't morning yet, the smell of coffee wafting upstairs told me otherwise. Infiniti's snores continued to fill the air. Footsteps creaked in the hallway. I shifted from my side to my back and rubbed the sleep from my eyes as the door to my room cracked open. Mom entered the room. She closed the door behind her and brought her finger to her mouth, silencing me.

The mattress shifted under her weight as she sat beside me. "Dominique, we can't stay here."

A blast of panic jerked me upright. "What?"

She brought her finger to her mouth again and eyed sleeping Infiniti. "It's not safe for us here."

My gut wrenched, my thoughts taking me to the others. "What about Farrell and Trent?" My gaze landed on Infiniti, her thick and wavy dark hair halfway covering her face. "And Infiniti? What about them?"

She gripped my arm and held me tight. "We stick with the plan: visit the past and gather clues. Once we have all the information we need, we're leaving." She dug her fingers into my skin. "Okay? And no one can know. We can't trust anyone."

I couldn't believe my ears. She wanted to leave the others behind? And what about Farrell? She and my dad were the ones who insisted I needed his protection, saying he could be trusted. And now that I had fallen for him, she wanted to up and bolt? It didn't make sense.

"Do you hear me?" she asked through gritted teeth.

Yeah, I heard her, but something was way wrong. Maybe the shock of losing Dad had sent her over the deep end. Or maybe, like Fleet had said, she was the traitor. My stomach turned at the thought of Mom's betrayal. Though after everything that had happened so far, nothing seemed impossible anymore. I had to keep cool and go along until I could figure it out. "I hear you."

"Hear what?" Infiniti mumbled, pulling the curtain of hair away from her face.

"Hear that breakfast is ready," Mom said with a smile. "I've been calling you girls to come downstairs."

Infiniti stretched. "Really? Wow, I didn't hear a thing."

Mom patted my leg. "You girls must've been exhausted. Now that the day is upon us and we have lots to do, it's time to get up." She made her way to the door. "I'll see you downstairs."

After getting ready, we made our way to the main floor and found Mom, Sue, and Richard at the kitchen table, drinking coffee. Farrell stood by the fireplace, his face set and arms crossed, obviously waiting for me to emerge from upstairs. His stance relaxed a bit when we made eye contact.

"Good morning," Sue said.

"Good morning," Infiniti and I answered.

Infiniti headed to the kitchen and the food while I searched the room for Fleet and Trent. "Where are the others?"

Richard handed me a glass of juice. "Fleet is in the study watching over Colleen. Your friend Trent went outside."

I sipped the bitter juice and made my way over to the study. Fleet snoozed in a chair in the corner. Colleen lay still on the sofa. The only sign of life was the slow rise and fall of her chest. I studied her model-like features and wondered why we couldn't reach her when we were driving from Houston to Michigan. Where had she been? And why had she appeared now? Her pale lips parted. Her throat moved up and down from a swallow.

"Caris," she whispered.

I let out a gasp and nearly dropped my glass.

Fleet woke and shot up to his feet. "What the hell?"

My gaze stayed on Colleen's still body. Her lips pressed together again. Did she really just utter Mom's name? Was it a warning not to trust her? Or was I imagining things? I backed up to the doorway and waited for her to say something else.

Fleet turned his attention to Colleen, then back at me. "Did she move?"

No way could I tell him Colleen had just whispered my mom's name. It would only aggravate the mounting suspicion already in the house. "No. I, uh, was just checking on her and almost," I raised my glass, "spilled my juice. Sorry."

I spun around and got out of there before Fleet could press me further. I plunked my glass into the kitchen sink and made my way to the sliding glass door behind the table. A bright blue sky had replaced the snowy downpour and a thick blanket of snow covered the ground. I spotted Trent's deep footprints leading down the path toward the river. Intense guilt at the thought of abandoning him and Infiniti and even Farrell burned inside me.

"He'll be fine," Mom said, apparently following my gaze. "Now come eat, Dominique. You're going to need your energy for the time-jumping."

I ignored Mom and continued peering through the glass. I thought of everything we'd done to Trent so far. Including how Farrell had erased his memories after our two confrontations with Tavion. If we were going to abandon him, he deserved to know exactly what we'd been through. With his memories back, he'd remember unleashing the energy in the bloodstone cross that brought me back to life, allowing me to finally end Tavion. He'd also get back moments of tenderness between us—moments I wanted him to remember. It was the least I could do for him.

"Farrell, can you give someone their memories back after you've wiped them?"

He shot Mom a curious look before answering my question. "Yes, I can."

"Good." I strode to the front door and yanked three jackets off their hooks. Back in the kitchen, I tossed one to Infiniti and the other to Farrell. "We're giving Trent his memories back."

Mom latched onto my arm and squeezed. "No, you're not."

I pulled away from her, certain that Colleen was warning me about my mother. "Yes, I am. If you expect me to—" I stopped. I wanted to say that if she expected me to dump my friends, then she better not stand in my way. Instead, I continued with, "—do what you want, let me do this one thing. Okay?"

A suffocating tension filled the room while Mom and I faced off.

"Fine," Mom said. "But be quick about it."

I stomped out of the house and down the path to the river, anger and confusion consuming me. I didn't even look to see if Infiniti and Farrell would follow, but heard their trudging footsteps behind me.

"Whoa," Infiniti said, now at my side. "You want to tell me what the hell happened back there?"

What happened was that my mom was forcing me to

do something I didn't want to do. That's what. But doing an act I knew she wouldn't like gave me a little control—no matter how small. And as much as I wanted to tell Infiniti the truth, I couldn't. "Nothing," I finally responded. "I guess I'm just tired of all this, ya know?" I lowered my voice. "And I want to do something for Trent."

Infiniti considered my words. "I see."

Farrell stayed silent.

The full heat of the bright sun warmed the air, and the three of us peeled off our jackets. When we got to the fire pit, we found Trent sitting on a log, staring at the charred wood. He glanced at Infiniti and me as we joined him. Farrell stayed on his feet, keeping his distance from the group.

Trent rubbed his hands across his jeans, almost gripping his knees. "So, you couldn't take the weirdness in there either?"

Infiniti's shoulders relaxed. "Oh my God! I know! Everyone in there is like freakin' nuts or something!"

"You don't even know the half of it," I added with a nervous laugh. I angled my body towards Trent. "But you can, if you want."

Trent gave me a puzzled look. "Huh?"

"Your memories," I said nervously. "The ones we took from you. You can have them back if you want."

He shifted his body to me. "Seriously? You can give me my memories back?"

"Well, not me." I motioned to Farrell. "But Farrell can."

"If you want them back," Farrell interjected.

Trent got up, shoved his hands in his jeans pocket,

and walked to the other side of the pit. "I don't know," he murmured. "I've done fine without them, so I'm not so sure I want them back."

Nervousness tightened my gut. I wanted Trent to remember everything. I needed him to know how he had saved me, longed for him to understand how special he was to me. Maybe then he'd forgive me for dragging him into this mess.

"It'll help you understand," I said.

He stopped in his tracks, as if considering my words. I bit the inside of my cheek as I waited for his answer. "Fine," he said. "I'll do it."

A feeling of relief swelled inside me, but faded fast because I had no idea how Trent would react to his stolen memories. "Thanks, Trent." I turned to Farrell. "I guess go ahead and do your thing."

Chunks of charred wood poked out of a round pile of snow. Farrell grabbed some fresh wood nearby and threw it on the pile. He flicked out a burst of white electricity, igniting the timber and creating a small bonfire.

Infiniti's jaw dropped. "Whoa." She leaned in and whispered in my ear. "Now he brings new meaning to the word hot."

I muffled a laugh and gave her a push. "Be serious," I whispered.

"I'm dead serious," she said.

"You just lit that with your aura," Trent said to Farrell, looking stunned and confused. "It's the same thing I saw back at my house before you brought me here."

"Yes," Farrell said. "I used my power source." He approached Trent with caution. "Some call it an aura, but it's really the manipulation of the energy in and around you. You'll understand everything in a minute."

Trent removed his jacket and threw it on a nearby bench. He fisted his hands at his side and clenched his jaw. "I'm ready."

The fire's crackling filled the silent winter air. Infiniti scooted next to me on the bench, pressing her body against mine. Even though heat burned from the logs, my body shivered with anticipation and fear. Would Trent be okay? And how would he react after getting his memories back?

I studied Farrell's perfectly sculpted face as white mist poured out of his hands and coiled around his arms. His bright green eyes started filling with flecks of white light. He lifted his hands and brought them closer to Trent's head. "Be still."

Trent nodded, his tan face and sapphire eyes set in deep concentration. He widened his stance and waited.

Farrell placed his fingertips on Trent's temples. Trent gasped while his body snapped rigid. His head flew back. His eyes rolled. I jumped to my feet, ready to break their contact, when Infiniti grabbed my arm. "Wait," she said.

Farrell's body blazed with a brilliant white blast. With a crackle, the white light streamed to his hands and shot into Trent's skin. Trent's body spasmed. Guttural groans sounded through his teeth. I lurched forward. I couldn't let anything happen to Trent. I just couldn't. Infiniti jerked me back. "He wanted this."

Trent wanted his erased memories, but did he want them back like this?

Trent's body seized. His feet left the ground. I was just about to push Infiniti away and charge for Trent when a blue misty hue trickled out of Trent's hands. It oozed over his skin and covered his entire body, like a protective force field.

"What the hell?" I whispered.

Infiniti tugged me away from Trent and Farrell. I stumbled back a little when an electrical humming filled my ears. The sound came from Trent *and* Farrell. It increased in volume as their auras grew bigger and brighter—one white, the other blue. I covered my ears—the buzz so loud it shook me through to my core.

With a thundering blast, a bolt of multi-colored light shot from them, flinging them apart.

Farrell landed on his feet, while Trent crashed to the ground.

I clasped my hands over my mouth. "Trent," I muttered.

Farrell rushed to Trent's side. "I didn't know," he whispered, checking for a pulse. Trent's chest didn't move. His breathing had completely stopped.

"No, no, no," I whispered.

Farrell blasted a stream of energy at Trent's chest, right over his heart. Trent's back arched and his legs kicked before going limp. Farrell waited a second and then blasted him again. This time Trent gulped for air. Relief covered Farrell's face as he got up, ran his fingers though his hair, and kicked at a pile of snow. "I should've known!"

Trent peeled open his eyes. He winced, rubbed his chest, and struggled to get up. Infiniti and I helped him to the bench. I knelt before Trent and studied his face, waiting to see if he was okay and wondering if his memories had been restored.

Infiniti backed away, giving me and Trent space. I rubbed his knees. "Hey, you okay?"

His bloodshot eyes were a million miles away—confused and unfocused. Singe marks riddled his shirt. I ran my fingers through his disheveled hair, waiting for him to notice me.

"Trent. Can you hear me?"

He zeroed in on me. His eyes softened. He leaned forward and cupped my face in his warm hands. "Dominique," he whispered. "You died. In that red desert. I saw it."

Tears spilled out onto my face as every single moment of our ordeal flooded my awareness. My palm throbbed where I had sliced it with my dagger. The taste of metallic blood filled my mouth. I even thought I could feel the desert heat stinging my lungs. And then I remembered how Trent had straightened out my splayed body and brushed the blood-matted hair away from my face.

Trent wiped the tears from my face. "I brought you back when I touched the cross."

Words escaped me and all I could do was nod.

"The energy source in it responded to my touch," he said, his voice in awe as if he were reliving the moment. "And you came back."

"Yes," I managed to squeak out. "And we wiped your memories to protect you."

He joined me on the ground and wrapped his arms around me, burying his head in the crook of my neck. "I'm so sorry, Dominique."

I slipped my arms around him and squeezed. The familiar soapy scent from him took me back to every minute I had shared with him in Houston. And for just a second there, I really missed him.

Trent released his hold on me and looked over my shoulder. "You said you should've known," he said to Farrell. He got up, helped me to my feet, and narrowed his gaze at Farrell. "Should've known what?"

A flash of pain and disappointment darted across Farrell's face, and I knew it was because of the moment I had just shared with Trent. He erased it quickly and straightened his back. "That you're one of us," Farrell said. "A Transhuman. We suspected it because of your ability to see auras. Now I know for sure."

Trent's eyebrows shot up. "What the hell are you talking about?"

"And not just any Transhuman, but a very powerful one," Farrell said. "You might even be—"

Farrell stopped. His body tensed. He looked around, as if hearing something none of us could. "They're coming."

Chapter Twelve

Farrell hurried over to me and frantically studied my eyes. I started to freak. "Farrell! What are you—?"

A blast of light shot up into the sky right over the cabin. Shock overtook me, followed by a sharp stabbing that pierced every nerve in my body. I collapsed to the ground, writhing in pain.

"Dominique!" Farrell called out.

My vision blurred. My head pounded. I closed my eyes and slammed my hands over my ears, screaming for the torment to stop.

A firm grip held my arms. Fingers dug into my skin. "Concentrate on your light!" Farrell hollered from right in front of me. "Make it dim!"

My light?

My hands shook. My body jerked. I brought my fingers to my face and cracked my eyes open. A glowing multi-colored mist shone through me. My energy source! My aura! It was bursting through my skin!

The pain permeated my insides, like a hot poker raking through me. I tried to concentrate on what Farrell had said, but couldn't. I grabbed my gut, and doubled over, the heat inside me unbearable. "Help. Me."

Trent's and Infiniti's faces came into view. They shouted out at me, but I couldn't hear them above the ringing in my ears and the searing pain ripping through my flesh.

Another blast sounded in the distance. I knew it came from the cabin. I knew something horrible was happening to the others.

Farrell's face loomed before me. His eyes blazed with anger and worry. "I'm going to use my strength to contain your shield!" he hollered. "Hold on!"

Warm white vapor encircled him, radiating from him like a soothing beam of sunlight. It seeped out of him and crawled over every inch of me, calming me until the pain subsided.

"My shield," I panted, desperately grabbing his shirt as I struggled to my feet. "My mom."

With Dad dead, Mom was the only one shielding me from the Tainted. And if my aura could be seen, that meant my protection was gone and Mom was in danger. Or maybe even dead.

"I know," Farrell said.

The ground shook beneath my feet. My body swayed. An explosion tore the soil around me, like an earthquake. Farrell grabbed my hand just as the earth began to split and separate. He pulled me away before the ground cratered open with a jolt.

"What is going on?" Infiniti cried.

"We need to get out of here," Trent said. "Now!"

"My energy source can only contain Dominique's for so long," Farrell said, his brow creased and his face strained. He stared in the direction of the house. "I need to go back. I need to help Caris."

I didn't want him to go, couldn't bear something

happening to him, but he was right. He had to go back for Mom. I couldn't lose another parent—even if she was acting weird. Plus, I needed her to shield me, especially since Farrell didn't look like he could manage it much longer.

Before Farrell could make a move, three black cloaked figures materialized in front of us—two bulky ones and a smaller petite one. I knew them right away. They were the same figures that appeared on the road and caused our crash. The petite one had even visited me on the plane.

They were members of the Tainted.

And they were going to kill us.

Farrell pushed me and Infiniti behind him. Trent sidled up next to him and together they shielded us with their bodies. Infiniti huddled beside me. "Oh, shit," Infiniti whispered. "Shit, shit, shit."

Farrell held his hands behind his back, hiding them from the Tainted. Small flickers of light burst and faded from his fingertips. His hands quivered. His body shook. And that's when it dawned on me. He was trying to release his power, but couldn't because he had diverted his energy to shield me!

Terror ripped through me. People were going to die again, I just knew it.

The young girl stepped forward and pulled back her hood. She leaned to the side, craned her neck, and made eye contact with me. "Come, Marked One." She extended her hand. "I promise we won't hurt your friends."

Our gaze connected while a multitude of emotions paralyzed me—fear and panic, followed by familiarity and warmth.

"Come," she said in my head. "You know you want to."

And I did. I wanted to go with her. I even longed to take her hand, despite the sliver of doubt and hesitation that fluttered inside me. I stepped out from behind Farrell, ready to leave my friends, when strong arms wrapped around me in a bear hug.

"Oh, no you don't," Trent said with a squeeze.

Before I could react, Farrell flung out his arms. A burst of light shot up into the air and descended on Farrell, Trent, Infiniti and me, encasing us in a protective bubble of shimmery white radiance.

The girl frowned. Her tiny innocent face turned deadly. "Get them!" she called out. The two bulky Tainted figures fired a barrage of flame-filled blasts at the shimmery dome. One after the other, the flare-like torpedoes careened off the shield, lighting the area in a bath of sparks and smoky blasts.

Trent wrapped his arms tighter around me. "Get us the hell out of here!" he hollered at Farrell. "Now!"

Farrell's legs buckled. His face paled over. He staggered a step to the left, struggling to right himself. Little red lines formed under his skin and streaked out like a web. He collapsed to his knees. "I… can't."

My desire to go with the girl lessened. My body eased up. My mind now consumed with worry for Farrell. "Farrell?"

His bloodshot eyes went in and out of focus, and I don't think he even heard me. "I can't hold them," he stammered. "Trent, you have to do it."

"Me?" Trent asked as a shower of sparks rained

down, repelling off the shimmery force that Farrell had created.

Farrell slammed his frigid hand on my arm. "Everyone, hold Dominique."

Trent kept his arms around mine. He twisted his hands and grasped my wrists. Infiniti reached in and grabbed on, too.

"Think of a safe place," Farrell mumbled to Trent, his eyes starting to roll back, his head drooping to his chest.

Trent closed his eyes, murmuring something over and over to himself. I knew he was trying, but I didn't think he could do it.

We were doomed.

Trent kept chanting while crashing blasts of energy from the Tainted slammed against our protective bubble. Effervescent sparks blasted overhead. The gleaming vapor started to disintegrate and stretch out in patches. With her eyes on me, the girl poked her fingers through a thin spot. She stretched out her arm, just brushing my hair with her fingertips, when everything went black.

A rush of warm air whooshed around me. My body slipped into a free fall. I squeezed my eyes shut, letting the weightlessness take me, until I landed with a thud on top of Trent and onto a flat surface.

His arms were still wrapped around me. A stunned expression covered his face. He released me and patted my arms. "You okay?"

I scrambled to me feet and helped him up. "Yeah, I'm fine."

Trent dusted off his jeans and surveyed the area. I followed his gaze and immediately recognized where we were—St. Joseph's, Trent's church in Houston. I had seen Abigail here, the Pure who had died for me so that her energy source could later bring me back to life. It made sense that this was Trent's safe place. But where were the others?

"Um, guys?" Infiniti sat up from an area just off to the left. She rubbed her head. "What the hell just happened?"

My eyes darted up and down the nearby benches. My chest tightened with terror. Where was Farrell? I dashed to the rear of the church—empty. I sprinted to the front. Trent and Infiniti trailed behind me, calling out his name.

Please, let him be up here.

He lay face down, just on the other side of the first pew. I pressed my fist to my mouth. Tears stung my eyes. My throat tightened.

He can't be dead. He just can't.

I crashed to my knees and stared at his lifeless body, afraid to touch him. Infiniti and Trent halted beside me, both of them staring open-mouthed at Farrell's still form.

"Is he dead?" Infiniti whispered.

I pressed my face down on the marble floor and leaned in to get a good look. The red lines under Farrell's skin were now splotchy and purple. Blood trickled from his mouth and nose. I reached a shaky hand forward, worried what touching him might do to me, but needing to anyway. Pressing my fingers to the side of his neck, I prayed for a pulse, even as his ice cold skin sent shivers racing through me.

Nothing.

I pushed harder, desperate for a sign of life, when a faint irregular throbbing thrummed against my fingertips. I exhaled. "He's alive."

"Oh, thank God," Infiniti said. She looked up at the looming crucifix above the church altar. "You, too."

"Maybe we should turn him over," Trent suggested.

Injury victims like this weren't supposed to be moved. Then again, Farrell wasn't a regular human. He had powers. He could heal himself. At least that's what I hoped, since he had done it in the past. We just needed to get him up and to a place of safety. Especially since someone could walk into the church at any moment.

The three of us worked our hands under Farrell and eased him over to his back. I stroked his clammy cheek and wiped the blood from his face with my sleeve.

"Now what?" Infiniti asked.

I scanned the church. A haze of sunlight trickled through the stained glass windows lining the side of the church. Even though I had been here just once, for midnight mass on Christmas Eve with Trent and his grandmother, I could tell right away that the place looked… different.

"This isn't right," Trent stammered. He pointed to the empty space on the wall over the altar. "There's supposed to be stained glass right there."

A door slammed in the rear of the church. Infiniti let out a startled yelp while my heart nearly shot out of me. We spun around to see who was coming.

A tall nun dressed in black from head to toe marched up the aisle toward us. A long silver rosary around her neck swayed back and forth with each stride. "What is the meaning of this? What are you doing in here? The church is closed!" Her long black skirt swished across the floor. A white collar went from her chest up to her chin. It stood out from the rest of her dark clothing, as did her pale face that streaked with permanent frown lines.

"Um, uh, we, uh—" I couldn't think of what to say when I studied Farrell's limp body on the floor and still out of the sister's view. Maybe this nun could help us. "My friend is hurt."

"Is he now?" She swung her arms with authority. "I will be the judge of that."

The closer she got the more familiar she seemed—her tall and commanding stature, her booming voice. Even a hint of vanilla wafted my way. That's when I figured it out. She looked and sounded exactly like Jan Kelly, my neighbor from back home. And the vanilla, I always smelled it around her. Even though she had visited me from the dead, this living person dressed as a nun couldn't be her.

Could it?

Infiniti let out a gasp and tugged my shirt. She recognized her, too!

"Jan?" Infiniti asked in a hesitant voice. "Is that... you?"

The nun came to an abrupt halt and studied our faces. "I am Sister Mary Johanna. There is no Sister Jan in my Order." She huffed. "Now which of you is injured?"

"My friend. Over here." I stepped back and pointed to the floor.

The nun glided around me and stopped when she saw Farrell. She crouched down and touched his forehead. As if in slow motion, she rose to her feet and closed her eyes, clutching the long rosary that hung around her neck. "There will be four of them, looking out of time. One will be injured. And they will need your help."

The nun's deep voice bounced off the walls, echoing all around us. Goosebumps cascaded along my skin. Trent, Infiniti, and I stood there, dumbfounded. After a few seconds, I broke the silence. "What did you say?"

She dropped her rosary and made the sign of the cross. She pointed at Trent. "You, take his upper body." She nodded at me and Infiniti. "You two, take his legs. And follow me. Quick."

I had no idea what was happening, and I definitely didn't understand what the Sister had said. All I knew was that she was going to help us. And we desperately needed it. I just hoped it wasn't too late.

Infiniti, Trent, and I lifted Farrell and followed the Sister back down the center aisle and to the church door. She motioned us to stay behind her as she cracked it, poked her head out, and looked both ways before opening it all the way. Sunlight poured into the church.

"To the left," she commanded.

We passed over the threshold, angling Farrell's long and muscular body just a tad, and curved to the left. The Sister quietly closed the door after us and slid back up to the front. "This way."

I kept my gaze on Farrell, waiting for him to snap out of it, when I noticed Trent looking around with a puzzled look on his face. I followed his line of sight.

The last time I was here was at night for Christmas Eve mass with Trent and his grandmother. I remembered the area being in a populated neighborhood with lots of trees near the downtown Houston skyline and a busy street. Looking at it now in full daylight, you'd think we were in a deserted town. Even the paved parking lot in the front of the church was covered over with dirt and gravel. Maybe the area was undergoing some sort of major reconstruction.

"What the—" Infiniti called out, dropping Farrell's leg. She snatched it up before it hit the ground. "Do you guys see what I'm seeing?"

I examined the area again, really studying our surroundings, when I spotted a couple of cars parked nearby. They were jet black with oversized wheels. The body of the car was boxy and square, with two small windows on each side. I had seen cars like this before, in old-timey gangster movies. I thought of what the Sister had said back in the church, about needing to help people out of time.

"Where are we?" I asked out loud, a sinking feeling settling in my gut.

Trent gaped at the nearby cars, his tan face now ghost white. "I don't know."

"Hurry along," Sister Mary Johanna ordered.

She led us across a grassy open space to a nearby house. The simple one-story, white house had a deep wrap-around porch. Another sister, dressed head to toe in the same black nun outfit, worked in the garden. When she saw us, she jumped to her feet.

"Mother Superior!" Her mouth dropped at the sight of us, and I couldn't blame her. Three teens carrying a limp body? Definitely not something you see every day.

"Sister Mary Catherine, I am taking this boy inside. He has fallen ill." She breezed past her up the steps to the front door. She held it open for us. A round brass plaque over the doorframe read Sisters of the Incarnate Word.

"And Sister Mary Catherine, you are not to speak of this. Understand?"

The young nun bowed low. "Yes, Mother Superior."

Infiniti's eyes widened as she mouthed the words Mother Superior to me.

Well, if we were going to get help, it might as well be from the head of a group of nuns. Perhaps, with divine intervention on our side, we'd gain some sort of advantage over the Tainted.

The interior of the house looked just as plain as the outside. All the walls were white, the floors a dull yellowed wood. The uneven planks creaked with each step, reminding me of the cabin back at the Boardman River. Immediately I thought of the blasts that erupted over the house. Worry for my mom and the others twisted my gut.

Please, let them be okay.

We followed the Sister through an empty sitting room, down a narrow hallway, and to a back bedroom. We lowered Farrell onto the small iron-framed bed. An oversized bronze crucifix hung over the headboard. I went to Farrell's side and placed my hand on his forehead. His skin had started to warm, the lines on his face fading.

"He's better," I said, relieved about Farrell, yet freaked about where we were.

The Sister crossed her arms, and studied us from head to toe. "Where are you from?"

"From?" Trent paced the room. "I'm from Houston, and St. Joseph's is my church. I've been going there since I was little. I was baptized and confirmed there." He ran his fingers through his thick brown hair and jerked his finger at the wall. "But that out there is not my church!"

I took his hand and squeezed, trying to calm him down. "I think the question is not where we're from, but when." My words lingered in the air. "Before arriving in the church, we were in Michigan, being attacked by these—" I stopped, unsure how much I should tell the nun. "Evil people. It was February, 2012."

The Sister's eyes darted to the crucifix on the wall as she made the sign of the cross over and over up and down across her chest.

"I'm freaking out right now," Infiniti whispered while she chewed on her nails.

"Mother Superior," I said, clearing my voice and trying to be calm and rational. "I know we're in Houston, I've been to St. Joseph's Church, too. But what… year is it?"

"It is the year of our Lord nineteen hundred and thirty."

Trent stumbled back onto a small wooden chair in the corner of the room. Infiniti slapped her hands over her mouth. My knees almost buckled. "What?" I asked, trying to wrap my head around the fact that we had just time-traveled. Not the time jumping Farrell and I had done with Sue. This was the real deal. "We're back in the thirties? As in the Great Depression? Big bands? Prohibition?"

The Mother Superior's eyes went wide before narrowing on us suspiciously. "That is correct, my child."

Infiniti moaned. "Oh, no. It can't be. There's no alcohol?"

I crossed my arms and glared at her. "Seriously?"

She shrugged her shoulders. "Dude! I'm just saying!"

Mother Superior backed away, as if afraid of us. "Let me get some water for your friend. Please, stay here."

She exited the room with a whoosh, followed by a clicking sound from the door. I rushed over and jiggled the small brass doorknob—locked.

Infiniti slammed her hands against the white door. "Hey! Let us out!"

I pushed and pulled the decorative knob. It wouldn't give. I slumped to the floor. Infiniti crashed down next to me. "Oh my God," she muttered. "We time-travelled, and now we're trapped in here by a creepy nun."

"She's not going to hurt us," Trent said. "She's just scared."

I wrapped my arms around my knees, unsure how Trent could possibly know that but going with his theory anyway. "We have bigger problems than a scared nun. Farrell is out. Something horrible is happening to my mom and the others back at the cabin. And now we're not even in the same century as them."

"Hey, your shield thingy," Infiniti said. "That light burst through you and Farrell stopped it." She picked up my hand and studied my fingers. "Now that he's out cold, how come the light isn't coming out of you again?"

My hand quivered. I pulled it back. "I guess my mom must be okay. Or maybe Farrell is still shielding me and we don't even know it."

Farrell shifted in bed. A small moan escaped his lips. Infiniti and I hurried to his side. He needed to wake up. He'd know about my shield and what was happening. He had to. And hopefully he could get us out of the thirties and back to our own time since we definitely didn't belong here.

Trent pressed his chair against the wall and

thrummed idle fingers against his thighs. Infiniti and I hovered over Farrell, waiting with baited breath for him to wake up. A series of groans escaped his lips, followed by mumbling.

"He's coming to," I said with relief.

Farrell sat up slowly and rubbed his head. The dark lines on his face had almost faded away. "Where am I?"

Relieved that he was okay, I stroked his arm. "When you told Trent to think of a safe place, we ended up in his church. In Houston." I stopped, not sure if I should mention the time change yet. "A nun brought us to her house. You were really out of it."

He pulled his arm away from me, tilted his head, and studied my face. "Do I know you?"

Chapter Thirteen

Shock muffled me. My breathing stopped. Trent joined me and Infiniti at the foot of the bed, alarm plastered across his face.

Farrell swung his legs over the bed and examined us. "Am I supposed to know the three of you?"

Infiniti lost it. "Are you kidding me? You're like the protector guy and now you don't remember us?" She grasped Trent's shirt and yanked. "He doesn't remember us!" Her voice rose until it reached a full out scream. "We're screwed! Completely and totally screwed! Stuck in a world with no alcohol! No cell phones!" She started to hyperventilate. "I'm supposed to graduate! Go to A&M! Date a ton of hot guys! And now I'm stuck in a time with shitty clothes and crappy makeup!"

She may have been right, but she needed to pull it together. "Infiniti! Calm the hell down!" I shouted.

She continued to rant, pulling at her collar and gasping for breath. I had never seen a panic attack before, but I was pretty sure this was it. I needed her to snap out of it. I grabbed her shoulders and slapped her cheek. She gasped, tears springing to her eyes.

"I'm sorry, Infiniti. But you need to get a grip."

Her bottom lip quivered. "O-k-k-ay," she whimpered.

Farrell hopped to his feet, his gaze still glued on us.

Suspicion filled his eyes. "I need someone to explain what's happening. Now."

My slap had muted Infiniti. Even Trent had gone back to the corner chair, his head down, and hands clasped around his neck. "Go ahead, Dominique," Trent muttered. "This is your story."

"Dominique?" Farrell asked.

Heartache, disbelief, and fear overflowed inside me. Did he really not know me? And then I thought of how in each life I had remembered him less and less until this life, life number nine, I didn't know him at all. Besides flashes of familiarity and moments of remembering, it was like we had just met for the first time. Now I understood the pain he had endured.

"Yes, I'm Dominique. That's Infiniti and Trent." I tried to hide my devastation while I eased myself onto the edge of the bed, my legs shaky. "We're your friends."

Farrell remained silent and studied me with attentive eyes while I explained everything to him—how the Transhumans split into the Pure and Tainted, how they were at war, how they decided to fight over just one soul, how that one soul was mine, how he had been my protector for lifetimes, and how Trent had ended up helping me kill Tavion. Lastly, I told him how we were still under attack and had time jumped to 1930.

I could've gone into a ton more, like how I kept hearing Tavion's voice telling me to kill people and how I had wanted to go with the creepy Tainted girl, but I didn't want to overwhelm him. Besides, other than what had happened back in the den at the cabin, the others had no idea about the voices in my head.

Farrell paced the room. "I know what I am. I just don't who I am," he mumbled to himself. He stopped and studied his hands while a white misty vapor oozed out and wrapped around his wrists. When the haze faded, he came up to me and took my arm, assuming his role as my guardian. "We need to get back to our time and regroup with the other Pures, especially since it may take a while for my memory to return."

Hope fluttered inside me. "It'll return?"

"It should," he said with a grave look on his face. "And if what you say is true, I hope it returns quickly. This is not our time and we need to get back right away."

"Whoa," Infiniti muttered. Still pale from losing it, she made her way to the center of the room. "Hold on a sec," she said, regaining her voice. "Nobody is going anywhere."

Farrell eyed Infiniti. He released my arm, yet stayed close. "Explain."

"It may sound crazy, but we're here for a reason." Color flooded her cheeks. She placed her hands on her hips. "Just before we zapped into this time, you said Trent was a powerful Transhuman."

Trent shifted in his seat. "Leave me out of this, Infiniti."

Infiniti ignored Trent. So did Farrell. "I said that?" Farrell asked. He furrowed his brow while he considered her words.

Infiniti continued. "Yep, you did. I'm telling you, Trent brought us to this place and time, and there has to be a reason. I can feel it in my bones." She wrapped her arms around herself, as if she'd gotten a sudden chill. "He must have some sort of power in him."

Trent leapt to his feet and held up his hands. "Okay, enough. I may be able to see people's auras, but I'm not a Transwhatever."

Farrell narrowed his gaze at Trent. "You're like me?"

"Pftt. I'm nothing like you."

Hostility from Trent oozed through the air, the tension so thick you could slice it with a dagger.

"There's a lot of anger in you," Farrell said to Trent, clenching his jaw. "And a strong energy supply." He took two long strides toward Trent. "You're not a threat, are you?"

"No!" I glided between them. "Trent's on our side. He's just mad because he—"

"Was kidnapped by you and taken away from my home," Trent finished, glaring at Farrell.

Farrell eyed me, waiting for validation. "He's right. We kinda took him from his home. But he's really one of the good guys, I promise." I wanted to add that Trent was also mad because I had chosen to be with Farrell, but how would that help? Farrell didn't even remember me.

"Enough of the drama, ladies," Infiniti said, rolling her eyes. "We need to figure out this whole Trent Transhuman thing and also why we're—" She stopped mid-sentence. "Wait. How did *I* get here?" She patted her chest. "I mean, when Farrell tried to mind thingy me back in Houston, it didn't work. So how did…"

Silence swallowed the room. Everyone turned to Trent. Infiniti had a point. How did he get us here, let alone Infiniti?

Trent shoved his hands in his pockets and lifted one shoulder. "I just did what Farrell said. I thought of my safe place. And I swear, I was *not* thinking of another century."

"Everyone, stand back," Farrell said. He widened his stance. "I need to check something." He held out his right hand. White misty vapor poured out of his fingertips and gathered into a ball. He tossed it and caught it with his other hand. "Energy, once created, can never be destroyed. It can only be relocated or transformed. And only a Transhuman can manipulate energy."

Farrell had used almost those exact words when he explained Transhumanism to me back in Houston. He had also said the only way a Transhuman can die is to be relocated or absorbed by another energy source.

Was he going to kill Trent?

"Farrell," I inched closer to him, my pulse quickening. "What are you doing?"

"Testing that human," he said. In a blink, he flung the energy at Trent.

Surprise choked me as the ball streaked through the air. Trent's hands jerked up. Amazingly, he caught the vaporized ball with ease. A stunned expression covered his face.

"Whaaat?" Infiniti asked in a whisper.

Trent studied the orb-like sphere while balancing it in his palm. He eyed it in fascination. "It's really hot, but it doesn't burn."

"Good. Now absorb it," Farrell commanded.

Trent raised his eyebrows. "Absorb it?" He brought the ball closer to his face. "How?"

Farrell crossed his arms. "If you can catch it, you can figure it out."

Nervousness for Trent built up inside me. Could he do it? And what would that mean? Trent coiled his fingers around the ball, closed his eyes, and held it tight. The light inside his fist illuminated under his skin, as if he had wrapped his hand around a bright flashlight. The glow dimmed until the light faded away all together.

I crept closer to Trent. "Did it work?"

He smiled, opening his hand. "Yep."

Infiniti and I gawked at Trent's now empty palm. I rubbed my fingertips across his skin. A warm tingling vibrated right through to my bones. "Trent, how did you—"

"Now you," Farrell said.

Huh? Before I could even figure out who he meant, Farrell formed and flung another energy orb, this time at Infiniti. She flinched, waiting for impact, but it dissolved before reaching her, as if it had slipped through a black hole or something. She peered through cracked eyelids, widened her eyes, and patted her chest.

"What the hell!" she exclaimed. "Where'd it go?"

"So you," Farrell pointed at Infiniti, "are a Void. And you," he motioned to Trent, "are a Transhuman. Maybe even a Supreme if you were able to manipulate a Void."

"Hold on a second," Infiniti snapped. "I may be a lot of things, but I'm no void."

Before anyone could respond to her or ask what he meant by Supreme, Farrell formed another orb and lobbed it at me. It bounced off, like a tennis ball hitting a concrete wall. "And you are shielded, but not by me. I'm not doing that."

The knob jingled. The door creaked open. Sister Mary Johanna entered with a silver tray, a large pitcher of water, and four glasses. "I apologize for my delay."

"Why did you lock us in here?" I asked.

She poured the liquid and handed out the glasses. "It was for your own protection."

Her rigid demeanor confused me. Was she really trying to help us? Or did she mean us harm? Either way, I didn't trust her. But I was dying of thirst. I eyed the others and then glanced at the water.

"Come on," Trent prompted, lifting his glass. "They're nuns."

Sister Mary Johanna peered at us, as if we were aliens from another planet, while we downed the cool water. She wrapped her hand around her rosary. "I have never been one to believe in science fiction. It has no place in the church. However, I knew of your coming." She lowered her voice. "And that you would be from another time."

"How?" I asked.

She rubbed the crucifix with her thick thumb. "An angel told me."

"Shut up," Infiniti whispered.

The Sister scowled at Infiniti. "You will not speak thusly in this dwelling or in my presence."

"Oh, um, no," Infiniti stammered. "I didn't mean it like that. I'm sorry."

"It's a common expression in our time," I explained, elbowing Infiniti. "It won't happen again."

"I should say not," the Sister said, smoothing out her long, black, dress. "I will have no trouble from you four, understand?"

"Sure," I said, motioning to the others. "We won't be any trouble, I promise." I straightened my shoulders and tucked my hair behind my ears. "Can you tell us about this angel?"

The Sister's gaze drifted to the ceiling. "It was a bright and cool day. Father Paul and Sister Mary Catherine had gone on a day trip to visit a new church in Corpus Christi. I decided to work in the garden, something I have always enjoyed."

Immediately I thought of Jan's front yard and its unusual and interesting art. Did this nun die and reincarnate into Jan somehow? Could that even be possible? The timing would be right since Jan had to have been born in the forties, assuming the nun would die in ten years or so. I shifted a little and spotted Farrell from the corner of my eye. Maybe he could figure it out. There had to be a reason why this nun looked and acted like Jan Kelly.

The Sister rubbed her forehead. "With the troubling times we are in, many children come to the Sisters of the Incarnate Word and to St. Joseph's for assistance. Some seek food for their families. Others seek clothing. So when this adolescent, blonde-haired girl approached and asked if I could read her a book, I was taken aback."

"Read a book?" I muttered under my breath. That's how Jan had met Abigail in my time. Back in Jan's hometown of Oracle, Arizona, Jan had volunteered to read to the kindergarten class. Jan described Abigail as wearing a white dress and having big green eyes. She even wore the same dress when she had appeared to me. I cleared my throat. "Was this girl wearing a white dress? And did she have green eyes?"

The Sister made the sign of the cross. "Yes."

I drew in a sharp breath, the realization hitting me like a whip.

Farrell crossed his arms and tilted his head. "You've seen this angel, too, Dominique?"

Abigail wasn't an angel. She was a Transhuman—one of the Pure. I didn't want to say so because we needed the Mother Superior to believe we were connected to some sort of religious calling. I'd have to tell Farrell later. "Yes, I've seen this angel. She saved my life."

The sister lifted her cross and kissed it. "She told me to keep you safe while you are here." Her hand trembled. "I told her I would." She stared off into the distance, as if caught up in that moment with Abigail.

"What else did this angel tell you?" I prodded, eager for as much information as we could get.

The nun's hand stilled. A warm smile spread across her face while tears welled up in her eyes. "She said she would return at my hour of need. And then she blessed me with a heavenly touch that sent peace coursing through my body—a bliss I have never known before. I implored her to stay, but she said she could not. She stepped away from me and a brilliant warm light radiated from her until she disappeared."

Infiniti linked her arm with mine. "We *are* here for a reason."

I didn't want to believe Infiniti's theory, but her wacky reasoning made sense. Abigail knew we were coming. She even arranged a safe place for us with these nuns. And Trent, somewhere deep inside, knew of her plan because he had brought us here. But what did it all mean? What were we supposed to do in 1930?

My head pounded. The room swayed. Farrell swooped in and placed his hands on my waist. "Dominique, are you okay?"

I wanted to tell him no, that I wasn't okay. That I

loved him and he loved me. That the Tainted were still after me, but this time instead of killing me they wanted me to be one of them. Maybe even their new leader. "I'm fine. I'm just exhausted, I guess."

Sister Mary Johanna backed up to the door, keeping her gaze on us. "I will do as the angel has asked." She looked us over from head to toe. "I will provide clothing, food, and shelter. And I will tell no one of your true identity. Not even Father Paul or Sister Mary Catherine." She opened the door. "I will fetch what you need. Please, stay here."

Farrell took no time barking orders when she cleared the room. "We must leave immediately."

"Are you serious?" I asked, surprised he would make such a declaration after hearing what the Sister had just said.

He avoided eye contact with me and paced the room nervously. "Yes. I am your Walker, charged with protecting you. I can feel the bond between us. But there are too many unknowns, and I cannot do my job without knowing what we are up against or who these people are, or what we are doing here."

Trent and Infiniti launched into a heated debate. Like Farrell, Trent wanted to leave. Infiniti wanted to stay, insisting we had been brought here to do something. As for me, I didn't know what to think, and listening to them argue wasn't helping.

I tuned them out, went to the window, and examined the world outside. A sea of emotions churned inside me. Back in my own time, Dad had been killed in a car wreck, Mom and the others were under attack, and someone in our camp was a traitor. Out of the blue, I thought of the first time I had met Infiniti back in Houston. She had invited me over for a party and we ended up playing a tarot-like card game. The writing on the card I had selected was etched forever in my brain—*There are heavenly forces behind the scenes working to help you, even if you don't see results yet.*

Heavenly forces… Abigail… the Pure who had saved my life after I had died in the red desert. She was a friend of Trent's grandfather. When they were little and playing at the Rice campus, Professor Julian Huxley had seen the grandfather fall from a tree and die. He witnessed Abigail bring him back to life with a touch. He ended up studying her brain by sending electromagnetic waves into her skull, accidentally killing her. What he didn't know was that Abigail had planned the whole thing. She had wanted to die so that her energy source could be absorbed into the cross and later bring me back to life. According to Huxley's journal, his encounters with her occurred around this time, the thirties, at Rice University.

A slow-moving wave of realization travelled through me. Abigail had saved me and Huxley wrote about her in his journal dated 1930. He had to be the reason for our time jump.

"Dominique, what is it?" Farrell asked, leaving Trent and Infiniti to their squabbling.

Everything about him took my breath away—his perfectly angular features, his tall and lean physique, his bright green eyes, the way he tilted his head and focused on me as if I were the only person on the planet. Now I was just a person under his protection. Nothing more. And even though the pang of loss pierced my heart, I didn't have time to worry if his memories would return. There were bigger issues at hand.

Infiniti and Trent's voices had silenced, their attention now on me.

"We're staying." I made eye contact with each of them before continuing, letting my words sink in for a few seconds. "And we're going to Rice to see Julian Huxley."

Chapter Fourteen

Mother Superior returned with a tray of food and a stack of clothes. When I told her we wanted to visit Rice University, she corrected me and said the school was called the Rice Institute. Then, when I told her we needed to borrow a car, she scoffed. Apparently, driving in the thirties was a luxury and only the rich owned cars. Since the church was definitely not rich, we'd have to ride bikes.

She left us with sandwiches and outfits pulled right out of the church donation box. Infiniti lifted a dingy white sailor-looking shirt with an oversized collar and ruffled blue trim. She held it by her fingertips. "No freaking way."

As I filled Farrell in on who Huxley and Abigail were and how Trent's grandfather factored in, I sorted through the clothes—baggy blue jean overalls for the boys with white undershirts, and sailor style shirts and long white skirts for Infiniti and me. Definitely not something any of us would've selected. Worse? The clothes reeked as if they'd been left in a gym locker all year.

"People are going to think we're hobos," Infiniti declared, tossing the shirt back onto the bed. She looked down at her brown Ugg boots. "With weird shoes."

"Maybe, but we need to blend in." I smoothed out the crinkly shirts, hoping to erase some of the wrinkles. "Skinny jeans and tight shirts would be worse."

Farrell's gaze landed on Infiniti. "We can't talk to anyone other than this Huxley person. Even then, we have to be careful with what we say. Understand?"

"Hey! Why are you looking at me?"

Trent had almost finished his sandwich. "You really have to ask, Infiniti?"

Infiniti placed her hand on her hip. "I watch sci-fi movies. I've seen Star Trek. I'm not an amateur, ya know."

The stale bread in my mouth clogged my throat. I forced it down with a swig of water and jumped to Infiniti's defense. "We *all* have to be careful with what we say, not just Infiniti."

Trent wiped his mouth with the back of his hand. "You're right." He surveyed the clothes. "I guess we should get on with this and see this Huxley guy so we can get back home as soon as possible."

After finishing our food, we took turns changing clothes. The result was something out of a bad Halloween party. We looked like orphans straight out of the movie *Annie*. And Infiniti looked like a little kid.

With a laugh, I poked her side. "Wanna be my little sis?"

She narrowed her eyes at me, Farrell, and Trent. "I really hate you tall people."

Trent wrapped his arm around her neck, pulled her in, and rubbed the top of her head. "Ya do, huh?"

For a minute it was like we were just hanging out, with nothing to worry about, until Farrell reminded us otherwise. "We have business here. And as Dominique's Walker, I will not hesitate to do whatever necessary to ensure her safety—including leaving the two of you behind should you hinder us."

Trent released Infiniti and sauntered up to Farrell. He crossed his arms. "Bullshit. You need me, and you know it."

The last thing I wanted was a fight, though I could totally understand where they were coming from. Farrell had no memories of us, and therefore no loyalty to Trent or Infiniti. He only knew that he was my protector. And Trent, well, he had brought us here and had some sort of power in him. We needed him to get home.

The door opened just in time to ease the budding tension in the room. Mother Superior glided in with the young nun behind her. I had seen her out in the garden when we brought Farrell into the house, but I didn't get a good look.

Until now.

She had a pale, oval-shaped face. Strands of blonde hair peeked out from the habit covering her head. Her shallow brown eyes zeroed in on me, and I immediately froze. The nun looked just like Veronica, Infiniti's best friend from back home. She had hated me, and Tavion had used her as a pawn to get to me. But she was the one who ended up dying instead. Infiniti noticed the likeness too, her mouth gaping open.

My mind gathered all the similarities from this time and my own. First, the Mother Superior looked like Jan. Now, this younger nun resembled Veronica. Back in Houston when Farrell explained lives to me, he had said many were connected over time. That had to be the case with these two.

"Sister Mary Catherine, these are our guests," the Mother Superior said. "We will extend them our hospitality until they leave on..." She lifted an eyebrow, waiting for one of us to finish her sentence.

"Um," I said, my voice cracking a little, "we should be leaving by tonight. At the latest, tomorrow morning."

She nodded her approval. "Very well. If you are finished with your lunch, I will take you to the bikes you may use for the day." She pushed up her black sleeve and glanced at a thin silver watch. "It is high noon. Please return by dusk. That is the house rule."

"Yes, Mother Superior," I said. "And thank you for the lunch."

The Mother motioned for us to follow her out of the room and we filed out behind her. The young nun stayed in the hall, her back against the wall. As I passed her, my hand brushed against hers.

"You have to kill them," a voice whispered in my head.

My footing caught as I stumbled to a stop. It was the voice of the young Tainted girl. My stomach clenched, my body tensed. "Did you hear that?" I asked in a half-whisper.

The nun pressed her back even further against the wall, her eyes wide with fear. "I beg your pardon, Miss. I did not hear a thing."

Farrell cupped my elbow from behind and steadied me. "You okay?"

"Um, yeah," I answered, picking up my pace to catch up to the others.

A bit of relief settled in me as we finally got out of the house. Even though the Mother Superior said she'd help us, something didn't feel right. I'd have to ask the others if they felt the same. But first, we needed to get out of there.

Four black bikes lined the grass of the front yard. They were rusted and worn, with oversized wheels. Overhead, the sun shone bright, yet a slight chill hovered in the air. I was just about to ask for jackets, when Sister Mary Catherine rushed up with a pile of sweaters slung over her arm.

"You'll need these," she offered.

She kept her gaze down while she handed out thick, white, wool sweaters. I did my best to avoid touching her, yanking the garment away in a single motion. "Thank you."

I straddled the bike and shuffled my way to Trent as I squeezed my body into the snug sweater. Since this was his church, he'd know the way to Rice. "You go first," I whispered. "And hurry."

He tied his sweater around his handlebars and casually peered at the nuns. "On it," he muttered under his breath. He pedaled away from the house, past the church, to a narrow two-lane road, and turned right. As soon as we had passed out of view from the Sisters, I called for everyone to stop. "Did you guys see—"

"Veronica." Infiniti finished my sentence for me, her eyes nearly popping out of her head.

Trent rubbed his head. "I know!"

Farrell stitched his brows. "Who is Veronica?"

I coasted my bike closer to him. "Let me first tell you about that head nun, Mother Superior Mary Johanna. She looks just like my old neighbor back in Houston—Jan Kelly. She was trying to help me figure out why I was marked by the Tainted, but died in a plane crash. And the nun who's our age? Sister Mary Catherine? Well, she looks just like Veronica, a friend of Infiniti's. She was killed when the Tainted used her to get to me."

"Souls linked over time," Farrell explained. "It's a common occurrence. Anything else I need to know?"

Panic laced my pounding heart. Should I tell him and the others about hearing the voice in the hallway? I mean, if someone told me they heard a voice telling them to kill me, I'd freak. Could I risk them fearing me? I didn't know. And then it dawned on me that I wasn't hearing Tavion's voice anymore, just the girl's.

Farrell placed his hand on my shoulder. "What is it?"

For a minute he seemed like the old him—the guy who cared for me and loved me for lifetimes, not the guy who had lost his memories and had turned into a complete stranger. No, I couldn't tell him or the others about the voice because I didn't know how they'd react, especially now that we were in a different time. Then I wondered if I should tell him about our feelings for each other, but what good would that do?

"It's nothing," I said, brushing him off with a smile. "Those nuns just freaked me out, that's all."

Infiniti shuddered. "Tell me about it. It's like *American Horror Story* meets *Back to the Future*."

Trent surveyed the 1930's Houston landscape. "This is Houston Avenue, or at least it used to be. Wait here while I check." He pedaled up to the nearest street sign and waved us over. "Yep, Houston Avenue. So if we follow this road, it should lead us into downtown, which is right over there." He pointed. In the future, the space would be littered with looming and reflective downtown skyscrapers, but now only a few smaller dull brown buildings jutted out from the flat landscape, about three miles from our location. "We should be able to travel down Main Street all the way to Rice."

He started to pedal on, keeping lead. Infiniti wobbled on her bike for a while, cursing under her breath, until she eased into a steady rhythm. I wanted to laugh, but Farrell's serious demeanor stopped me. Besides, I wasn't too comfortable on the bike either. The handlebars were pure metal, with no soft rubbery ends. Even the hard and flat seat had no cushioning and rammed me with each bump.

This sucked.

After about five minutes, and already with a sore butt and burning thighs, I decided to initiate small talk with Farrell. Maybe talking would spark something in him. "So, um, Farrell, you really don't remember anything?"

Farrell kept his attention on our path. "That is correct."

Our rusted bikes clamored over dirt and patches of grass as we followed Trent and Infiniti. "You mentioned feeling a bond with me, right?"

"Yes, my energy source recognizes yours. But that's not a memory. It's a state of being. Like a magnet drawn to metal."

Heat crept into my cheeks. Knowing his energy source recognized mine made me feel even more drawn to him, but also more hurt that he had forgotten our past. My eyes blurred with tears. I forced them down and concentrated on my tarnished metal handle bars, hoping he wouldn't catch on to my emotions, when my bike veered into his.

He grabbed my handle bar, averting a collision, and

then tilted his head slightly while studying me. "Are you okay?"

"Yes," I said, regaining control of my bike. "I'm just not used to riding a bike, that's all."

Trying to have a conversation with him wasn't easy, so I gave up and instead focused on Huxley as we made our way down Houston Avenue and closer to downtown. What would we say to the Professor when we found him? A cool breeze swept over me, sending doubt and shivers up my spine. What if we didn't find him? My stomach knotted with tension and my legs ached from all the pedaling until finally we turned a corner and emerged onto a busy road.

"This is Main Street," Trent announced.

Infiniti whistled. "It's like a movie set or something."

The pristine white concrete sidewalks were filled with people on both sides of the street, mostly men in three-piece suits and hats. Old-timey cars parked on both sides of the street, lined up and angled in perfect rows, while others cruised up and down. Thick black electrical wires, hung much lower than I was used to, crisscrossed from one structure to another, like a giant spider web.

"This is amazing," I whispered while examining the multitude of store signs and awnings dotting the fronts of the buildings as far as the eye could see.

"We need to keep moving," Farrell said.

"After we get some water," Infiniti tacked on. "I'm dying of thirst."

Sweat dampened the dark hair around her red face. She took off her sweater and tied it around her waist. I pulled my hair away from my neck, wishing I had a hair tie or something. "I could use something to drink, too."

"Come on," Trent said. "We should find something up here."

We biked slowly down the sidewalk, staying away from the shop doors and closer to the parked cars. We passed a bank, a hat store, and a shoe store. The further into downtown we went, the more crowded the sidewalks. We hopped off our bikes, opting to walk them through the throng. As we did, a path cleared for us. The pedestrians turned up their noses at us, frowning and averting their eyes. That's when I remembered our old and shabby clothes. And the smell. The people on the sidewalks probably thought we were homeless.

After a couple of blocks, Trent stopped under a wide green awning at the corner.

Liggett's Drug Store.

One glass display case featured an array of cough drops for ten cents. Another featured an assortment of chocolates for five cents. There was even a sign for a soda fountain. My mouth watered. Looking down at my rags, I realized we didn't have any money.

I rested my bike against my body. "Guys, we have no cash."

"I've got this," Trent said. "Stay here."

Trent leaned his bike against the brick facade and slipped through the store door. Infiniti and I parked our bikes with his, glad to be on our feet if only for a little while. Farrell kept his stare on the crowd, like a hawk searching for an enemy. Fear prickled the back of my neck. Were we in danger? Or was he just being cautious? I grabbed Infiniti's arm and scooted closer to Farrell, just in case.

The sidewalk buzzed with activity. Cars rumbled up and down Main Street. A cop with a long coat and tall hat blew his whistle in the middle of the intersection, directing traffic. I turned back to the store. Raising myself up on my tiptoes, I craned my neck as I looked through the window display, eager for Trent to come back out.

That's when I spotted her.

The Tainted girl.

Dressed in all black, she looked like a creepy kid straight out of a scary movie. Her cropped brown hair framed her pale face. Her stare fixed on me as she made her way through the store and to the front door. I backed into Farrell, waiting for him to react, but he didn't budge. It was like I had bumped into a wall.

"Holy shit," Infiniti whispered. "Farrell?"

I tore my gaze away from the girl and shuffled around to face Farrell, shocked at what I found. He had frozen in place, like a statue. I spun around and saw that everyone in the area except for Infiniti and me had stopped moving, as if someone had pressed pause on a giant remote control.

"What's happening?" Infiniti whispered, pressing her body against mine and digging her fingers into my arm.

"I-I don't know," I muttered, knowing damn well the Tainted girl was responsible. I whipped my head back around to the store entrance. The girl had come out of the building and stood just steps away from me. I tugged at Infiniti's shirt and pointed. "Do you see that girl?"

Infiniti searched the area. "Huh? What girl?"

"Nobody can see me," the Tainted girl said in my head. *"Just you, Marked One."* She stopped inches from me and

stretched out her tiny hand. *"Are you ready to come with me?"*

My body trembled. Even though she scared the hell out of me, a part of me wanted to go with her. As if I belonged with her. Needed her. Mounting desperation rose inside me. I pried Infiniti's grip from my arm and shoved her away from me.

"Hey! Dominique! What are you doing?"

I ignored Infiniti and instead focused on the girl. I reached out. "I'm ready."

"Who are you talking to?" Infiniti asked, fear thick in her voice. "Dominique!"

The girl smiled, her tiny white teeth gleaming like square pearls, her olive-colored eyes flashing black. I started to pull my hand back when she reached out, grabbed it, and held me in an icy death grip.

She grinned. *"Too late."*

Chapter Fifteen

There are moments in your life that define you. Alter your course forever. For me, my life changed forever when we moved from Elk Rapids, Michigan to Houston, Texas. And now that I had taken the hand of the young Tainted girl, it was about to change again. I felt it in every bone of my body, like a giant gavel had landed and announced my life verdict.

"Do you know where you are?" the girl whispered.

I had just been in front of a drug store in 1930's Houston. Now I stood in pitch black nothingness. A haunting chill ran up my spine; my childhood fear of the dark stealing through me. When I was afraid as a child, I would yell for Mom or Dad. Other times, the fear of the unknown would strangle me and I couldn't even call out for help. One day I had mustered up the courage to talk to my dad about it. "There's always a sliver of light in the dark," he used to say. "You just have to find it."

My pulse raced. My heart slammed against my chest. I widened my eyes and searched for the light, but couldn't find one. I stretched out my arms, fumbling around for something solid.

"Do you know where you are, Marked One?" the girl asked again, more forceful this time.

Dread invaded me. Thoughts of death filled my mind.

I forced myself to breathe deep, praying I wouldn't lose it. "No."

"Look harder," she said.

A streak of light appeared at my feet. I inched forward until my boots bumped against something solid. A door? I rested my palms against the surface before sliding them down to a small, round knob. Yes, definitely a door. My hand gripped the smooth knob. Instead of turning it, I hesitated about my next move, my mind imagining a multitude of dangers that lurked on the other side.

Terrified of what I might find, yet knowing I had no other choice, I turned the doorknob and flung the door open. The barely lit room reeked of dirt, like a musty gardeners shed. To the right, rows of clay pots lined thick wooden shelves. My gaze flitted over a small cot jammed into the corner. I stumbled forward as someone shifted on it, my mind racing with the impossibility of who I thought I was seeing.

I stretched out my neck and squinted for a better look, my legs almost going numb. Could it be?

"Dad?"

He sprang to his feet, surprise evident on his face. "Dominique?"

Shock flooded me, followed by utter disbelief. The last time I had seen him was at the car crash. Images of his crushed legs flashed before me. Farrell and Mom said he had died. "Dad?" I repeated, hot tears stinging my eyes.

His face softened. "Dominique." He shuffled over to me and wrapped me in his arms. Soft weeping sounds escaped his lips. "I thought I'd never see you again."

I hugged him back, tears spilling down my cheeks. "You're alive," I choked out.

He released me, stepped back, and studied my face. "Alive? So you thought I was dead?"

He sported a full beard sprinkled with gray hairs. He wore the same clothes he had on when we had crashed, complete with blood stains and ripped fabric. He covered his face and collapsed on his cot. "Your mother," he whispered. "She's the one."

I crashed down on my knees in front of him. "What?"

His eyes darted back and forth as he searched the room. I followed his gaze, expecting to see the Tainted girl, but she was gone. "We don't have time, so please listen," he whispered, his eyes desperate and worried. "We've known of a traitor in our midst. We've known it for lifetimes. We thought maybe it was Colleen, or even Fleet." He rubbed his forehead. "Now it's all making sense. It's her. Caris. It's been her this whole time. She arranged the car crash. She had her followers bring me here. And now..." His bloodshot eyes glazed over. "She's trying to get you to switch sides. Maybe even kill you."

His words lingered in the air for a moment before sinking in and stabbing my heart as fiercely as a knife. My brain scrambled as it searched for evidence that Mom could have turned against us. She knew our route from Texas to Michigan. She wouldn't let us help Colleen. But could she really be a traitor?

My body trembled, not wanting to accept the harsh truth. "No. It can't be."

Dad studied me through a broken gaze, his strength and confidence emptied. "It's the only thing that makes sense."

Something inside me said to believe him. That all this

time she was directing my choices. She had even gone so far as to order me to abandon the others. My stomach dropped. "What do I do?"

He cupped my face and ran his rough thumbs across my cheeks. "My sweet girl. So many lives, and so much heartache. And now it comes down to this."

The dirt floor began to shake. Clay pots from the shelves tumbled and crashed to the ground. The light in the room dimmed. I knew I didn't have much time.

"Dad. I'm scared."

He brought me in close. His tears had left a trail through the grime on his face. "Trust no one but Colleen." His lip quivered while the room rocked. "When you get back to the cabin..." He leaned forward and whispered in my ear. "Kill your mother."

My arm jerked. "Do you hear me?" A girl's voice penetrated my ears as Dad's face misted away. "You're freaking me the hell out!" The voice said again.

I turned to see Infiniti yanking me by my forearm. As soon as I realized it was her clutching me, the street sprang to life. Farrell snapped his attention to me. He narrowed his eyes. "What just happened?"

His words repeated in my head. What *did* just happen?

Trent burst into view. Four soda bottles clanked in his hands. "Hey, I had a really strange feeling in the store."

"Uh, no shit," Infiniti said. "Everybody in sight stopped moving. Everybody except for me and Dominique." Heat rushed to my face while she studied me, as if I were a total stranger. "You asked if I could see a little girl, but there was no little girl around. And then you totally zoned out. Like the way you did back at my house when we played the card game Jan had given me." She stepped even further away from me, terror evident on her face.

Back at her house in Houston when I had touched her magical cards, the vision of the red desert zapped into view. It was like I was hallucinating, but I wasn't. The red desert was real. I had been killed there in each of my past lives. So that meant Dad had to be real, too. And if what he said was true, Mom was holding him captive somewhere back at the cabin. And he wanted me to kill her.

An urgency to get back to the cabin and find him flooded me.

Trent lifted my chin, forcing me to focus on him. "Hey, you all right?"

Farrell slammed his palm against Trent's chest. The glass bottles in Trent's hands tumbled from his grasp and shattered against the concrete sidewalk. Farrell's eyes stormed over. "Stay away from her."

Trent got up in Farrell's face and raised his chin. "And if I don't?"

Before I could tell them to stop fighting, a whistle blasted in my ears. The cop from the intersection strode our way. He pointed a long, sleek, black baton at Trent's chest and pressed it against his overalls. He turned his attention to Infiniti and me. "Is this Mexican bothering you young ladies?"

Mexican? I gulped, realizing for the first time that Trent was the only one in the area with tan skin. "No, Officer. Not at all." I stepped closer to Trent and took his hand. "This is my friend, and we were just leaving when I, uh, tripped, and dropped our drinks."

The officer eyed Farrell, keeping the long stick on Trent. "Is that right, young man?"

Farrell nodded. "Yes, Officer. That's correct."

The cop lowered his baton and slipped it back in its sheath at his side. He held us in a steely glare. "Move along," he commanded in a deep voice. "Out of my territory."

The four of us hopped on our bikes and pedaled away without looking back. Trent took the lead again with Infiniti, followed by Farrell and me. My heart ached for Trent. I knew he was only worried about me, but to be attacked by Farrell and confronted by the cop had to have been hard on him.

As soon as we traveled out of downtown, the sidewalk ended and morphed into dirt and grass. Trent continued on for a bit before biking through an overgrown field to a boarded up and dilapidated house. He biked to the rear, hopped off his seat, and tossed the bike by its handlebars. He kicked at clumps of dirt and debris, muttering to himself in Spanish.

Infiniti chewed her nails. "This is so not good," she said. "He only breaks into Spanish when he's really pissed. And even then, I've only seen him do it a handful of times."

Trent stomped over to Farrell and got up in his face. "Don't you ever touch me again, got it?"

Even though Farrell stayed perfectly still, his jaw clenched. He fisted his hands at his sides. Crackling sparks burst from his fingertips. "Don't threaten me."

Trent inched closer. "Or what?"

Dad had said not to trust anyone. That included Trent and Farrell. But I didn't need them fighting. If we were to see Professor Huxley and get back home, I needed them to work together. My life depended on it.

"Stop!" I yelled. "Please!"

I spotted a nearby tree stump and slumped down, exhausted from all the distrust and doubt wracking my brain. A small rusted ax poked out from the tall grass. I gave it a kick. "We're never gonna make it like this."

Back in my time, Mom had warned of a traitor. Now Dad warned of the same thing, claiming it was Mom. I just didn't know who to believe. In fact, I wasn't sure of anything anymore.

Trent crouched down next to me. He picked up a small branch and scraped at the dirt. He kept his gaze down. "I'm sorry. I shouldn't have lost my cool like that." He tossed the stick. "I promise I'll stand by you. No matter what."

Right now I needed people I could count on. And that included Trent. He took my hands and helped me up. I dusted off my stupid white skirt and pulled at my snug collar. "Thanks, Trent."

Farrell tilted his head slightly while he looked from me to Trent. His brow creased. He rubbed his neck, as if confused about something. I bit my lip. Were his memories coming back? He shook his head, turned away from Trent and me, and studied the skies. He turned back around. "I know you," he said to me.

My heart skipped. Hopeful excitement budded inside me. "You do?"

He tilted his head again. "It's more of a memory." He stepped forward. "We were at a beach. You told me if you ever changed..." He paused and moved closer to me, "That I should kill you."

"Whoa!" Infiniti called out. "Are you crazy?"

Farrell ignored Infiniti. White misty vapor poured out of his hands. "You begged me."

Trent pulled me behind him. "Back the hell off, asshole! You're not touching Dominique!"

My mind raced. I didn't remember any of my past lives, so how could I know if he was telling the truth? And if he wasn't, why would he lie?

I pushed Trent aside. "Listen, I don't know what to believe anymore," I said to Farrell. "Everything is," my voiced cracked, "lost." Infiniti whispered for me to get back. I ignored her because in my heart I knew Farrell would never hurt me. We had been through too much, and somewhere deep inside him there had to be a piece of me. I held up my hands and approached him. "You don't remember anything and I don't remember any of our past lives. So you see, how can you even know if I've changed?"

The misty vapor faded from Farrell's fingertips. His face started to relax. "I will continue with my duties," Farrell said. "One of them is to follow the orders of my Charge. And if I discover you indeed want me to end you, I will."

A hard shudder rippled through my body. This new, colder Farrell scared me. I told myself he only acted like this because he didn't remember me. But other thoughts crept into my imagination. Scary ones. And I knew that one way or another, more people would die. The only question was, who?

Chapter Sixteen

Trent trudged through the tall grass to get his bike while the rest of us surveyed the run-down house. The one-story structure had a pointed roof with dark, moldy shingles. There were even a few holes where the roof had caved in. Chipped white paint sprinkled the wood exterior, and the closer we got to the house, the worse the smell—like a toilet that hadn't been flushed in days. I covered my nose and mouth with my sleeve. "This is disgusting," I mumbled.

Thick pieces of timber crisscrossed the windows. Broken shards of glass splintered through the openings. Farrell grabbed a piece of lumber and pulled. It snapped off with ease. He peered through. "Empty," he said. He dropped the wood and dusted off his hands. "I'm going to take a look around the grounds. Make sure we're alone."

"Knock yourself out," Infiniti said. "We're gonna stay here." We found a spot far enough from the stench of the house, yet still hidden from the street, and plunked down.

Infiniti ripped a piece of fabric from the bottom of her frayed skirt and tied her hair back. She eyed Farrell as he walked to the rear of the lot. "What the hell do you make of what Farrell said about you telling him to kill you if you changed?"

My gut had twisted so hard it hurt and the last thing I

wanted to do was talk. But Infiniti couldn't help herself. She ripped off another piece of fabric, handed it to me, and went on. "I mean, shit. And what about what happened back at the drug store? Everybody froze back there except us. I get that I'm this Void and the Transhuman whatever energy has no effect on me, but what the hell happened to you?" She gulped. "And who did you see?"

I let out a sigh as I tried to work the strip around my straight hair, but it wouldn't hold. I tossed it instead and thought of what Dad had said in the shed about not trusting anyone. Even though he had warned me for my own good, something told me I could confide in Infiniti. Plus, if I didn't say something to someone, I'd burst. I just needed to be careful with what I told her, and seeing Dad was definitely not on the list of things to share.

"Look, I don't get any of it either." I scooted closer to her and lowered my voice. "But I swear I saw the Tainted girl—the same one that attacked us out in the back of the cabin right before we transported here."

She stitched her brows and tilted her head. "Huh?"

Even though she had told me back in Houston that she'd quit smoking, her regular trips to the "garage" must've permanently killed some of her brain cells. I blew out a breath. "You know, we were ambushed by the Tainted back at the cabin—two large ones and one small petite one. A girl. Remember? She even reached out to me."

"Uh, I saw the two figures, but there was no girl there."

Fear and disbelief raced through my veins. "What?" I asked, not believing what she had just said.

She raised two fingers. "I saw two cloaked figures."

"You didn't see..." My voice trailed off. My throat suddenly bone dry.

"Oh my God," Infiniti whispered. "I think I know what's happening here." She scanned the area. Trent still labored on fixing the damage done to his bike. The rattle of the chains as he worked them back into shape tinkled throughout the quiet air. Farrell had joined him as they tried to make sense of the metal mess. "I've heard of spirits that only reveal themselves to certain individuals," she continued in a low voice. "Like there's a link between you two or something."

I thought of every time I had seen the girl. Each time, no one else had mentioned her presence. When she appeared to me on the plane from Houston to Michigan, not even Fleet noticed her. He'd even called me a liar when I mentioned I'd seen her.

An icy chill shot down my spine and spread over my body. "You're right," I murmured, realization hitting me like a fist. "But what does it mean?"

"What does what mean?" Farrell repeated, looming over Infiniti and me. I startled and Infiniti let out a surprised yelp.

I shot Infiniti the 'don't say anything look,' convinced that seeing the Tainted girl would put me in jeopardy with Farrell. "Um, well, uh," I stammered, struggling to come up with something to say.

Infiniti huffed. "Not that it's any of your business, but we were trying to figure out why the hair tie I made works in my hair and not Dominique's."

"Uh, yeah," I said with a forced laughed. "That."

"And what it means is my hair is thick and wavy and

Dominque's is straight and smooth." She flicked her bushy ponytail. "See?"

I tried to act like Infiniti's cover-up wasn't the dumbest thing I'd ever heard. "Oh," I said, pointing at her hair and trying to act casual. "I didn't realize that. Thanks, Infiniti."

Of course, Farrell knew we were lying. It was written all over his face. "Fine," he said with a tight-lipped frown. "If that's the way you want to play it."

Infiniti rolled her eyes. "You used to be pretty cool, ya know," she said to Farrell.

"Yeah right," Trent said in the distance as he worked on his bike.

They could say all they wanted about the new Farrell, but deep down in there was the guy I had fallen in love with. And even though this new version of him frightened me, I couldn't give up on him. "Cut it out," I said.

Trent paused before clanking away even louder at his task while tension oozed from him and filled the air like an invisible toxic cloud. I got up, resigned to the fact they'd probably always hate each other, and noticed Farrell staring at me. His eyes softened. Even his shoulders eased up, but only for a moment. He snapped back to scary mode—his body tense, his face devoid of expression. Dude had turned into a split personality overnight.

He shielded his eyes and examined the bright sun that loomed closer to the horizon. "If we're to return to the nun's house before dark, we better get moving."

"Got it!" Trent exclaimed, pushing the last link of chain into place. He hopped on his bike and pedaled around. "I'm ready."

"Me too," Infiniti said with a huff, peeling herself from the ground.

I groaned, my legs aching while I got up, when the rusted ax came into view. *"Get it,"* the young voice in my head said. *"Hurry."*

Without hesitation, I took hurried steps to the ax. I reached for the small tool and balanced it in my hands. Bits of rust rubbed off on my palm, leaving a streak of dark orange residue. It reminded me of the cuts that laced my skin when I had confronted Tavion back in the red desert. I wiped it off, suddenly needing to kill again. Trent pedaled over to me.

"Kill him," the voice instructed.

I raised the ax, aimed for Trent's head, and threw. It flew directly at him, cruising straight for the spot right between the eyes. Trent started to duck, a look of sheer terror filling his eyes, when a streak of light blasted out of nowhere and ricocheted the flying weapon off course. It landed with a hard thud onto the ground.

"What the—" Trent exclaimed, not even able to finish his sentence, his gaze glued on me.

Farrell grabbed me from behind and held me in a chokehold, an electrified tingling emitting from his skin. "Why did you do that?"

Disbelief and guilt over what I had done descended on me. "I don't know!" My hands shook at my sides. "I didn't do it on purpose! I promise!"

Infiniti came into view. "What's happening to you?"

I waited to see if I would hear the Tainted girl's voice in my head again, but there was nothing. Only silence and regret. "I don't know," I answered.

Trent hopped off his bike. "Ease up," he said to Farrell. "She's telling the truth."

Farrell released his hold, but kept one hand latched around my arm as if I were some sort of criminal. My thoughts flooded with the idea that I was indeed changing, against my will, and trying to hurt my friends.

"How do you know she's telling the truth?" Farrell asked Trent.

Trent rubbed his neck. "My family has always been able to sense things, and I can too."

I thought of his grandmother's cloudy blue eyes, the strange things she seemed to know about me, and the cross she had given me.

"My family name, Avila, is linked to a powerful line of curanderos." Trent said. "What you would call healers. Some of us are even psychic."

"Whoa, really?" Infiniti asked. "Why didn't I know?"

Trent shrugged his shoulders. "People usually don't understand or believe. And besides, it's not exactly something that comes up over text."

An eerie stillness settled around us, as if the entire universe was holding its breath, waiting to see what we would do next.

"I think we should cut our losses, go back to the church, and try to get home," Trent suggested. "This is all becoming way too dangerous."

"No!" I interjected. "We're almost to Rice. We can't go back now." Trent and Infiniti gave each other questioning stares. "Come on, guys. We've come this far. We need to see this through. We need to find Huxley." Desperation mounted inside me with each word. "Keep a close eye on me, tie me up, whatever. But please, we've got to keep going. It's my only hope." In my mind, seeing Huxley had become some sort of salvation for me. As if he held the answers to my troubles. As if he could change my fate.

Trent came up close and peered into my eyes, as if searching my very soul for a reason to go on.

"Please, Trent. We're almost there." I took his hands and held on for dear life. "Don't give up on me," I whispered.

He rubbed the back of his neck. "Okay," he said. "But let's hurry. I have a really bad feeling about this."

"Fine," Farrell said to me. "We continue on. But my eyes are not leaving you for one second."

"Fine," I said in a shaky, yet relieved voice.

I hiked up my skirt, hopped on my rickety bike, and followed the others through the tall grass and back to Main Street. Farrell stayed close, so close I almost steered my bike into his several times. He even reached out and touched my arm from time to time, as if making skin contact would keep me in check. Grateful to have him near me, yet still paranoid I'd hear the Tainted girl again, I focused on my surroundings. Maybe if I didn't think of her, she'd leave me alone.

The last time I'd been in this area, in the twenty-first century, buildings filled the air. Hospitals mostly, along with busy neighborhoods and even a few churches. Now the landscape looked mostly deserted. Other than a few buildings here and there, the area reminded me of the Wild West.

After what seemed like forever, Trent slowed his pace. He coasted while he looked over his shoulder at Farrell and me. He pointed to the right.

Despite the missing trees and residential homes, I recognized the main structure of Rice University right away. The long, rectangular building loomed out of the barren fields like an alien structure—completely foreign to the desolate surroundings.

Trent turned right onto a nearby street and made his way to the building. As we got closer, the white columned arches came into view. Perfectly manicured shrubs dotted the mowed grass. Trent stopped. "We should probably stash our bikes somewhere out here and continue on foot."

A clump of thick trees, like a small forest, clustered nearby. "How about in there?" I asked.

We found a perfect spot in the wooded area for our bikes and made our way to the campus. The closer we got, the more my stomach tumbled with nervous energy. What if we didn't find Huxley? Or worse, what if the Tainted girl came back again? Invaded my mind? Too many doubts raced through me.

Farrell matched my stride, his hand brushing against mine. Instead of pulling it back, he got closer, as if sensing my fear. Or maybe he worried I'd attack again. I wondered if sharing a memory would help him remember things, especially since I needed him now more than ever. "We've been here before. Twice." I gulped, recalling how we'd been attacked here. "It didn't go so well."

He tilted his head, concern etched in the lines of his forehead, and stopped. "Is that why you're so afraid?"

Even though he scared me, he was still my protector, so I knew he could sense my feelings. It's something he'd always been able to do. "Yes," I whispered so Infiniti and Trent ahead of us wouldn't hear me. "You could say that."

I pushed my hair behind my ears. "I'm also freaked about you honoring some so-called order of mine to kill me."

"I see," he said. He pulled my arm, brought me in, and looked down on me with his striking green eyes. "I would never hurt you unless you wished it."

A myriad of emotions swept over me—fear of him killing me, worry for my dad, anxiousness over seeing Huxley, and a touch of excitement at being so close to the most gorgeous guy I'd ever known. I steadied my breathing, trying to keep my feelings in check.

He tilted his head. "Anything else?"

A desperate urge to tell him we had loved each other for lifetimes surged in me. But as much as I wanted to tell him, I didn't think I should. At least, not now. "Yeah, one more thing. I need you to know that I want to live. Okay?"

A strange expression swept over his face. Something like surprise mixed with sadness. I prompted his reply. "Okay?"

His eyes softened a tad. "Okay."

We caught up with Trent and Infiniti, stepping through the big archway of the main school building. We stopped and stared. There weren't any students or professors around. In fact, I was wondering if we had emerged onto a ghost campus when a group of five guys dressed in suits rushed past us. They each carried a stack of books and didn't even notice us. Another student walked by, eyeing us with disapproval.

I smoothed out my grimy skirt. "Now what?" I asked, afraid that looking homeless would get us kicked off campus.

"We find someone and ask for Huxley," Trent said. "Someone around here must know where he is."

We started combing the grounds, searching for someone to talk to, when I noticed movement from the corner of my eye. I shifted my gaze, expecting to see another passing student. Instead, the Tainted girl flashed into view.

"It's almost time, Marked One."

My skin prickled with fear. My heart nearly jumped out of my chest. Her voice echoed in my mind as she faded into nothingness, her evil smirk the last thing to disappear.

Farrell halted the group and moved me behind him. He peered at the spot where the girl had been. "What is it?"

Infiniti and Trent examined the area too, and then glanced back at me with fear and distrust in their eyes.

"Nothing," I answered fast. "Let's keep moving." I pushed Farrell on, thinking that if we kept looking and if I focused on the grounds, I wouldn't see her again.

The four of us continued our search. With each passing minute, any hope of finding Huxley, or anyone who might help us find him, started to wane. But then we spotted a guy around our age. Dressed in dark green overalls, he raked at a pile of leaves. He stopped when he spotted us, and looked our way.

"You no belong here," he said, a thick Spanish accent lacing his words. "Go. Vaminos. Es collegio. No for you."

Trent stepped forward. His mouth hung open as he stared at the guy. "You're the gardener," he fumbled out.

"Oh my God," I whispered, catching on to Trent's dumbfounded reaction.

Trent had told me his father, grandfather, and even great-grandfather had tended the grounds of Rice. Since Trent's grandfather was a little boy during this time period, this gardener had to be his great-grandfather. And that's when I fully noticed their striking resemblance. Trent and the worker had the same muscular build, identical unkempt hair, and the same tan skin coloring. The only difference between them was that Trent had blue eyes while the gardeners were brown. Seeing him was sure to screw up the whole Star Trek space-time-continuum thing.

I yanked Trent back. "Let's go."

The gardener dropped his rake. "¡Espera!"

While I didn't know any Spanish, I could tell the gardener wanted us to stop—and we did. He approached slowly. Wonder and amazement flooded his face. He reached out to touch Trent, but his hands shook so badly he had to drop his arm. "¿Trenius?"

"Trenius? Who's Trenius?" I asked.

Trent shuffled back, his stare locked on the gardener. "Me. That's my full name."

An army of goose bumps broke out along my arms. If Trent hadn't been born yet, the gardener could not possibly have known his name. Trent must've thought the same thing.

"¿Cómo sabes mi nombre?" Trent asked.

"This isn't good," Infiniti whispered to my left, tugging my sleeve.

Farrell came up and positioned himself in front of me and Infiniti.

The gardener's eyes glossed over. He held out his arms in a gesture of welcome. "I sorry. Perdón. I no scare you. I am your great-grandfather." He patted his chest. "Julio. Julio Avila." He waited for a response, but we were too stunned to say anything. "Trenius, your great-grandma, mi esposa, tell me you come. Her name Carmen. She sees things."

My knees nearly buckled. We weren't here for Huxley after all, but for Trent? To meet his great-grandparents? I didn't understand.

Trent raised his hand, giving Julio the universal sign for hold on, and turned to face the rest of us. The color had drained from his face. "Somebody wanna tell me what the hell we do now?"

Infiniti chewed her nails. Even Farrell looked confused. "I wipe his mind and we get out of here," Farrell offered.

"No!" Infiniti exclaimed. "There are no accidents in the universe." She glanced at Julio from the corner of her eye. "We were meant to find him." She let her words sink in. "I say we go with him."

She had a point about things happening for a reason, but this was something else. We were in a different time now. Our actions could have huge consequences later down the road. "I don't know," I said. "Sounds dangerous."

"Duh," Infiniti said. "Everything we're doing is dangerous. Shit, our whole futures are probably all screwed up by now. But we're here. Right now. We gotta see it through. We can't just leave."

Her words prodded me like a poker, forcing me to go along with her theory. "I guess we could do the mind wipe if things go wrong." I imagined a completely different future when we returned to our own time. "Right, Farrell?"

He hesitated for a few seconds, his mind obviously processing our predicament. "Right. Just give the word and he won't know what hit him."

Trent rubbed his forehead and pinched the bridge of

his nose. "Fine," he muttered. "But no one gets hurt, man. Okay? Not unless," he paused, "absolutely necessary."

Farrell gave a slight nod of agreement which made me think he really didn't care at all about Trent's ancestors. Trent countered with a threatening look before he turned back around to face his great-grandfather.

"Julio," he murmured, as if getting used to the name. "Can you help us? ¿Puedes ayudarnos?"

Julio smiled. "Sí. Come. Todos."

We followed the gardener across a grassy area lined with long rows of squared shrubs, through a wide field, across a narrow two-lane road, and finally to a small, one-story house. The simple, wood paneled structure sat alone, separated from a newer neighborhood not far in the distance. A cool breeze swept across the area, gathering around my legs like an invisible snake. A makeshift wind chime sounded from a lone tree in the yard. I peered at it, trying to figure out what it was made of as I wrapped my arms around myself.

"A teapot with hanging spoons," Infiniti whispered, following my gaze.

The swinging silverware and their tinkling held my attention, when again I noticed movement through my peripheral vision—a black streak darting by. I followed the flash, terrified that I'd see the girl in black, but didn't. My eyes had to be playing tricks on me, or maybe I was losing it all together. I edged closer to Farrell and looped my arm through his, my body shivering uncontrollably.

"We don't have to do this," Farrell whispered.

"Yes, we do," I answered, wondering if my body shivered from the coolness of approaching evening, fear that the Tainted girl would appear again, or the mounting tension as we approached the one-story shack. I looked back at the Rice campus. The sun had sunk so low we'd never get back to St. Joseph's church before dark. I wondered what the Mother Superior would do.

Julio opened the faded front door. It moaned like a lonely cat. "Come," he beckoned Trent. "Pasa."

A blast of doubt wracked my senses. My legs stopped moving. I thought of telling the others about my reservations when Trent made his way up two small concrete steps and through the narrow doorway. We had no choice now but to follow him.

"You," the great-grandfather said to Infiniti with a wave. "Come."

She shuffled ahead, her body movements making it clear she didn't really want to go in, but did anyway.

"Qué bueno," Julio said. He held his dirty hand out to me with a smile, his teeth crooked and brown. "You."

Farrell released his hold on me so I could step ahead of him but kept one hand on my lower back. I took Julio's rough hand and moved forward—my steps slow and heavy.

"Es okay," he laughed.

Holding my breath, I crossed the threshold and plunged into a dark room. My eyes blurred as I blinked them to adjust to the dim lighting. Furniture came into view, along with a shadowy figure just to my left.

The girl!

Before I could do anything, the figure beside me whipped a cold piece of metal up against my neck. The sharp edge pressed against my skin.

Panic rushed through me as a startled gasp escaped my lips.

An ambush!

Chapter Seventeen

A burst of electricity crackled from behind me. It blasted my hair forward with a whoosh, illuminating the room in shimmery light. My skin tingled. Fear gripped my insides.

"Let her go!" Farrell commanded from behind me. "Now! Or you're all dead!"

"Farrell, don't!" Trent warned. "They've got a knife to Dominique's throat!"

A thin, coarse hand crept up the back of my neck, to the base of my skull, and pulled my hair taut. The pressure of the knife against my skin rooted me in place. I flicked my eyes back and forth, trying to make out the scene.

Trent stood six feet in front of me. To the right, a Hispanic guy dressed in work overalls like Trent's great-grandfather gripped a struggling Infiniti by her arms. To the left, and pressing up against me, I made out the profile of a Hispanic girl. A sliver of relief settled in me when I realized that she wasn't the Tainted girl. But then confusion set in again. My skin crawled with panic.

Why would Trent's relatives attack us?

Trent raised his hands in the air and approached me and my captor one step at a time, as if walking a tight-rope. Julio swooped in, stopping Trent in his tracks. He grabbed Trent's shoulders and pointed at me. Terror etched across his face. "Hay maldad en su interior." He pointed behind me at Farrell. "Dile a dar marcha atrás."

Trent almost did a double-take before translating. "He says there's evil inside Dominique. He wants you to back down, Farrell."

"Like hell," Farrell growled.

The light from Farrell's energy grew brighter and saturated the room, yet the warmth couldn't stop my blood from turning cold at what Julio had said about me. My throat throbbed under the serrated blade. I was imagining the knife running me through, my head toppling to the floor, when a small shadowy figure emerged from the back of the room, behind Trent.

"You're going to be fine," her voice said from inside my head. *"I'm here now."*

The Tainted girl!

Farrell continued to radiate threatening power. The sleek knife held fast at my skin. Warm moisture trailed down my neck. And the Tainted girl slithered closer.

"You need to kill them," she said. *"All of them. Especially the Walker."*

"Farrell, ease up," Trent pleaded, holding his hands palm up. "Please. Let me talk to them."

"You've got thirty seconds to talk your people down," Farrell said through gritted teeth. "After that, they're mine." Farrell's light faded until the room grew dark again. The shuffling of feet sounded around me. A dim yellow light appeared. My gaze shot to the source. It was Julio. He carried an oil lamp across the small room and into an adjacent kitchen. He grabbed another lamp, lit it, and set it on a square wooden table.

My eyes adjusted to the new lighting while I searched for the Tainted girl. I couldn't see her, but I could sense her presence. I had to warn the others before I lost myself to her.

"Sh-sh-she's here," I squeaked out, my neck pulsing with fear against the cool blade. "The girl."

Infiniti whimpered. "Oh my God! The girl?"

"Who?" Trent asked. He spun around, searching the room. "Who's here?"

"I sense it," Farrell warned. His light brightened the room again. Before anyone could say another word, a cold wind blasted through the house. The glass hurricane lamps shattered, their destruction plummeting the room into pitch darkness. Infiniti shrieked. Boots thudded across the floor. The knife at my neck clanked to the ground. And the face of the evil girl appeared before me, an unearthly glow surrounding her features.

"I've always been inside you," she said. *"Because I am you. The real you. And if you won't accept who you are, I'll have to force you."*

Her face dissolved into a thick purple haze that sank into my body. My eyes stung. Razor sharp pain stabbed my skin. My insides burned like a sizzling inferno. My entire body wanted to ignite, when just as quickly, the pain subsided.

"Dominique!" Infiniti screamed.

My tense body relaxed. My mind cleared for the first time in months. Nearby, someone lit another lamp that barely penetrated the darkness of the room.

A strong arm wrapped around my waist and drew me in. I didn't even have to look to know who it was. Farrell. My protector. Chosen to walk beside me in each of my lives. Even though he suffered from amnesia, deep down he still loved me. I could tell. He had always loved me and would do anything for me.

And that was why I needed to kill him first.

"You okay?" Farrell asked.

I wiped the sticky trail of blood from my neck. "Yeah, I'm fine."

Before I could make my move, I examined the room. A petrified Infiniti huddled next to Trent, five feet away from me and to the left. Trent's great-grandfather, Julio, took his place next to them, one hand on Trent's shoulder. Behind them stood the other Hispanic guy, holding the newly lit hurricane lamp in a shaky hand. Standing apart from the others, hands clenched at her sides, the lean and small-framed Hispanic girl glared at me. I recognized her right away as the knife wielder. Carmen—Julio's wife and Trent's great-grandmother.

She glowered at me, and pointed. "*Ella no es la misma.*"

"She's not the… same?" Trent repeated, questioning her statement.

"Shit," Infiniti whispered. "Dominique? You, um, okay?"

Okay? I was more than okay. Strength coursed through my veins. Power beckoned at my fingertips. An immense force I'd never known gathered inside me. And I loved it. I needed it. They had kept it from me—these so-called Pures who had me under their control. But not anymore.

"I'm great," I answered.

I felt the energy vibrations from Farrell shift. He released his hold on me and stepped back. I turned and met his stare, studying his hot body for a second. I thought of asking him to join me, but his stormy green eyes told me he never would.

I widened my stance, ignoring everyone else in the room. Farrell and I were combatants now, waiting to see who would strike first.

And that would be me.

A surge of anger flared inside me. It warmed my body from the inside out, working its way through each blood vessel and every muscle. Suddenly I could do anything—including kill the powerful Pure before me.

"Don't!" Farrell blurted.

A blast of purple hued vapor exploded from my hands directly at Farrell. He swooshed his arm in a circular motion, deflecting my blast and sending it up to the ceiling. The house rocked. Pieces of sheetrock showered down. Screaming filled the room. Furious at my miss, I blasted again, over and over, unsure of how to wield the newfound power in me, yet certain of my hatred for the Walker in the room—and anyone else who stood in my way.

In a flurry of action, he dodged, deflected, and absorbed each attack. The house roared with my strikes and rocked with his defensive blocks. The stench of sulphur and ash flooded the air. I started to advance, thirsty for his blood, when out of nowhere, a body slammed into me from behind. Arms wrapped around my torso, holding on tight.

"Holy shit," the person muttered.

Fury exploded inside me. This time it failed to materialize outside my body, as if my light had been snuffed out.

With a grunt, I craned my neck at the person who had somehow muffled my energy source. It was Infiniti—eyes wide, terror splashed across her face. I had forgotten she was a Void, one immune to Transhuman abilities, and now the person impeding my assault.

I jerked my body back and forth, trying to fling her off. "Let go!"

Another body smashed up behind Infiniti. Together they secured me in a double body hold. "Hold tight," Farrell grunted to Infiniti.

"You're dead!" I screeched.

Infiniti whimpered. Farrell squeezed. The room lit up with more lamps. Carmen scurried up to me and pressed a hand against my forehead. Her rough fingertips moved in a circular motion while she mumbled something indiscernible. I tugged my head back and spit in her face. "Get the hell away from me!"

She wiped the dribble from her cheek, unfazed at my outburst. *"Ponla en la cama."*

Trent's worried gaze glued on me and he did a double take. "Huh? Put her on the bed?"

"Sí, bed. *Aquí,"* she said, motioning to a small bed crammed into the corner of the room.

Together, Farrell and Infiniti shuffled me over to the spot while the Hispanic girl disappeared into the kitchen. I had no idea what they were up to, but I needed to act. Fast.

"Trent?" My voice softened. "Wh-wh-what's happening?" I forced tears to spring into my eyes and quivered my lip. "I'm scared."

Trent darted in front of me, blocking the path to the bed. "Stop!" He stepped closer and peered into my eyes, as if he could see something in there. "Is it you? Are you back to normal?"

"Yes, it's me," I lied. "What's happening?"

"Let her go," Trent commanded.

"No way," Farrell said. "She's playing you. I can feel it."

Trent crept closer to me, narrowing his eyes in what looked like confusion. "She is?"

"I'm not," I whispered, shaking my head, wrenching sobs now shaking my body. "Please, help me."

Farrell gripped me tighter, forcing an "ouch" out of Infiniti. "Back away, Trent," Farrell commanded. "Now!"

Trent hesitated, doubt filling his eyes. "Okay," he mumbled. Before he could step aside, I swung my leg back and slammed my foot into his crotch. He groaned, grabbed himself, and dropped to the ground. I kicked both legs into the air, trying to wrestle away from my captors.

"Let go!" I yelled.

"Shit!" Infiniti called out, her legs buckling for a second before Farrell lifted her upright.

"Keep moving," Farrell commanded. He shoved Infiniti forward, forcing me closer to the bed. When we got there, they stopped.

"Now what?" Infiniti asked, her voice cracking with fright.

Trent scrambled to his feet, struggling to catch his breath. All the color had drained from his face. *"¿Ahora qué?"* he asked his relatives who were obviously in charge now.

Carmen rushed up to us. *"Aquí."* She pointed at my body and then pointed at the bed.

Julio approached with a bundle of rope. *"Hay que atarla,"* he said.

Trent kept his distance from me. "They want us to put her on the bed and secure her."

Fear spiked in me. I couldn't let them tie me up! I gathered all the hate inside me and tried to push it out and blast them away from me, but nothing happened.

The Hispanic trio disappeared from view. Shuffling sounded behind me. I stretched my neck, trying to see what they were doing, when hands clutched my calves from behind. A rope laced around my ankles and cinched tight.

My fury shaped itself into words. "I'm going to kill you! Kill you all!"

Carmen reappeared with two glass bowls filled with water. She placed them on the floor next to the bed and motioned for Farrell and Infiniti to place me on the mattress.

"Voy a quitar el mal," she declared solemnly, with narrowed eyes.

Trent froze. *"¿Quitar el mal?"* he repeated to the girl, as if he couldn't believe what she had just said.

"What?" Infiniti asked in a hushed tone. "What did she just say?"

Trent swallowed. "She said she's going to take the evil out of Dominique."

"No!" I hollered. "She can't do shit to me!"

Julio and the other guy wound my legs tight. Carefully, they threaded the rope between Infiniti and me. They secured my arms to my torso, wrapping me over and over with the thick cord. Farrell relaxed his hold, placed his hands on top of Infiniti's, and moved her arms up to my head. He pressed her palms against my temples. "Don't lose the connection," he warned.

"I don't know if I can do this!" Infiniti burst out.

"Infiniti!" Trent barked. "Just do it!"

"Fine! I'll try!" she snapped. "But I can't guarantee anything!"

"You're all going to die," I taunted them. "All the Pures are going to die." I eyed my captors. "Including the humans who align with them."

Farrell released his hold on my now bound body and circled to my front. He glared. "If these people can't get the Tainted out of you, the only one who'll die is you." White vapor oozed from his fingertips and wrapped around his hand. He paused, working his jaw before adding, "That's a promise."

My mind raced with ideas on how to escape. Then it hit me. If I could trick anyone into getting me out of this mess, it was Infiniti. Her hands trembled against the sides of my head as the men lifted me and placed on the bed.

"Infiniti, you're my one true friend," I said, gulping. "Please, get me out of here."

"Ignore her," Farrell commanded while he and Trent secured my already bound body to the bed with even more rope.

"Infiniti…" My voice broke. "Please," I said, turning pleading eyes on her. She darted her gaze away from me. "Don't let them hurt me," I begged.

She knelt behind the mattress, her arms stretched out on the bed, and her hands on my skin. I tilted my head back and lifted my chin, trying to make eye contact with her. The tips of her long wavy hair brushed against my forehead. "You have to help me."

She looked up at the ceiling and bit her bottom lip.

"You can't let Farrell kill me."

"La la la la la," she started to hum, blocking out my pleas. Her gaze frantically roamed from one side of the room to the other.

I needed her to look at me. It was the only way to get to her. A sob escaped my lips. Tears streamed down my face. Her gaze flitted across my face and I didn't waste the opportunity. "You're my best friend."

"Farrell," Infiniti whispered. "Maybe she's—"

"No, she's not," he said. He and Trent finished with the rope and stood over me. Farrell reached over to Infiniti, grabbed the sleeve of her shirt, and tore it off. He balled up the fabric and shoved it in my mouth.

"There." He ignored my grunts and groans. "Now what?" he asked Trent.

Trent, still doubled over a little from my kick, glanced at his great-grandparents. "They do their thing, I guess."

Trent shuffled away from the bed and cleared a path for Carmen. She studied my face with distrustful eyes before lowering herself onto her knees. Cracking her knuckles, she started making the sign of the cross by moving her hand from her forehead to her chest, and from one shoulder to the other. *"Diós nos ayude."*

"God help us," Trent mumbled.

Chapter Eighteen

The strike of a match sounded, followed by the smell of strong woody incense filtering through the air. Heavy wind whistled against the thin windowpanes, prompting a cascade of shivers over my body.

Carmen spit into her hands, rubbed them together, and placed them on my cheeks. I tried to wrench my head away, but she tightened her grip and dug her fingertips deep into my cheekbones. She started chanting in Spanish, her rough fingers pressing hard as they moved across my face. Her skin stank of grass and mud.

I must get out of here. I must kill them.

I focused on my hate, concentrating on lashing out at them. Still nothing happened. The girl brought her tanned and weathered face close to mine. She blew a soft trail of warm breath over me. *"Limpia,"* she whispered.

Mesmerized by her dark skin and brown eyes, I hardly noticed the egg she held up to my face. She closed her eyes, chanting again, and brought the egg to my skin. She moved it over my cheeks, down to my chin, up the bridge of my nose, and to my forehead without losing contact.

"What the hell?" Infiniti murmured, her hands still pressed against my temples.

"It's an ancient ritual people from my culture do to

eliminate bad energy," Trent whispered. "Like a spiritual cleansing. But I've never seen it done."

At first I thought the Hispanic girl was crazy, but then my upper lip started tingling. Warmth spread across my skin and gathered inside my throat, itching my esophagus and tightening my airway. A hundred thousand tiny needles poked me from the inside out. The jabbing intensified, forcing my stomach into a tight ball. The girl broke contact, cracked the egg, and plopped the contents into a glass bowl of water Julio held over me. What should've been a yellow yolk came out gray and dirty. Panic seized me, my entire body growing rigid as I studied the murky contents of the water.

"Whoa," Infiniti muttered. "What the heck?"

Farrell and Trent inched closer as they studied the bowl, both of them staring in disbelief. Trent shook his head. "It's working," he said.

The girl picked up another egg. This time she pressed it against my shirt, right over my pounding heart. She rubbed it around the itchy fabric. Even though a layer of cloth lay between the egg and me, my skin burned where it traveled, like a lit match scraping against me. My body seized and my gut wrenched, as if someone had leveled me with a massive kick. A silent scream filled my throat.

The girl jerked the egg away and cracked it. The sharp stench of rot burst into the air. Dark brown contents spilled out. She quickly grabbed another egg and pressed it against my navel. Her chanting grew faster and more urgent as she ran the egg over my torso.

My body scorched. The burning pain ran through me, up and down my entire body. It filled every inch of me, jerking my limbs and crushing my lungs. I gasped for breath, choking on the fabric that jarred my mouth open. Tears of agony stung my eyes and blurred my vision.

They were killing me!

"Stop!" Infiniti yelled.

I concentrated on Infiniti—the only person standing between the others and me. Her hands quaked against my skin. Her palms slicked with perspiration. If I craned my neck and jerked hard enough, I knew she'd let go.

"Hold tight," warned Farrell.

But it was too late.

I yanked my head and Infiniti's hands lost their hold. A flash of hate poured out of me, blasting an explosion of energy through the room. Like a violent wind, it hurled the Hispanic girl away from me and flung her across the room. Hollering filled the air. The ropes around my body disintegrated. I tugged the cloth from my mouth when a body crashed down on top of me.

Farrell!

He wrapped his arms around me and held me in a death grip, his face just inches from mine. His angry green eyes glittered with white flecks. Every muscle in my body flexed when yellow-hued crackling light blazed from his skin. It hovered over me like a ton of invisible bricks, pinning me down and driving my energy blast back inside.

My body shook. My hands fisted. I met his enraged stare with my own and gnashed my teeth, hell bent on forcing my power back out and killing him. Finally, my sizzling aura seeped out. It poured out of me and hissed against his, crashing against him with a showering burst of sparks.

"Infiniti!" he grunted, forcing his weight against mine. "Hold her!"

I lifted my chin and narrowed my eyes. "I'm going to kill you, Walker."

"I don't think so," he groaned. Sweat beads dotted his forehead. The veins in his neck popped out. Infiniti must've pulled herself together because tiny hands slammed against my temples. The force that I had unleashed vanished, rendering me helpless again.

Fresh terror over being tortured again by the Hispanic witch and her crazy voodoo descended on me. I surveyed the room for her and spotted her on the ground. Trent and the others huddled around her limp body.

Good.

"Is she okay?" Farrell hollered at Trent, his body still pressed against mine and his arms wrapped tight around me.

"She's out, but breathing," Trent panted.

"Can anyone else finish the ritual?" Farrell asked.

"¿Puedes limpiar?" Trent frantically asked his great-grandfather and the other Hispanic guy.

Terror-stricken, the men could barely look at me, as if making eye contact would kill them. I glared at them and furrowed my brow, jerking my chin in their direction. They jumped a little and backed up against the wall.

Superstitious idiots.

Farrell's body bore down on mine. The white sparks in his eyes intensified as he studied me, his face so close our lips almost met. Damn, he was hot as shit, and for a second there I thought of kissing him, but what the hell for? He was on the other side and as good as dead to me anyway.

"I guess we'll have to do this my way," he threatened with a cock of his head.

Infiniti's hands twitched against my head. "What?"'

Trent crept up to the side of the bed. "What will happen to Dominique?"

"He's going to kill me, dumb ass," I spat out. "And it'll be all your fault!"

Like a slap to the face, my words made Trent flinch. He avoided eye contact with me, focusing on Farrell. "Do it," he whispered.

Farrell bought his gaze up to Infiniti. "I'm going to extinguish the negative energy in her. So when I say let go, you let go, okay?"

"Oh my God, oh my God, oh my God," she whimpered, her voice laden with fear.

"Infiniti! Let go when I say!"

"Fine!"

"And if something goes south—" Farrell took a long pause. "Slam back down on her." He leveled Infiniti with a serious stare. "Got it?"

Her teeth chattered as her hands trembled against my head. "O-k-k-k-ay."

Farrell looked over his shoulder at Trent. "Be ready to help her."

Trent nodded and moved behind Infiniti.

This was it.

Fight back or die.

As soon as Infiniti let go, I had to do everything in my power to kill the Walker. If I didn't, he'd end me. I squirmed under his muscled body. I even tried to jerk my legs and kick him until hands grabbed my ankles. I lifted my head a little and saw Julio holding me.

I growled like a wild animal. "The second the Void lets go, you're all dead! You hear me? Dead!"

A hard look of determination swept across Farrell's face. His jaw clenched. He eyed Trent and Infiniti. "Let go."

Infiniti yanked her hands away. In one fluid movement, Farrell released his hold and straddled me, squeezing his legs against my torso to keep my arms down. Blinding white light exploded from his body, forcing my eyes shut. A howling wind whipped through the room.

I had summoned all my hate, was focused on killing every single person in the room with my own energy blast, when something cool and smooth traced my forehead. My eyes snapped open. It was the voodoo witch! She hovered over me, running an egg across my forehead.

"No!"

Excruciating pain erupted inside me like a volcano. Darkness blotted my vision. A hard seizure lifted my body from the mattress.

Just before I thought my body would split in two, a warm yellow glow filled the room. A feeling of peace crept over me, and suddenly, I was me again.

With a thud, I landed on the concrete floor of the house. A tiny hand stretched out to help me up. A lifeline. I held it tight, struggling to my feet. When I caught my balance, I discovered Abigail and Jan before me.

"What's happening?" I whispered.

"Well, my dear, quite a lot." Jan placed her thick strong hands on my shoulders and turned me toward the corner of the small house, to the bed where my body lay under attack by Farrell and Carmen.

Tears covered Infiniti's face while she pressed her

hands against the sides of my head. Trent braced himself behind her, helping to keep her palms in place. Julio and the other Hispanic guy held my legs. Carmen knelt beside me, rubbing her egg all over my chest. And then I gaped at Farrell. He sat on top of me, his legs pressing against my sides and immobilizing my arms. His brilliant aura filled the room like a burst of sunlight. He held his hands down, pointing them at me, while a thick stream of shimmery white vapor lasered into the middle of my forehead.

I patted my upper body, and then covered my mouth. "They're killing me," I mumbled.

"Since you are in the space between, that seems to be the case," Jan said sorrowfully.

Abigail squeezed my hand. "But they're not trying to."

She was right, I knew they weren't trying to kill me, but getting the evil Tainted girl out of me could mean my death whether they wanted it or not.

Wait...the evil Tainted girl. She claimed to be part of me. I whipped around to face Jan and Abigail. "The Tainted girl. Who is she?"

Jan looked down at Abigail before meeting my gaze. "We have come to the conclusion that she is a manifestation of a part of you that's been buried all these lifetimes. Perhaps by your own doing, or by the shielding of your parents, we don't really know."

"We don't," Abigail whispered in agreement.

"My dear," Jan went on. "The spot at the back of your neck—the mark Tavion placed there—we think it is more than just his brand."

My hand wandered to the birthmark at the back of my neck, just under my hairline.

"We think Tavion injected his spirit through that mark. Gave you a part of his soul, if you will."

My hand covered the splotch, as if smothering it would make it go away. "His soul?"

"Yes," Jan answered. "We think his plan all along was for you to kill him and take his place."

I suddenly thought of what the Tainted girl had said about my blood mixing with Tavion's back at the red desert. I brought my palm to my face and studied the faded scars laced across my skin. "The Tainted girl confronted me on the plane from Houston to Michigan. She said Tavion's essence was taking me over because our blood had mixed together."

"Ah," Jan said. "So that's how he did it. His blood mixing with yours awakened the part of him he had left inside of you."

Dread swept over me, followed by sheer panic. Shivers raced across my skin. I turned back around to witness my ordeal in the real world. My face had paled over. My body lifted from the bed in a contortion of pain. My hands clutched at Farrell's legs.

Abigail and Jan flanked my sides and held me. "It'll be over soon," Jan said in a soft voice.

Abigail rested her head against my arm. "I hope you live," she said in her tiny voice.

A flood of tears sprang to my eyes and blurred my vision. "I hope so, too."

Jan and Abigail stayed close while we watched my corporeal body take a beating from Farrell and the others. And when I didn't think the real me could take it anymore, a massive explosion of purple vapor exploded from every pore in my body. Mesmerized, I watched as Carmen hollered at Farrell to send the energy into the egg. With a whipping of his energy stream, he forced the purple haze into the small egg. The room shook. The light from the hurricane lamps flickered. Finally, the evil from inside me disappeared completely through the shell.

The house settled. The room fell quiet. Carmen's hands shook as she carefully held the egg. Julio rushed away to the kitchen and returned with a glass bowl of fresh water. The girl cracked the egg over it. Thick black ooze dribbled out, like oil, followed by wisps of dark smoke. Infiniti rushed to the corner of the room and vomited while the others covered their mouths in disgust.

Carmen rubbed her face and tucked her long dark hair behind her ears. After catching her breath for a few seconds, she stooped beside my still body. She checked my pulse. *"Está limpia."*

Trent crashed down to his knees and ran his fingers through his hair. "It's done. She's clean."

Jan rubbed my back. "Now we wait."

Wait to live or wait to die. Stuck in some strange place in between my two fates, I quivered in fright. Not really knowing what to do, I worked my way through the room and watched as the others took care of me. Carmen placed a wet washcloth over my forehead. Infiniti smoothed out my dress and combed my hair out of my face. Trent sat by my side and held my hand. Farrell stood on guard at the foot of the bed with arms crossed and stance wide.

"They both love you," young Abigail whispered. "I can tell."

Grief had taken over me. It invaded every inch of me,

overflowing my heart with such immense guilt and despair I wished I had died. I loved Farrell even though he didn't remember me. Trent held onto his love for me, even though I had chosen Farrell. My best friend Infiniti stayed by my side.

And I had tried to kill them.

The worse part of it all was the uncertainty of what lay before me. Back in my own time, Mom and the others were under attack. Maybe even dead. Dad, who warned that Mom was a traitor, was being held somewhere on the premises. If I didn't wake up, my friends would have to face them alone. And if I did wake up, I didn't know if I could face the unknown, let alone face the others after what I had done. If they didn't hate me, maybe they should.

Without even realizing it, I started making the sign of the cross over my body. I stopped short, my hand hovering over my chest for a second before I finished the motion.

Chapter Nineteen

Seconds turned into minutes. Minutes turned into hours. Trent's relatives sat at the kitchen table, my friends kept watch over me, and Jan and Abigail, in our space between, left me alone. My only companions were feelings of remorse over having tried to kill my friends and anguish over their fate if I didn't wake.

"You shouldn't think that way," Abigail said, breaking the dread-filled silence and making her way over to me.

I brought my knees up to my chin and wrapped my arms around my legs. "If you're reading my thoughts, don't. Okay? They're all I have left."

Abigail sat next to me on the floor. She crossed her legs and studied the scene that had riveted me in place. "I don't have to read your thoughts to know of your despair." She laid her tiny hand on my leg. "But you have much more than that."

Jan joined us. "She's right, my dear."

Their words offered no comfort, but I faked a smile anyway. Abigail scooted over and positioned herself in front of me, blocking the earthly me and the others from view. She tilted her head to the side while her big green eyes examined mine. Her gaze dropped to my neckline. "Your cross."

I grabbed the top of my shirt and bundled the fabric into my fist. "I lost it." A lone tear escaped and traveled down my cheek.

Abigail wiped it away and smiled at me reassuringly. "It's okay. You'll find it."

There was no way, but I didn't tell her that. All I could do was nod and secretly hope she was right. It was the least I could do.

"I hate my life," I mumbled.

"Dominique, don't waste your words on such thoughts," Jan said, interrupting my self-despair. "When one's life path is chosen and laid out in all its beautiful and sometimes terrible glory, all we can do is journey forward and hope for the best."

That was it? The best advice she could give me? Hope for the best? I desperately needed more. If not for me, then for those connected to me. I started to say so when my vision narrowed and my body swayed.

"She's waking," Abigail said.

Jan helped me to my feet and steadied me with her strong arms. "Are you ready to continue your journey?"

No, I wasn't ready. Not at all. I wanted to be normal. I wanted a life without a stupid mark at the back of my neck. And how I wished I hadn't killed Tavion after all.

"Jan," I whispered, my sight blurring. "I want a different path."

Jan's face zoomed in and out of focus. The space around her started fading to white. She leaned forward. "Go where the love is."

Darkness surrounded me. The floor below my feet slipped away, sending my body into free fall. Just before I crashed to the ground, my eyes snapped open.

"Dominique?"

Trent's worried face hovered inches over mine. I wanted to answer him, but couldn't. My mouth felt glued shut and stuffed with cotton. I rubbed my head and tried to sit up. Trent wrapped his arms around me and held me tight. "Dominique," he said again. "You're okay."

He buried his face in the crook of my neck. I hugged him back and held on for dear life, afraid something horrible would happen to me if I didn't. Then I remembered the others in the room and slowly let go. He propped me up and repositioned the pillow at my back.

Infiniti closed in and took my hand. She squeezed. "Don't ever scare the shit out of me like that again, you hear me?"

My throat burned. My heart hurt over what I had put them through. "I hear you," I croaked out in a scratchy voice. I pointed at my mouth. "Water. Please."

Carmen handed me a glass. I took it with a nod of thanks and sipped as the cool liquid soothed my rough and dry throat. By now, everyone in the house had circled around me, except Farrell. He stayed at the foot of the bed, arms still crossed. His gaze probed me as if he didn't trust I was me again.

I handed the glass to Infiniti but kept my gaze down, afraid of looking them in the eye after everything I had done and said to them. "I'm really sorry," I said, my voice hushed. "I didn't mean to—"

"It wasn't you," Trent cut in. "We all know that."

Infiniti rubbed my leg. "Yeah, no apologies. Okay?"

"Okay," I muttered, yet unable to shake the horrible feeling inside me.

Farrell crossed his arms and glared at me. "We need to know what happened to you," he ordered. "In case you attack us again."

Trent jumped to his feet. "Man, back off!"

While I had turned back to the real me, Farrell still hadn't. And for some reason, I knew, really knew, his memory would never return.

"It's okay," I blurted, tired of the tension between them. "Farrell is right. You guys need to know what happened to me."

As best as I could, I explained everything about the Tainted girl, how she had been a part of me, and how Tavion's blood mixing with mine triggered my change. Infiniti practically chewed her fingernails off while I spoke. Farrell stared at me in cold silence. And Trent did his best to translate everything to his relatives. But I could tell they were all confused.

My gaze shifted from Trent to his relatives. "So, that's really your great-grandfather?"

"Yeah, can you believe it?" He gestured at the Hispanic girl. "And this is my great-grandmother." He smiled at them, warmth lighting his deep blue eyes. "Carmen and Julio." He patted the other man's back. "And this is my great-uncle, Javier. Apparently, Carmen had a premonition we'd be visiting her today. Weird, huh?"

"Yeah, totally weird, but kinda normal for us," I said with a laugh, amazed to be in the presence of his ancestors while we were all the same age. My attempt at humor faded fast, drowned out by the seriousness of what had just happened. "Now that they've saved me, I guess we should tell them everything."

"Yeah," Trent agreed. "I guess we should."

We gathered in the tiny kitchen and Trent explained our story to them going back to the first time I met him in Houston. With intent eyes, they took in every word. My gaze glued on their expressions: wonder, fear, surprise. But most of all, I saw worry, concern, and love for Trent. I could see it in the way they stayed by his side and the way Carmen would reach out and touch Trent at certain parts of his story.

When Trent finished, no one said anything for a while. Farrell broke the silence. "We need to get back to the church."

Now that we had done what we needed to do in this time, our own time needed us since back home a major battle raged at the cabin. I just prayed we'd get back in time to help the others—and save Dad.

Trent's family loaded us up with a supply of food and water. They walked us through the cold, dark night to our bikes. There, under the moonlit and starry sky, they pulled Trent in for a hug. I turned away and thought of my own family. Would I ever see them again? If I did, would they be okay? And could Mom really be a traitor?

I shoved down the lump in my throat and forced my tears away. I didn't have time to get emotional. I needed to focus on getting back home because the sooner we got back, the quicker I'd know the truth about Mom, and hopefully save Dad.

We had hopped on our rides, ready to pedal away, when Carmen collapsed to the ground. Julio called out her name. Trent leapt off his bike and hurried to her side. Carmen's frame went rigid. Her hands tightened into fists, her eyes were wide open and glazed over.

"What's happening?" I asked, terror-stricken.

Julio cradled her head. *"Tiene una visión."*

"She's having a vision?" Trent asked out loud, surprise and fear in his voice.

Infiniti slammed her hand over her mouth and knelt down on the ground next to the girl. I started to join them, but Farrell stopped me. "Stay back," he cautioned.

Carmen's stiff body started to quake. Bursts of warm vapor puffed out of her mouth into the cold air. The bright moonlight revealed a cloudy blue film creeping over her eyes. I gasped, remembering how Trent's blind grandmother had the same hazed-over eyes and the ability to sense things.

Trent looked back at me. His lips parted in shock. "Like *abuela,*" he whispered.

Too freaked out to speak, I nodded, knowing exactly what he meant, then glued my attention back on the girl. Julio rubbed Carmen's forehead, mumbling comforting words in Spanish. After about a minute, the girl's breathing steadied. Her body relaxed. Her eyes closed, as if she had slipped into a deep sleep, and then flew open. Infiniti jumped.

"Estoy bién," Carmen said, scrambling to get up. She steadied herself on her wobbly legs and combed her long black hair away from her face. With eyes that had morphed back to their normal brown color, she leveled a serious look at us.

"Dolor y la muerte les esperan a todos en su propio tiempo."

Trent gulped. "She says sorrow and death wait for us back in our time."

A terrified hush hovered in the cold air. The gravity of Carmen's premonition muffled us. She approached Trent, placed her hands on his shoulders, and whispered in his ear.

I waited for Trent to translate, but he didn't. Instead, he placed his hands over hers, lowered his head, and mumbled something to her in Spanish.

A lone tear slid down Carmen's cheek. Trent wiped it away and stepped back. Julio placed his arm around Carmen, and both of them watched helplessly as Trent picked up his pack of supplies and got back up on his bike.

"Let's go," he said to us, refusing to look back at the Hispanic teens.

We followed him back to Main Street, pedaling fast to keep up the pace, when Infiniti stopped. "Trent Avila, slow the hell down!"

He coasted. "Infiniti Clausman, hurry the hell up!"

She huffed and then crossed her arms. "Not until you tell us what just happened back there!"

My gut coiled because if Trent wouldn't tell us what his great-grandmother had said, I knew it had to be bad. Real bad. Luckily, Infiniti would have nothing of it. "You better tell us what the hell she said!"

Farrell and I slowed, and eventually Trent did, too. Instead of joining us and explaining things, he called out, "It has nothing to do with you guys! Okay?"

A tiny crack in Trent's voice told me to jump to his defense. That and the guilt for dragging him into my nightmare life and attacking him at the house. "If he wants to tell us, he will."

Trent muttered something like thanks and continued on.

Infiniti cursed under her breath. "Fine, but I don't have to like it." She worked to build momentum with her oversized and squeaky tires and the four of us trekked back the way we had come.

I could tell Farrell had a problem with Trent's silence. I could see it in the tight grip around his handlebars and the way his arms flexed. Or was something else up? I didn't know, but tension mounted inside me.

More than halfway to our destination, and in the middle of downtown, Infiniti's leg cramped. We made our way down a dark alleyway and to the back of a building so she could work it out. She stretched and walked around for a bit, grunting and groaning with each step. I slumped down for a rest, but couldn't relax. Trent's silence was still thick in the air.

"Hey, Dominique. What are you going to do if we get out of this whole mess?" Infiniti asked, pulling an old tin canister from Trent's bag and taking a swig of water.

She passed it to me and I took a small sip. "I don't know." I wiped my mouth, wondering if Trent would come around and tell us what his great-grandmother had said. "I guess be normal. Keep my head down." I shrugged because I had no idea how to be normal. Plus, I really didn't believe we'd live beyond whatever lay in store for us back in our time. "Maybe go to college. You?"

She ripped a piece of fabric from the hem of her skirt and started tying her long wavy hair back. She sighed. "Get laid by a hot dude."

"Infiniti!" I laughed.

"Are you serious?" Trent asked, taking the canister from me. "That's what you want to do?"

"Yep, that's what I want to do. I mean shit; we almost died back at that house. And I know it sounds crazy, but I kept thinking about how I'd never had sex before." Her voice trailed off for a second. "Never fallen in love."

Love—that's what Jan had said. Go where the love is. My body shuddered. I had no idea what she meant, but it seemed Infiniti was searching for love, too. Or something close to it.

"We're wasting time," Farrell cut in. He paced around like a wild animal, jumpy and agitated. "Can you ride?" he asked Infiniti.

"Yeah, Mr. Impatient," she rolled her eyes. "I can ride."

Everyone got on their bikes except for Trent. He knelt down to inspect one of his wheels. I hopped off my ride and joined him. "Hey, you okay?"

He kept his focus on the spokes of his tires, bending them here and there. "I'm not gonna make it, Dominique."

His words cut straight through me, almost stabbing the very life out of me. "What?"

He shoved his hand in his pocket and pulled something out. "Here." He opened my hand and wrapped my fingers around a smooth, round object. "For you—just in case."

Before I could say anything, he got back on his seat, leaving me crouched down in a fog of worry and shock. Making sure no one was looking, I uncurled my fingers. There in my palm was the Petoskey stone I had given him for Christmas.

"What's that?" Infiniti asked, looking down on me.

I fisted the treasure and plopped it into my boot leg, hopping back on my bicycle quick. "Nothing. Come on."

Infiniti grunted. "Everyone has a damn secret but me."

Back on track, we continued on to the church. The cold night wind forced my eyes into a permanent watery squint. Cloudy white vapor from my labored breathing puffed in front of my face. The closer we got to St. Joseph's, the faster I breathed and the harder my heart pumped. Doubts flooded my thoughts. Dread gripped me tight. What if we got there and we couldn't jump back to our time? What if an evil still lurked inside me? What if something horrible happened to Trent?

Before I knew it, the church loomed into view. Trent, who had taken the lead, slowed down. He hopped off his bike and the rest of us followed. "Stay in the shadows," he warned.

We moved slow and close together, staying as far away from the street as possible. My nerves skyrocketed. My body trembled. When we got to the church, we hesitated and studied the abandoned-looking building. The dark windows looked eerie. Creepy silhouettes from a nearby tree slithered along the brick exterior. Just beyond, the nun's dark house sat in silence. We stashed our bikes behind a row of bushes, careful not to make a sound.

"Now what?" I asked in a low voice. The breeze rustled the leaves from the nearby shrubbery, making me jumpy and nervous.

"We go in," Farrell said, declaring the task like it was the simplest thing ever, as if breaking and entering were an everyday occurrence. I guess after time travel, an exorcism, and a near-death experience, sneaking into someone else's property was no big deal.

"And get back home," Infiniti muttered.

"Yeah," Trent chimed in. "Home." His doubt rang clear in my ears, but I knew the others didn't hear it.

Trent and Infiniti crept to the front door of the church. I started to follow them, when Farrell held me back. "Something's off," he whispered in my ear.

The fine hairs on my body stood on end. My stomach knotted. "What do you mean?"

He brought his face closer to mine. "I'm not sure. Just stay close."

Horrifying thoughts and images popped into my head as we caught up with the others. No matter how hard I tried to push them out of my mind, I couldn't. We were all screwed.

Trent rested one hand on the wooden door and the other around the brass doorknob. He glanced over his shoulder at us. "Here we go."

He turned the knob and swung the door open. We hesitated for a second, waiting to see if anyone was inside, then scurried in and pressed our backs against the wall. A haunting stillness filled the church, sending a tip-toeing shiver down my spine. Traces of woodsy incense lingered in the air. Minimal lighting from above cast long shadows across the white marble floor. Even the oversized figure of Jesus hanging on the crucifix at the front of the church looked menacing. It was as if we had just entered the creepiest haunted house.

Infiniti edged up beside me. "I have a bad feeling about this."

Crap. Not her, too.

I shot an uneasy look at Farrell. "There's nothing to worry about," I said, trying to sound convincing.

"That's right," Farrell added. He scanned the church, taking it all in. "Where did we cross over?"

Trent pointed to the front. "Up there." We made our way up the center aisle, to the front benches. "Dominique, Infiniti, and I ended up around these pews."

I stopped and stared at the open area in front of the first long, wooden bench. I could almost see Farrell's listless body on the ground, his face covered with splotchy red veins. "And you ended up on the floor," I said, pointing at the spot by my feet.

Farrell examined the area for a minute, as if willing himself to remember who he used to be and what had happened. He looked away and rubbed his hands together. "All right, let's get in a circle and hold hands." He eyed Trent with a serious look. "If I told you to think of a safe place and we ended up here, you should be able to do the same thing and get us back."

"And you're sure you can't do it, right?" Infiniti asked Farrell, as if desperate for him to say yes, not fully trusting Trent's untapped abilities. "I mean, you know, since you've got experience."

"No, I can't. Not without my memories. But Trent can."

A sliver of doubt flashed across Trent's eyes. He pushed it away fast and replaced it with determination while we all held hands, but I had seen it. I wondered if the others had, too. I squeezed his hand. "You can do it."

He exhaled and gripped my hand back. "The Boardman River," he whispered. "The cold. The snow. The attack." He closed his eyes, muttering the same words over and over.

Infiniti's terrified eyes practically bulged out of her head. Farrell's gaze kept darting around the church, as if any second something horrible might happen. I tried to remain calm, even though my mouth had dried and my heart pounded like a massive drum.

A minute ticked by, and then another. My hope for an exit back home started to wane, when crackling sparks blasted through the air. Infiniti let out a high-pitched scream. Farrell jerked me close.

"There you are!" a deep voice called out.

We whipped around to the back of the church to find Fleet. Dressed in all black and wearing his usual scowl, he sauntered over to us. I glanced at Farrell, wondering if he'd remember they were brothers, but he made no sign of recognition.

"Where the hell are we?" Fleet barked, scanning the Catholic surroundings. He eyed our clothes. "And what the hell are you wearing?"

"We're at my church," Trent said. "And we're wearing 1930's clothes because—"

"We're in freaking 1930!" Infiniti finished for him.

Farrell moved me behind him. "Who the hell are you?" he asked, glaring at Fleet.

Fleet froze, shooting me a puzzled look. "Huh?"

"Farrell, that's your brother—Fleet," I said, moving out from behind Farrell. "He's a Pure, like you, and a Tracker."

Farrell kept his gaze narrowed on Fleet. "If he is, then why can't I read him?"

"What?" I asked, more confused than ever. "You can't—"

"Enough," Fleet blurted. "We need to get back, and fast, before everyone's killed."

"Killed?" Farrell repeated, keeping one arm wrapped around me and pressing me up against him. "By who?"

Fleet inched closer. His face softened as he turned his attention to me. "By Caris, Dominique's mother. That's who."

Alarming silence filled the room. A chill raced along my spine. I didn't want to believe that Mom could turn on me and Dad, but here was the evidence. "My mom? Are you sure?"

Fleet nodded. "Yeah. And if we don't get back, like right now, we're all dead. Every last one of us."

Chapter Twenty

Dead? My Mom the traitor? She definitely had been acting strange, and Dad had warned me about her, but could it really be true? My stomach knotted so tightly I wanted to double over.

"I don't believe it," I mumbled.

Fleet ran his hands through his thick dark hair. "I know. I was surprised as hell when she attacked. It took all my strength to get away and track your signature. Now that I've found you, we gotta get back. Now." He jerked his chin at Farrell. "Come on."

"He can't," I murmured.

Farrell shifted. "I can only transport to a place I know. And I don't remember where we were."

Fleet let out an exasperated laugh. "What? Are you kidding me?"

Nobody spoke. We were all too shocked at our messed up situation. At least, I was.

Fleet paced. "So you brought everyone here, and now you can't get anyone back?"

"Not exactly," Trent offered. "*I* brought everyone here, but not on purpose."

"You?" Fleet asked, in disbelief.

"Yeah, me. Apparently, I'm something called a Supreme."

Fleet stumbled back a step. He let out a whistle. "Really?"

The abrupt sound of a door slamming open rang through the church. "What is the meaning of this?!" The booming voice that called out sent an echo bouncing off the sacred walls. I didn't have to look to recognize the voice of Mother Superior Mary Johanna. She swung her arms briskly as she moved with purpose toward us. Sister Mary Catherine trailed in her wake. "You have broken the rules! No one is allowed in the sanctuary at night!"

"Holy mother," Infiniti said, mouth hanging open.

"I told you they were of the devil!" Sister Mary Catherine declared.

Great, so the young nun had turned our ally against us. I tugged on Trent's shirt. "This would be an excellent time to get out of here."

"Everyone, hold hands," Farrell barked. "Trent, focus on where we came from. Fleet, you and I will help him direct his energy."

"Stop what you are doing, you hoodlums!" Mother Superior ordered. "The police are on the way!"

Sirens wailed in the distance. Farrell held my hand in an iron-clad grip. Trent took the other, squeezed his eyes shut, and started moving his lips. My worry that something would happen to Trent was replaced with fear that none of us were going to make this time jump.

My frantic gaze alternated between Trent's silent chanting and the swishing of Mother Superior and Sister Mary Catherine's long black robes. The Mother Superior wore a deeply etched frown while the young nun stared directly at me with a look of pure hatred in her eyes. I glanced at Farrell to see if he noticed, but he was focused on Trent and Fleet. Then I shifted my attention to Infiniti. She gaped at the young nun, a baffled expression covering her face. Good, she had to have noticed the young nun's hateful gaze that had glued on me. But what did it mean?

Trent hummed under his breath. Fleet and Farrell joined in. Smoky vapor poured from their hands like wispy tendrils. My palms grew sweaty. My legs started to wobble. I knew we'd be gone soon, but what about the nuns? They were almost on top of us!

The Mother Superior had quickened her pace when Sister Mary Catherine shoved her out of the way, drew a butcher knife from her sleeve, and flung herself at me. In a blur of motion, she dove for me just as the marble floor dissolved beneath my feet. Flashes of black and yellow filled my vision. Curses blared in my ears. With a thud, I landed on my back amidst a crunchy layer of snow. In a blink, the nun appeared in the air above me. She collapsed onto me, knocking the wind right out of my lungs.

"You're the devil!" she spat out, wrapping her long fingers around my neck and digging into my windpipe.

"Get. Off," I choked out, clutching her wrists and trying to pull her from me, keenly aware she wasn't using a knife and grateful that she must've dropped it.

She had half strangled me when a body tackled her, hurling her from me. Coughing and gasping for air, I caught a glimpse of Farrell as the nun tumbled to the ground. Her headpiece flew off her head, exposing long blonde hair tied high in a ponytail. She scrambled to her feet, ready to lunge at me, when she noticed her foreign surroundings—freezing white snow and tall naked trees.

"Where am I?"

Before I could even worry about the nun, I did a quick scan for Trent and saw that he had made it! We exchanged knowing looks of relief, and he helped me up. We all stared at the out of place nun and I couldn't believe she had tried to kill me just like the Veronica version of her in my time.

"What sorcery is this?" the nun whispered, her lip quivering. Suddenly I felt sorry for her, even though she had attacked me.

"We have to send her back," I said to no one in particular.

Fleet stood next to Farrell now, both of them close to the nun and eyeing her as if they really didn't know what to do with her. With a quick flick of his wrist, Fleet shot a thick stream of energy at the nun's forehead. Her body gave a hard jolt before flopping over, lifeless.

I gasped and hit his back. "Why did you do that?"

He spun around and towered over me. Farrell and Trent pulled me back. And that's when I noticed the quiet air. When we had left, crashing booms rocketed from the cabin. Even the ground had shifted and split under our feet. Now, everything looked weirdly normal.

I inched further away from Fleet, my stomach tight and my pulse racing. "What's going on?"

Colleen burst into view. "Is that them?" She marched toward us from the cabin, her long staff in hand. "All of them?"

"Yes," Fleet answered. "All of them."

She was the oldest Pure and a friend to my parents. Before we time jumped to 1930, she had appeared and cautioned us not to trust anyone before she fell into a comatose state. And when I had seen Dad, he had said to trust her. But the look on her face and the way she advanced forward didn't match Dad's directive.

"This is all wrong," I whispered.

Infiniti pressed up against me. "I don't like this."

Farrell, Trent, Infiniti, and I moved back even further, confused by the turn of events.

"Colleen, you're okay," I said to her as she neared. Her long black hair and blunt bangs framed her perfect, pale face.

She ignored me, her gaze focused on Fleet. "Which one?" she asked him.

Fleet pointed at Farrell who had now pushed me back behind him. "That one," he said.

Everything seemed to slow down as my jumbled mind processed the unfolding scene. Colleen raised her staff at Farrell. It morphed from an ordinary brown walking stick into a blazing white weapon. Farrell brought his hands up, sparks shooting from his fingertips. Trent tugged me back, my screaming echoing through the woods, while Infiniti stumbled to the ground. Before Farrell had a chance to defend himself, a green blast of electricity exploded from the tip of the staff. It lasered straight into Farrell's forehead, boosting him off the ground. His head jerked back with a snap. His limbs gave a hard twitch before going limp. Colleen lowered her weapon and Farrell slipped to the ground.

A rush of frigid air blew over me. Uncontrollable shivers wracked my body. I wrenched myself away from Trent and rushed over to Farrell, sinking to my knees beside him. His emerald green eyes were wide open, his lips slightly parted. I touched the side of his neck, checking for a pulse, but couldn't find one.

"You have done well," Colleen said to Fleet.

Done well? Rage brewed inside me. An overwhelming need for revenge took over. With fisted hands, I jumped to my feet, ready to attack Fleet and Colleen with my bare hands, but froze. Crackling vapor oozed from Fleet's palms. It traveled up his body in a circular motion, roping him in a misty fog. When the haze cleared, he wasn't Fleet anymore, but Dad.

I stumbled back, confusion knocking me off my feet. I crashed into Trent and Infiniti who held me upright. Dad had said Mom was the traitor. If that was true, where was she? Why was Dad disguised as Fleet? And why did Colleen kill Farrell? That's when I knew the ugly truth.

"It's you," I whispered, my heart dying inside me. "Both of you. You're the traitors."

Colleen nudged Farrell with her stick, making sure he was really dead. And he was.

"You have no idea what you're talking about, Marked One." She flicked her fingers in my direction. I cringed, sure of my death, but instead she hurled a shimmering blast of energy at Trent, Infiniti, and me. It cascaded over us, imprisoning us in a bubble of vapor. Trent slammed his fists against the glistening sphere, over and over; banging so hard his hands started bleeding.

I grasped his shoulder, letting him know it was no use, while deep despair trickled through every inch of me. Farrell had died trying to protect me. He had really died this time. And if Dad and Colleen were going to kill the rest of us, then I wanted answers. After everything I'd been through, I deserved that much. For me, for my friends who would probably die, for Mom and the others who were held captive somewhere or dead. And especially for Farrell.

I folded my arms over my chest, hiding my trembling hands—hands desperate to choke the man who was my father. "Fleet was never the traitor. And neither was Mom." Even though I knew the answer, I had to ask the question. I had to hear the truth.

"Correct," Colleen answered.

Tears sprang to my eyes again. My vision blurred. I blinked them away fast, gritting my teeth, determined not to show her any weakness. "Dad, how could you do this?"

He gave me a blank stare, as if he didn't even hear me talking to him.

"Dad!"

His eerie stillness and the faraway look in his eyes struck me. Something was up, and Colleen was responsible.

"What have you done to my father," I demanded. "And where's my mom!"

"YOU will listen to ME!" Colleen ordered, pointing her staff at me.

My breath hitched at her outburst. Trent, Infiniti, and I stepped away from the edge of the shimmery force-field and huddled in the middle of the dome.

"Tell them," Colleen ordered my dad.

He took cautious steps toward our glistening prison. "My sweet daughter, don't you see? We're doing this *for* you."

"What are you talking about?" I asked, more confused than ever.

He ran his fingers across the sizzling energy field, almost taunting us. "Tavion became a part of you when his blood merged with yours during your confrontation at the red desert. With Colleen's help, I'm going to undo that moment. All we need to do is go back to that time and change things. By doing so, you'll be saved."

Goosebumps lined my skin. My body shook with ice cold fear as I tried to make sense of his reasoning. I looked at the nun's dead body and then Farrell's.

And yet they wanted to save me?

The pieces slowly started falling into place.

If they undid my killing of Tavion, someone else would have to do it. And if someone else did it, that person would probably end up like me, their blood mixed with Tavion's. If that happened, that person would be the new leader of the Tainted—just like I was supposed to have been except Trent's great-grandmother had rescued me from that fate.

I glared at Colleen. She wanted to be the new leader of the Tainted and she had somehow turned my father. My stomach sank. My hands shook. "This is not about saving me. This is about Colleen taking Tavion's place."

Dad smiled. "Always the smart one."

Colleen marched to the hazy bubble. She stepped in with ease and touched Trent's chest with her staff. "Move," she ordered. She pushed him out, gripping my wrist and yanking me along.

I got that they needed me, but why did they need Trent? As if reading my thoughts, Dad said, "At first I thought we'd use the Walker to help transport us to the conflict at the red desert, but since he couldn't remember anything, he was rendered useless."

I thought of how back in the thirties we had told Fleet that Farrell had lost his memories. We had even mentioned that Trent was a Supreme. But we weren't talking to Fleet! We were talking to my possessed Dad!

Colleen continued. "Plus there was the whole binding protector thing that would've gotten in the way." She motioned at Trent. "Luckily for us, we have a Supreme in our midst."

"Okay, fine, I'm a Supreme," Trent said, wrapping his arm around me and holding me close. Poor Infiniti was now alone in the sphere. "That means you don't need Dominique or Infiniti. Just me."

Colleen laughed at Trent's attempt to be a hero. "No, no, no. It doesn't work that way, boy. Without Dominique's presence in the desert, Tavion will be tipped off, and we can't have that." Colleen grabbed my chin. "You see, she's the bait."

Bait? Oh, hell no! I tried to jerk away when Colleen sent a blast of pulsing electricity at Trent. He thudded to the ground, his body seizing and shaking. Dad held me in death grip. After a few seconds, the zapping stopped. Dad brought his mouth to my ear. "Do that again and it'll be much worse."

Trent staggered back to his feet, holding onto me for support.

"I'm so sorry," I said.

He put his hand on top of mine and squeezed. "Don't be," he said between labored breaths.

Colleen started clapping her hands. "How touching. Now let's get on with this."

Dad and Colleen pushed Trent and me until we

formed a circle with them. They forced us to hold their hands.

"I'm not gonna do it," Trent said. "I'm not gonna help you get back to that red desert."

Trent was right. We had to do whatever we could to stay out of the red desert because if we went back there, we'd never make it out.

I nodded in agreement with Trent. "He won't," I said firmly.

"You're going to do what we want you to do," Colleen cautioned. She dropped my hand and poked Trent's forehead. Sparks burst from the spot and streams of vapor oozed into his skin. Trent flinched and blinked, and then acted like nothing had happened.

"Trent?"

He ignored me and kept his focus on Colleen, his eyes taking on the same faraway look as my dad.

"What did you do?!" I tried to wrestle my hand away from Colleen's grip. "What did you just do?!" She squeezed my hand so hard I thought my fingers would break.

"You remember the red desert, yes?" Colleen asked Trent.

"Yes."

"And the confrontation between Tavion and Dominique?"

"Yes."

"Good. We need to go there."

Like a robot following orders, Trent closed his eyes.

"No!" I hollered, swinging my arms all over the place trying to break free. "Trent! Don't do it! Don't listen to her! Don't take us to the red desert!" My head spun. My legs started turning to jelly. "They're going to kill us!"

Chapter Twenty-One

My body drifted into weightlessness. The pulsing of my heartbeat whooshed in my ears. The white snowy landscape whirled out of control, and a hard surface appeared beneath my boots. Darkness surrounded me. My eyes adjusted and Farrell, Trent, and Infiniti popped into view!

"What the—" Infiniti muttered.

The four of us were standing at the wood door of St. Joseph's church. Trent spun around and grabbed my arms. "Dominique! I heard your voice and I knew we couldn't go back to the red desert!"

"Oh my God," I said, wrapping my arms around his neck and kissing his cheek. "You saved us!"

I whipped around to face Farrell. "And you're alive!" My heart soared. I wanted to grab him, kiss him, and tell him I loved him. Instead, I bit my tongue and nervously clasped my hands together. "I'm so glad."

Farrell circled the walkway that led from the church to the nun's house, examining the area. "Trent rewound time," he snapped. "But not by much."

I pushed my emotions for Farrell out of my head, forcing myself to study our surroundings—the dark night, the empty church. Farrell was right. Trent didn't buy us a lot of time, but I'd take it any day. "We still have time to change things." I yanked the church door open. "Let's get inside."

We huddled just inside the church foyer, antsy and on edge. I stayed close to Trent, suddenly feeling safer closer to him than Farrell. "Any second now my dad is going to appear disguised as Fleet. And we need to—"

"Kill him," Infiniti offered, sounding more sure than I'd ever heard her. "Before he kills Farrell again."

Kill my dad? I couldn't do it, especially since he probably didn't even know what he was doing. I rubbed my temples. "He's still my dad, Infiniti."

"Dude, you're right. I'm sorry. I'm just freaking over here."

"I know. Me too." I patted her arm, and then looked to Farrell for an answer.

Farrell paced. "What if we go along with your dad's plan? We pretend he's Fleet and go back with him to our proper time. Once there, we take him and hold him hostage. Make him tell us everything so we can find the others. Use him against Colleen."

Thick silence filled the air while I thought of Farrell's idea, my mind racing in desperation. Before anyone could offer another option, sparks of light streaked all around and Dad appeared in Fleet form. But a new fear formed in my mind. We had all remembered what had just happened, so would my dad too?

"There you are," the fake Fleet said, coming over to us, and acting as if he didn't remember anything. He eyed the church. "Where are we?" He looked us over in our little orphan Annie attire. "And what the hell are you wearing?"

Those were the same words he had used before, so he

definitely didn't remember what had just happened before Trent brought us back to this point. I eyed Trent in amazement. He definitely had a lot of power in him.

Infiniti started coughing. "Nuns," she squeaked out through spurts of hacking.

Crap. The nuns. They were going to show up any minute.

"We're in 1930's Houston at Trent's church," I rushed out. "And we need to get back to our own time and do that thing that Farrell said." I eyed Farrell, okaying his plan to hold Fleet—or Dad—hostage as soon as we got back. "Everyone hold hands."

Fake Fleet raised one eyebrow, came into our circle, and joined hands with us. "That thing?"

"Yeah," I said. "Help the others because when we left they were under attack."

I casually shot the others a "don't say anything" look because I didn't want my dad to know Farrell had lost his memory, Trent was a Supreme, or that we knew his true identity. "Farrell," I nodded. "Get us back."

"Back to the cabin," Farrell said, glancing at Trent.

"Yeah," Trent added. "The cabin." Trent kept his face down, while flashes of yellow hued mist oozed from Farrell's hands. Farrell's display was a cover for Trent's power. I prayed Dad wouldn't catch on.

While Farrell continued with his distraction, I snuck a peek at Trent from the corner of my eye, suddenly remembering his great-grandmother's premonition that he wouldn't make the time jump. Did she mean now?

Sparks emitted from Trent's hands, slowly at first and then more rapid-fire, until the sizzlers crackled and popped. A glowing hue of blue emanated from his body.

Holy crap, I could see his power!

"Hey," the fake Fleet said, catching on that something was up. "What's—"

The church door slammed opened. Mother Superior and the Veronica look-alike nun surged through. Sirens wailed in the distance. The Mother Superior raised her fist. "No one is allowed in the sanctuary at night!"

"You devils!" Sister Mary Catherine added.

The nuns rushed our way. Closing in, the young nun brought up her arm. I waited to catch a glimpse of her butcher knife, but this time she brought out a long, narrow pistol and aimed for me.

What?

My attention snapped to Trent. He gave me a haunting look, telling me this was it.

The vision.

It was coming true.

He broke the circle and lunged in front of me. The popping of a bullet leaving its chamber chilled my blood. A force slammed into Trent and something wet splattered against my face. His body started to crumple. I reached for him, when the floor beneath me slipped away like grains of sand blowing in the desert. The feeling of being suspended in mid-air overcame me. My stomach dipped, followed by a rush of cold air as my feet landed on snow.

Farrell stepped in front of me. He raised his hands palm up at the fake Fleet and shot out a barrage of shimmering energy that clung to him like a glistening web.

Fleet's face and body changed into Dad's. He jerked his shoulders back and forth, trying to break the barrier holding him hostage. He cocked a brow at Farrell. "How did you know?"

I frantically searched for Trent, but didn't see him. The cold realization that he had been shot and left behind slammed down on me. I wiped my face and eyed my bloodied hand. It shook with a fierce tremble, leaving me enraged and out of control. I rushed Dad and slammed my fist into his face.

"You did this!"

He laughed. "Why, Dominique, I didn't know you had it in you."

"Guys!" Infiniti said, mascara streaking her face. "Trent's gone, okay? But we're here, and she's coming!"

A glowing mist laced Farrell's fingers. He eyed the path to Richard and Sue's log cabin. "She's right. Colleen will be here any minute." He worked his jaw, eyeing the space around us. "We'll make our final stand right here." He took Infiniti by the shoulders and positioned her in front of me. "You block whatever blasts you can."

"What?" she exclaimed. "I mean, I know I'm a Void whatever thing, but what if—"

"What if nothing," he growled. "You will deflect any blasts that get past me. Got it?"

"Oh my God," she whimpered.

I held her hand and squeezed. "We'll do this together," I whispered. "Okay? You and me."

"O-k-k-ay," she chattered.

Farrell positioned himself in front of Infiniti and me. He clenched his fists. He had protected me for lifetimes, and had failed each time. Why would this time be any different? Especially now that he didn't even know me? I whipped my head around and studied the nearby trees, looking for a place to hide in case things got out of control.

Tall and naked, they didn't offer much cover. I continued scanning the area, when I spotted a thick cluster of bushes not too far away. Heavy with snow, I figured we could bolt over there if we needed to.

"Your final life is going to end like all the others," Dad taunted.

A hard chill seized my body. My already mounting doubt and fear spiked. I ignored him, telling myself he wasn't my dad anymore while I forced my gaze to stay on the path to the cabin.

"Your final stand will be your last before your inevitable death," he added.

"Shut up!" Infiniti yelled.

"And if he doesn't?" Colleen called out.

You could hear the collective gasp from me and Infiniti as Colleen's menacing voice cut through the cool, quiet air. She tramped toward us, her glowing staff held at the ready.

Farrell flexed his hands. "Where are the others?" he demanded.

"Now!" Dad shouted.

Colleen's staff ignited like a massive solar flare, washing the white landscape in a sea of emerald. The energized hue hovered in the air for a second before it pulsed out in waves, ringing in my head like a supersonic shrill. I ducked and covered my ears, but kept my sights on the skies that had suddenly turned dark grey.

Infiniti pressed up against me. "What's happening?!"

The thick clouds clustered together. Bright flashes lit up the dark puffs, as if a massive jet plane threatened to break through and crash down on us. What emerged instead were bolts of dark crackling energy. They streaked down, landed next to Colleen, and took on the form of two black cloaked figures. My gut twisted tight. Those figures had attacked me twice already. And now they were back for more.

"Surrender the Marked One," Colleen commanded, her staff pulsing with power. "And we'll spare the others."

"Like hell you will," Farrell answered.

Slow and easy, I started backpedaling toward the large cluster of bushes, pulling Infiniti with me. "When I say run, run," I whispered, linking my arm with hers, our footsteps sinking into the thick snow as we moved backward.

Trying not to make a sound, and holding my breath so tight my chest hurt, I eyed Dad. With a look of sick hunger on his face, he stared at Colleen and the Tainted assassins that were almost on top of Farrell. Worry spiked inside me—not just for Farrell, but also for my taken-over dad.

"Now?" Infiniti whispered.

Farrell unclenched his fists and stretched his fingers. Sparks shot out into the cold air. Colleen leveled her staff at Farrell, the tip covered in a shimmery haze.

Holy hell.

This was it.

A white and gold-laced blast erupted from Farrell's hands. A green shimmery beam exploded from Colleen's staff. Power meeting power, their auras collided midair like crashing waves. I spun around, digging my fingers into Infiniti's arm, the word RUN blaring from my mouth but drowned out by the screaming energy filling the frigid air.

We raced to the thick cluster of bushes. The cold air stung our faces and the thick snow slowed our pace. Just a few feet away from cover, a flash of black zipped overhead. It singed the nearby tree branches and sent a burning stench into the air. Infiniti stumbled over a fallen log, barely regaining her footing, before we found ourselves face to face with one of the black cloaked figures.

We were dead. I knew it.

And then something weird happened. Every ounce of fear in me melted away until only rage remained. Colleen had turned my dad into a traitor. Trent was dead. Mom and the others were probably dead, too. And Farrell was under attack.

"For Trent," I muttered.

I knocked Infiniti away and tackled the Tainted. I wrapped my arms around its tall thick frame and knocked it to the ground. I tucked my chin in and slammed my head down, head butting it so hard my skull jolted with pain and my vision darkened before exploding with stars. He grunted and twisted under me as a slow humming of electricity emanated from him. *Crap*. I tucked my chin in again, ready for another slamming, when Infiniti dropped down in front of me. She pulled the hood from the Tainted and pressed her hands against the temples of the pale-faced killer. The power that had started to come out of him vanished, the buzz in the air completely gone. I studied his black eyes and his white skin, afraid to let go, wondering how I could kill him without a weapon.

"You're dead," he threatened in a guttural voice.

"Not yet she isn't," a voice called out from behind me.

I glanced over my shoulder to see Fleet racing over to

me. In one fluid movement, he zoomed to my side and plunged his energy pulsing hands straight through the Tainted's chest.

"Back away!" he roared at Infiniti and me.

We scooted away as fast as we could, our attention locked on Fleet. His face contorted with pain. His arms flashed with different hues of light—gray, green, blue, purple. The pulsing colors sped up until he looked as if he might burst. The Tainted below him writhed and seized, bone-chilling moaning filling the air. I pressed a fisted hand to my mouth, terrified for Fleet, when the Tainted exploded like a massive firework. Infiniti and I covered our eyes while Fleet fell back onto the ground.

I rushed to his side. "Fleet!"

He scrambled to his feet, working to catch his breath.

"Where'd you come from?" I pressed.

"The house," he huffed. "The others. Attacked. By Colleen." His breathing started to steady. "I barely got away." He stared in the direction of Farrell who was under heavy attack. Dad was still bound. "I'm going for Farrell." Dumbfounded, Infiniti and I stared at him. He grabbed my shoulders. "Get to the cabin. Now."

Fleet took off, flinging an array of blasts at Colleen and her remaining cloaked ally as he joined his brother's side. Infiniti grabbed my arm and started dragging me away. I dug my heels in. "I'm not leaving."

"You're not?" Infiniti exclaimed, stunned.

Colleen and her Tainted accomplice were powerful—so powerful that even though Fleet had joined Farrell, they seemed way outmatched, especially with that long and deadly energy rod against them.

Courage swept over me. I straightened my back and raised my chin. Farrell may not have remembered me, but I knew him. And there was no way I wasn't going to help him. "Go back to the cabin and get help. I'm going for that staff."

Chapter Twenty-Two

Energy blasts sizzled and exploded in the air. Clumps of snow dropped from nearby tree branches. Even the ground beneath my wet boots shook. I had no idea what Infiniti would do, but I had to give her the option to get away because I was going to stand by Farrell no matter what. Even if it meant my death. And nobody could stop me.

"Uh…" Infiniti hesitated. "I'm staying." Sheer terror laced her voice before she gave a weak smile. "I mean, what kind of sidekick would I be if I bailed on you right before the big battle?"

A warm feeling of love and gratitude for her overwhelmed me, and I brought her in for a hug. Maybe even our last hug. I glanced over my shoulder at Farrell and Fleet. They were losing ground while Colleen and her cloaked partner advanced. We had to act, and fast. "Let's get that bitch," I snarled.

We followed a narrow path up a small slope and through a heavily wooded area. Our footsteps crunched against twigs and patches of snow. Luckily the sound was muffled by the explosive exchange happening just yards from us.

I quickened my pace, thinking of what Farrell had said about Infiniti being a Void. So no matter what happened, she should be okay. Then I thought of my shield. I peered through the rows of tree trunks we were passing and caught a glimpse of my still captive dad. If my shield still held, it wasn't by him because he wasn't himself anymore. Mom—if she still shielded me, I should be able to attack Colleen and not get obliterated.

I hoped.

Mustering up my last bit of resolve, I crouched down behind a barrier of dense underbrush. It was the last place for cover before the open space where Farrell and Fleet fought for their lives. I placed my palms flat on the snowy ground. The cool touch calmed me, gave me strength even.

"Now what?" Infiniti asked.

"We charge." I locked eyes with her. "And go for that staff."

My attention snapped back to the deadly rod blasting out currents of energy. From here, Colleen and the Tainted had their backs to us. If we swept in quick enough, we could jump them from behind before they even had a chance to react.

"We can do this," I whispered.

Infiniti's face hardened. "Shit yeah, we can."

Hope surged inside me as I huddled with the best friend I'd ever known—a friend who had risked everything for me and wanted to risk more. With one last glance at her, I drew in a deep breath and took off like a runner at the starting blocks.

We burst into the clearing, my plan for a surprise attack failing immediately as Farrell's attention zoomed to me. Horror swept across his face. His electrified blasting wavered. In that split second, Colleen's stream landed square at his chest. He was flung into the air and onto his back, Colleen's flow lacing his body from top to bottom like an electrified cocoon. Fleet dodged to the side, but not quick enough to escape Colleen's sweeping attack that immobilized him, too.

My heart lurched. "No!"

Colleen spun around to face me. She pointed the tip in my direction. The end glowed in a dark hue of emerald, pulsing like it had a life of its own, and stopped me in my tracks.

She took two steps forward. "They can never save you, did you know that? Never have. Never will."

"Don't listen to her," Infiniti whispered. She hovered close to me, but I hardly even noticed. The despair of the moment had taken me.

"Colleen! Set me free!" Dad bellowed.

Colleen ignored him, a cruel smirk spreading across her face. Her gaze locked on mine. "Dominique." She held out the last syllable of my name, her tongue clicking like a snake. "Do you want to know how I turned your father?"

Infiniti started pulling me back. I refused to budge because I wanted to know the truth about Dad. I needed to know. Besides, where the hell could we go now?

"Yes," I whispered.

She rubbed her hands up and down her staff. "After your Walker transported you and your mother to the Boardman after your most unfortunate accident, your broken father was left all alone and on the brink of death. So I saved him." She moved even closer to me. "Want to know how?"

Her diabolical evilness had left me too shocked to answer.

"I sucked the Pure out of him. Every last drop." She licked her lips. "If I had known he tasted so good, I would've turned him lifetimes ago."

I envisioned her vile mouth over his, drawing the good energy out of his body.

She moved closer to me. "And now you're going to help me take the throne as the new leader of the Tainted—a position that should've been mine from the beginning. A position I've waited patiently for."

Tingles of shock and horror raced through me. She had wanted to take over as the Tainted leader from the beginning? Pretended for lifetimes to be friends with my parents? And then we had gone and left my dad on that road, giving her the perfect opportunity to turn him into a Tainted so that he could help her. A dark rage seethed deep inside me. I eyed her deadly staff, determined to snatch it, praying my mother's shield still held, resolved to go down in a freaking blaze of glory if this was to be my end.

I shoved Infiniti away and slammed my hands around Colleen's staff. Heat oozed from the smooth wood and sank deep into my skin, traveling like lava through every inch of me. But it didn't kill me! I tightened my grip, the surge from the rod suddenly familiar, like I had been in this position before. And maybe I had in one of my past lives, but I didn't remember any of them. But I knew this.

She had to die.

Colleen's eyes widened. Her mouth twitched. I jerked the staff and thrust it at her, ramming her in the chest and digging against her shirt and into her skin. She sneered, re-gripped her weapon, and pushed it back at me. Blazing energy crackled from the staff in the space between us, as if it didn't know where to go, the two of us equally matched in strength.

She grunted. "You! Always! Die!"

My legs started to shake. I struggled to gain an advantage, when my foot slipped on a patch of icy snow. Colleen smiled. "You see?"

Defeat loomed over me, my end in sight. The glowing energy pulsing between Colleen and me flashed bright, and then crept closer to me. I braced myself for destruction when I spotted Infiniti behind Colleen, her lips pursed, her eyes afire with courage. She grabbed Colleen from behind in a bear hug. "Die, you psycho bitch!"

The pulsing energy in the rod flickered and then went out! Infiniti beamed in shock surprise. "It worked!"

Colleen let out a growl. Before she could make a move, I forced the rod into her with my full body weight, but pressed too hard. We toppled to the ground and right on top of Infiniti. Infiniti grunted. Colleen thrashed about. I scrambled to get up when Infiniti lost her hold.

"Shit!" she yelled.

Colleen struck out at me. She grazed the side of my head with her fist and then kicked me off of her, rolling away from me and Infiniti amid a flurry of dusting snow and a misty green current. The vapor grew in intensity until the snowy landscape was awash in an emerald glow. I turned my face away from the flash and shielded my eyes. After a few seconds, the heat started to fade.

I blinked my eyes to clear the splotches from my vision, struggling to catch my bearings, desperate to see where Colleen had gone, when a body collided into me.

"Watch out!" Infiniti yelled.

I thought it was Colleen, but a muscular arm wrapped around my neck and placed me in a choke-hold.

"Don't move," my dad commanded.

My body froze, and a chill settled in my heart.

"Dad?"

"Back off, Stone," Farrell threatened. "Now."

He and Fleet moved in and pulled Infiniti behind them. They raised their electrified palms at Dad.

Caught in a stand-off, I desperately searched the area trying to figure out what the hell was happening. Colleen had vanished. Only a black-streaked stain remained. Even her rod had disappeared. That had to have been how my dad, Farrell, and Fleet had been freed from her electrified web. But now *I* was held captive. And my dad still wanted to kill me.

A soft whisper sounded at my ear. I closed my eyes, straining to make it out.

"Go where the love is."

My heart skipped. My eyes flung open. I halfway expected to see Jan or Abigail, but didn't. I focused on my dad. There was no love from him now, but there had been. He had loved me so much he had spent all of his lifetimes trying to protect me. And even if he didn't remember, I'd never forget. Maybe that was the key. Maybe I needed to remind him of who he really was.

"Dad, this isn't you."

His arm muscle relaxed and he loosened his grip enough that I was able to turn and face him.

"What are you doing?" he asked, suspiciously.

"I'm thinking about you, and how much you loved Mom and me." As if slapped in the face, he winced. "When

I was little, you used to come in my room in the middle of the night to check on me. I faked sleeping because I didn't want you to leave. I'd hear your footsteps every night—waited for them even. Sometimes you'd come so close to my bed I could hear you breathing."

"Shut up," he sneered.

"Remember all those times we'd go to Dock Road and look for Petoskey stones?" I could almost feel the cold water around my legs, could almost see the fossilized rocks in my hands. And then I remembered the Petoskey stone I had put in my boot and thought of Trent. A weight of guilt and responsibility sank deep inside me. "We'd search for hours until we'd found a bucket of treasures. And then we'd spend days polishing our finds." Tears spilled out onto my face. "That was our time, Dad. Just you and me."

Dad scowled. "Not another word."

If I was going to die, I wanted my last thoughts to be of love. Maybe that's what Jan had meant when she had said to go where the love is. Maybe if I thought of love, I wouldn't be so afraid. So alone. And so I thought of my friendship with Infiniti and Trent, my deep feelings for Farrell, and lastly I thought of everything my parents had done for me. Before I could lose my nerve, I wrapped my arms around my dad and held on tight.

"I love you, Dad."

His body stiffened. His muscles jerked. Like a furnace, a surge of heat radiated from him. I stepped back, suddenly afraid of being so close to him, when Infiniti latched onto my arm and yanked me back.

Together with Farrell and Fleet, we moved away from Dad. The color of his face changed from a normal hue, to pink, and finally to a deep scarlet in a matter of seconds. His eyes bulged, his face swelled, and a suffocating gurgle escaped his lips. He stumbled about before doubling over and collapsing to his knees. I wanted to rush to him, but fear held me in place.

"Dad?" I whispered, inching forward.

Farrell grabbed me. "Stay back."

Even though he had tried to kill us, I couldn't stay away. I lunged forward and crashed down on the ground next to him. "Dad?"

He continued to groan, his body shivering uncontrollably. I touched his forehead. His flesh burned like an inferno. I whisked my hand away, the fiery touch lingering on my fingertips.

"He's on fire."

Dad raised his head, his eyes glazed over. He pounced on me, pinning me to the ground. His blazing hands wrapped around my neck, his body on top of mine.

Farrell and Fleet rushed us. They tried to pry him off me, but they couldn't break his grip.

"She told me what to do," he growled. "She said you were supposed to die." He dug his fingers into my windpipe. "Once and for all."

He tightened his grip even more, pressing his full body weight onto me. His burning saliva dripped onto my face. The smell of charred flesh flooded my nostrils. "Dad," I managed to croak out. "It's me, Dominique."

He hesitated. His hands loosened and trembled against my skin. "Dominique?" He lifted himself off of me. "What am I doing?"

Fleet slammed his foot into his face, sending him

rolling off me while Farrell swooped in and carried me away.

"No!" I hollered. I watched my Dad struggle to his feet, stumbling about in pain, bursts of electricity shooting out of his mouth.

"He's expelling the Tainted," Farrell yelled. "Run!"

Dad crashed down onto his knees and grabbed his stomach. *Hold on Dad,* I thought to myself. *Please.* His body jerked back and forth. His face turned crimson again. His mouth opened with a silent scream and out blasted a thick, black stream of energy.

The gush shot up in to the air, then plummeted down like a massive tornado. The gale force winds flung us into the air and then knocked us to the ground, whipping all around and stabbing our skin with jabs of electricity. I covered my face and peered through my fingers looking for Farrell, but the dark wind blinded me. I clawed around me, searching for anyone who might be near, when I found Infiniti's petite hand. I held on tight, trying to comfort not just her but me too as I whispered over and over, "I'm so sorry."

Chapter Twenty-Three

Remorse and guilt flooded my senses while my body burned with pain from the wind's electrical shock. We were stuck in a hell hole because of me. Dying because I had killed Tavion and had some sort of connection to him. I prayed for death, begging for all of this to end, when Infiniti's hand went slack.

No!

I tightened my grip and shook. Nothing. Not even the slightest twitch. My chest squeezed from the inside as my heart shattered. She was all I had left, and now she was gone. Desperate to stay with her, I clutched her hand and scooted closer. She deserved so much more than this, so much more than a deadly friendship with me.

Tears trickled down my face. My body went numb from pain. I wasn't sure how much more I could take, when the whipping electrical current came to an abrupt stop.

I stayed perfectly still, my sweaty body molded against the ice cold ground. I strained my ears, trying to make out any hint of noise. I lifted my chin and stared at Infiniti's lifeless form. I brushed the wild hair away from her face.

"Hey," I whispered, my heart pleading for her to be alive.

A low groan seeped from her lips. "Hey."

"Infiniti?" I yanked her arm to make sure I wasn't hearing things.

"Ouch!"

"Infiniti! You're alive!" I kissed her cheek, then propped myself up on my shaky forearms. My gaze darted to Dad. He was crouched on all fours, singe marks streaked across his clothes. I sucked in my breath, waiting for him to make a move. Did he get the Tainted out of him? Or was this another trick? I had to find out.

My body still reeling with pain, I crawled over to him. Farrell and Fleet raced over to me as I neared. I halted them with a flick of my hand. "Wait!"

Farrell cast me a worried glance. Sparks crackled from his hands. "I don't think so," he said.

"Damn straight," Fleet added, gathering his own energy. "He tried to kill us."

Dad rubbed his head, his gaze fixed on the snowy landscape. After a few seconds, he scrambled to his feet, stumbling around a bit. I pushed through the pain in my legs and stood, eyeing him carefully. His face had relaxed. The crazy look in his bloodshot eyes had disappeared. He scanned me before a spark of recognition settled in his face. "Dominique?"

"Dad," I answered, exhaling the breath I had been holding. "Is it you?"

"Yes," he said in a confused tone, his gaze taking on a faraway look. "It's me. I have no idea what just—"

"Is it really you?" I asked again, wanting to believe it but needing some sort of proof. "How?"

Dad's gaze wandered over the snow. After a moment,

he raised his watery eyes and studied me. "Dominique," he said, his voice full of wonder. "You did it. You brought me back." Dried blood stained his lips. Bruises dotted his cheeks. "You said you loved me. And your words, they echoed inside my head while memories of you and Mom flooded my mind. Everything we've sacrificed and everything we've been through surged through me, sending the Tainted out of me and expelling Colleen's poison."

"Go where the love is," I muttered to myself.

"Love? Bullshit," Fleet said. "Something else is at work here. And if we don't figure out what, then we're fucked because that dark energy is somewhere...and so is that bitch."

"She's gone," my dad said. He pinched the top of his nose. "The connection between us is severed, but I can still sense her and she's not here."

"What about the dark smoke that came out of you?" Infiniti asked.

Suddenly I remembered what Farrell had said about energy and repeated his words. "Energy, once created, can never be destroyed. It can only be relocated or transformed."

"What?" Infiniti asked terrified. She spun around and studied the skies. "So where the hell is it?"

A ray of sun streaked down from the sky and blinded me for a second. I shielded my eyes and searched the clouds. "I don't know," I murmured, looking around, thinking I'd see some sort of evidence of where the Tainted energy had gone, but I didn't.

"Dominique," Farrell said in a low tone. "My memories. They're filtering through."

"They are?" Hope and excitement budded inside of me, relieved that he was going to remember me again. I started for him, but Fleet held me back.

"Wait," Fleet whispered.

"Our first life," Farrell added. "It's coming back. And I'm sorry for this." His eyes misted over as he shifted closer to my dad. Pain and regret flooded his face. "Really sorry."

He blasted a laser-like beam at my dad's neck. Fleet knocked me to the ground. Streams of sizzling power exploded overhead. Infiniti's screaming pierced my ears. And as quick as the lightning barrage erupted, it ended.

"Dominique," a voice called out to me. My body shook. My head pounded from slamming against the snowy ground. Strong hands gripped my arms. "You okay?" the same voice asked.

I peeled my eyes open, not even aware I had shut them, and gazed up into Fleet's now solid green eyes. I couldn't speak. Couldn't even move my lips. My mind had gone blank.

"Hey," Fleet repeated, giving me a shake. He brought his face closer to mine. "Can you hear me?"

"She's in shock," Infiniti said from somewhere behind me.

Fleet helped me to my feet and turned me so that I was facing the cabin. "Get her out of here, Tiny" he commanded.

My brain had muddied and I had no idea what had just happened. Couldn't filter it through any logical reasoning. My teeth chattered from the frigid air that had sunk deep into my soul. "W-w-what's going on?"

Infiniti grabbed my arm. "We need to get to the cabin," she said in a half-whimper.

My body cemented in place. My mind so jumbled that it couldn't communicate with my legs. Infiniti pushed forward, leading my near comatose body back to the cabin. My feet dragged across the snowy ground.

"I don't know what's happening," I whispered, my mind on the brink of insanity. All I could think about was Dad. Farrell. The laser beam. "I need to see my dad."

"No!" Infiniti pleaded. She nudged me forward, but I wouldn't budge. She darted in front of me. Panic filled her red-rimmed eyes. "Let's get out of here. Okay? Please? For me?"

Farrell, my protector who had loved me for lifetimes. The guy who had my heart. He had…

My breathing stopped.

My heart crushed inside me.

He had killed my dad.

I pushed Infiniti away and spun around. My gaze settled on Dad's brown boots, drifted up his splayed legs, and stopped on his chest. Blood soaked his shirt and oozed through the snowy patches around his upper body. A rush of heat filled my forehead. My gut spasmed. I doubled over and vomited, splashing watery bile all over my shoes. My vision narrowed until darkness took me away.

***

Somewhere between a restless sleep and plaguing nightmares, a lone voice came to me.

"You have to leave."

I didn't know who the voice belonged to, or where it came from, but it played in my head like a song on repeat, followed by my name. *"Dominique, Dominique, Dominique…"*

My eyelids fluttered open.

"Dominique?" Infiniti hovered over me. Her worried face relaxed when we made eye contact. "Dominique," she said, letting out a sigh. "Thank God."

I found myself stretched out on the long sofa in the den of the cabin. Every muscle in my body hurt, as if I'd just been beaten up.

"There she is," Sue said with a smile, coming up behind Infiniti.

Mom perched on the edge of her seat opposite me. Richard and Fleet stood by the windows. Outside, the sky had darkened to black. A hard chill traveled through my body. "How long have I been out?"

"Not long," Mom answered. "Less than an hour."

I rubbed my arms, realizing I still wore my musty and wrinkled 1930's attire. That's when everything that had happened to me in the past and back here in the present sifted through my thoughts, ending with the horrifying reality that Farrell had betrayed me.

He had killed my dad.

Mom rested her hand on my knee. "Let's get you cleaned up and we can figure everything out later, okay?"

Figure everything out later? How the hell do you figure out that the guy who used to love me just sliced my dad's head off? And right after I'd finally gotten my real dad back? "No. We talk now," I said in a firm voice, swinging my legs around the edge of the sofa. "Especially since Colleen is out there and so is that Tainted energy that was in Dad."

Arguing erupted, but Richard's voice cut through the din. "Fleet told us what happened and as best we can tell,

Colleen is gone. Probably nursing her wounds somewhere. As for that Tainted blast, it must've gone into Farrell." Everyone silenced, as if waiting for my reaction. And right then, I had none to give. I was beyond lost.

"Let's go through what we know," Sue offered.

Everyone gathered close, including Fleet. Even though he had turned out to be on my side, I still didn't completely trust him. After what Farrell had done, how could I trust anybody?

Mom cleared her throat, focusing on me. "Well, let's start with what happened here in the cabin after you, Farrell, and Infiniti left to restore Trent's memory." She paused for a good while before continuing, and that's when I noticed that her eyes were puffy and red. "After you left, we were attacked by Colleen and… your father." She gulped, gripping her hands together on her lap, her knuckles turning white. "Fleet managed to get free. When the explosions broke out down by the river, I ordered him to your aid. There was no time for him to free us first."

Sue rubbed Mom's back reassuringly. "Dominique, what happened after you all left the cabin?"

I rubbed my face and focused on every detail, trying to figure out when Farrell had turned against me and overcome with grief at what had happened to my dad. "After we restored Trent's memory, we were attacked by three Tainted—a young girl and two others."

"The creepy invisible girl," Infiniti said with a shudder. "No one could see her except Dominique."

Fleet furrowed his brow. "The same one you thought you saw on the plane?"

"Yes. Only I could see her because she was a part of me. A manifestation of some sort of evil lurking inside me from something Tavion had done to me from who knows when. Maybe since birth."

Mom edged closer, her hands now trembling.

"That's not even the worst part," I said, my insides wound up so tight it hurt. "Fleet was right. She was trying to turn me to the other side. She said I was meant to take over after Tavion died. When she attacked us, Trent ended up taking us to 1930."

"Trent?" Fleet asked.

"He's a Supreme," Infiniti explained.

"Come again?" Fleet asked, his question laced with surprise and maybe even a hint of awe.

I thought of how Trent had been shot and left in 1930. "He *was* a Supreme," I clarified, swallowing a sob. "He was shot before we time jumped back."

Before sorrow and grief could set in, I had to finish. I had to get it all out. "Back in the thirties, we met up with Trent's ancestors. They did this ritual thing to expel the Tainted out of me. When they finished, we came back to our time."

"You're leaving out that Farrell lost his memory," Infiniti said.

Suddenly I thought of everything Farrell had said to me in the thirties, zeroing in on the statement he had made about me asking him to kill me if I had changed. "Yes, he couldn't remember any of our past lives. But he did say that he thought I was changing."

Mom sucked in a hard breath. She unclenched her hands and dug her fingers into her jeans. "He said you were changing?"

"Yes." A host of shivery tingles raced across my skin. "Mom, what does that mean?"

Her eyes started to water. "If a Walker believes their charge has been corrupted, they have an obligation to switch directives. They don't even have a choice. It's genetically hard wired into them."

Fleet ran his fingers through his hair. "Oh, shit." He paced in a small circle. "If that's true, then Colleen is the least of our problems."

The quivers racing over my body multiplied until my body shook, realization hitting me like a freight train. I slowly rose to my feet. "Switch directives?" I asked, already knowing what that meant but needing my brain to catch up with my heart.

Mom stood and took my hands. Deep lines I had never noticed before etched across her forehead. Her green eyes telling me that we were doomed. "Walkers are different than the rest of us. They protect or they destroy. And if he thinks you're changing it means instead of guarding you, he's now required to eliminate you. Whether he's a Tainted or a Pure."

Infiniti slapped her hands over her mouth. "So that black blast could've gone into him?"

"Yes," Mom said. "It could've. And it probably did."

My breathing stopped. My gut coiled, her words devastating me.

I searched Mom's face, praying she was wrong, hoping for her to say something I could hold on to. Her hand squeezed mine, the hopeless expression on her face saying everything that needed to be said.

Farrell was going to kill me.

Chapter Twenty-Four

Fleet snatched his jacket off his chair. "We need to get the hell out of here."

Everything inside me said he was right, that we had to get out, until I remembered the voice in my head telling me I needed to leave. *I.* Not them. Not us. Just me.

That's when I knew what I had to do.

Pushing down the fear churning in my stomach, I resolved to save the others. And the only way I could do that was to leave. My very presence put everyone at risk, and I couldn't take that on anymore, couldn't live with myself if someone else I cared about died. Even if Farrell and Colleen were out there somewhere plotting my end.

Mom hurried about the room. She barked orders on what to take, when to leave, and possible places to go while I strategized my next move in my head. If I told them I had to leave, they'd never let me go. So I'd have to slip away. I wondered if I could really get away without them knowing. Was it even possible?

Richard cleared his throat. "Caris?" He threw her a look. Mom came to a standstill, meeting his somber gaze. "Sue and I aren't leaving the cabin."

Mom's jaw dropped. A hush fell on the room. "What?" A stunned expression settled on her face. "You can't be serious."

Richard wrapped his hand around Sue's. "We've never known anything but the cabin," he explained. "This is our home, Caris. We built it from the ground up. We've spent lifetimes here. You know that. And if this is it, we want our end to happen here."

Mom started to object, but Sue cut her off with a wave. "Please, don't. This is something we've thought long and hard about and we're ready for it."

A jolt of fear jarred me. They were bailing on us because they knew we were doomed. I couldn't believe my ears. At the same time, I could relate because I had decided to ditch, too. I just needed to figure out how.

"Suit yourselves," Fleet said, shoving his hands in his jean pockets. "But we're not waiting for death to come knocking on our door." He looked to Mom. "Right, Caris?"

Death? Farrell now equaled death?

Mom hesitated before answering, as if Richard and Sue's decision to stay diminished her determination to leave. Her hands fell to her side and her gaze drifted over the room before focusing on the night sky outside the window. I wondered if she secretly hoped Dad would somehow magically appear and save the day. And for a second there I thought he would. But he didn't.

Mom brought her attention to me and raised her chin. "That's right."

"Damn straight," Fleet muttered. He made his way to the kitchen and started shoving supplies into a grocery bag.

"Get your things," Mom commanded to Infiniti and me. "We leave right away."

Once upstairs, Infiniti paced the room, her breathing short and labored. "Holy shit. This isn't happening" She pulled at her shirt collar. "Not only is that crazy psycho going to hunt us down, but so is Farrell. I mean, we're dead. Like, really dead. For real." She slumped to the floor. "Just like Trent."

A fresh wave of sorrow overcame me, but I pushed it aside. I had to focus on my task. There was no time for tears. Not yet anyway. "I know, Infiniti. That's why we need to get out of here."

She slowly rose to her feet and moved around the room like a zombie, mumbling and crying. I tuned her out and started shoving her stuff in her duffle bag. If I left Mom, Fleet and Infiniti, maybe they'd have a chance. I pulled off my stupid old-timey clothes, when the Petoskey stone fell out of my boot. I scooped it up and held it tight, picturing Trent's face in my mind. Grief was now a permanent emotion for me. But I had to let it drive me and not hold me back. I had to use it to my advantage because right now that was all I had left.

I put on my black, long sleeved shirt, yanked on my jeans, and shoved the stone in my pocket. I tried my best to focus on how I could get away and save the others when an idea came to me. Since they never left me alone, I'd have to slip away at night while everyone slept.

"Hey!" Infiniti burst out. "Are you listening to me?"

"Not really," I confessed, tossing her pack at her and slinging mine over my shoulder. "You ready?"

She huffed, clutching her things to her chest. "Ready to die?" she asked, sarcasm lacing her voice. "Yeah, no."

"Nobody's dying, Tiny," Fleet snarled from the doorway. "At least not anybody who's coming with Caris and me."

I hated Fleet. Hated him for not being a traitor. Hated him for still being here with me instead of Farrell or Trent...or even Dad. And how dare he not give a damn about Richard and Sue! I stomped out of the room and slammed my bag into him as I passed. "You're still an asshole."

"Wouldn't have it any other way," he called out to me.

A solemn mood hovered in the air downstairs. Mom kept her face blank, her lips pursed together. Richard paced the room while Sue nervously moved her hand from her face to her neck and back again. And even though the fire crackled bright, it was the dying embers that spoke to me as I prepared myself for the goodbyes we were about to exchange—goodbyes that were forever.

"Well," Richard said, interrupting through the silence. "You guys just got here and now you're leaving!" He laughed, trying to lighten the mood, but his chuckling faded fast. His long face took on a serious expression. "Dominique, you may not remember us, but we'll never forget you." He opened his arms and motioned for me to join him and Sue. "Come give your Uncle Richard and Aunt Sue a big hug."

A feeling of knowing them crept through me. Not a memory, or a recollection of me with them, but a deep sense of familiarity that made me so homesick that suddenly I didn't want to leave the cabin. Richard and Sue must've seen it on my face because they wrapped me in their arms and squeezed tight.

"We love you, Dominique," Sue said, rubbing my back.

"Sure do," Richard added.

Mom joined our hug and we stood there for a few seconds locked in a group embrace. My heart so devastated I thought I could die. With my head hung low, I let tears fill my eyes.

"Well, I want in," Infiniti said. She dropped her bag and entered our circle. "I like hugs."

Richard started laughing again, as did everyone else. Except Fleet. He stayed away from our group and I was glad. He didn't belong with us. I could tell the others felt the same way because no one invited him over.

Mom broke away and the circle disbanded. I spotted Fleet by the door, arms crossed, supplies at his feet. Instead of looking like his usual jerk self, sadness covered his face. His shoulders hunched over. He straightened his stance right away when he noticed me looking at him.

"You guys done with your farewell episode of *Friends*?" he asked, irritation lacing his voice and cocky arrogance filling his eyes.

I kept my gaze on him, wondering what kind of person he really was. Mom redirected my attention when she rubbed my arm. "Yes. We're ready," she said.

Richard handed Mom his car keys, followed by Julian Huxley's worn and tattered journal. "You may need this."

Mom eyed it for a second before taking it. She must've forgotten about it like I had. But there it was. She tucked it in her bag. "Thank you, Richard. Thank you for everything. You and Sue."

Nobody spoke as we drove away from the cabin. Only the rumbling of the engine as it labored through the snowy path broke through the stillness in the car. When we finally emerged from the woodsy and snow riddled road and onto the open highway, Mom told us we were heading south and driving through the night. She didn't mention Dad, Farrell, Trent or anyone else for that matter. She didn't even talk about a plan to survive. We were just going to drive. And that was plan enough for me because I was moving on. I just had to find the right opportunity.

We drove for hours, deep into the night. The droning of the car's heater mixed with Infiniti's soft snoring. Even though my body screamed for sleep, my mind refused to shut off. Thoughts of getting away kept me awake. I lifted my duffle bag from the floorboard of the car, trying to give myself more leg room, when I spotted a small outside pocket halfway unzipped. For some reason, I hadn't noticed it before.

I placed the bag on my lap, eyed Infiniti sleeping next to me, and then glanced at Mom and Fleet in the front. Everyone was zoned in their own little world, leaving me to explore the newly discovered pocket.

Afraid to make any noise, I poked my fingers through the opening instead of unzipping it all the way. Empty. I shoved them in a little farther, swiping my fingers back and forth, when I felt something hard and stiff. A stick? I pinched the tip between my index finger and middle finger and pulled. And what I saw floored me. It was a beautiful, long, white feather with golden hued edges. My feather. The one I'd seen off and on back in Houston—Farrell had said I'd seen it in a past life and called it a symbol of hope. This had to be a good sign!

With my spirits raised, I held the feather in my fist, closed my eyes, and concentrated on the beach Farrell had called my safe place. *Go there*, I repeated in my head. *Get away*.

My head started to spin. My stomach dropped. My body swayed. The sensation of falling overcame me, my spirit soaring to someplace else. When my feet came into contact with solid ground, I slowly peered about. Bright sunlight, brilliant blue waters, soft brown sand—the beach! I'd done it! I had made it to Elk Rapids Beach!

My gaze darted around the coast, making sure I was alone, and I was. I drew in a deep breath and let it trickle out. A soft wind caressed my face. The rippling whisper of calm waves filled my ears.

"Whenever you're here, I'm here," a voice called out from behind me.

Panic seized me. My body prickled with fear. Little by little, praying it wasn't really him, I turned around.

A ray of light illuminated Farrell's gorgeous face. His golden hair sparkled under the sun. "I knew you'd come," he said.

Defenseless, I scanned the nearby area for a weapon. A rock, a stick, anything.

"I'm not going to hurt you, Dominique." He shoved his hands in his pockets and approached. "At least, not here anyway."

Anger quickly erased my fear. He had turned against me! He had killed my dad! I raised my hands. "Stay the hell away from me!"

He stopped mid-stride, his perfect face taking on an expression of sadness mixed with something like regret. "I brought you here to explain things."

"Bullshit," I said, backing away from him until my boots were fully immersed in the cool lake water.

"I remember everything," he rushed out, his voice cracking a little. "All of it."

My heart skipped. He remembered our feelings? That we had loved each other? If so, how could he be doing this to me?

"My memories came back after what happened to your dad."

My fury spiked. "After what happened? As if you had no responsibility in his death?" I rushed him and slapped his cheek so hard my hand stung. "How dare you!"

He grabbed my arms and held me tight. His eyes glistened, his face filled with remorse. "I know, I'm sorry. Just let me explain things." I tried to wrestle away, but couldn't. "I have to do this, Dominique. I have to kill you." He shook me and I held still. "You're changing!"

I started to cry, completely losing control of myself. "No, I'm not. Not anymore." I thought of how Trent's ancestors had helped me. Remembered the look in Trent's eye when he took a bullet for me.

"You are," he whispered. "What happened back in 1930 was the first sign. I just didn't realize it because I didn't remember. When my memories came back, I knew." Tears filled his eyes, and suddenly I believed him. He couldn't lie about something like that. My muscles slacked and he loosened his grip on my arms. "You don't remember this, but it was told to us in our first life that this would happen."

His words lingered in the air for a second before they sunk in. "Our first life?"

"First will be the changing that comes from within.

Second will be the changing that comes from without. Third will be the demise of those linked to the One."

The deadly prophecy that he quoted chilled me to the bone.

"We talked about this, Dominique. We planned for me to end you should this happen. You just don't remember."

My lip quivered. My body shook. I had no idea what to think or what to do. Misery and hopelessness had swept me away.

Farrell cupped my face in his hands and I looked up into his eyes that had turned from a brilliant green to a dark olive—just like mine. "Your eyes, they're—"

"Mixed," he finished. "Like yours. Part Tainted, part Pure." He moved his hand to the back of my neck and rubbed it across the spot where Tavion's mark was. "A part of him has always been in you. I understand because the Tainted is now a part of me, too."

"Part Tainted," I muttered, thinking of the blast from Dad. It had to have gone into Farrell. "That dark energy from my dad is now in you."

"Yes," he whispered, stroking my cheek. "It is. I also know why we lost our connection." I thought of how I had tried to mentally connect with him on the plane but couldn't. "The changing inside of you wouldn't let me, Dominique."

I searched for words to describe the anguish consuming every inch of me, but couldn't find any.

"Once we leave this place..." He gulped, struggling to finish his sentence. "I will have to hunt you and kill not only you, but anyone connected to your survival—whether I want to or not."

"Like my dad."

The wind around us picked up, the sky overhead darkened, and terror raced through my veins.

"I'm so sorry, Dominique. Please believe me. I never wanted it to come to this." He wrapped his strong arms around me and held me. "I love you," he whispered in my ear. "I have always loved you." He buried his face in my neck. "But I have no choice."

My heart shattered. Icy loneliness swept over me until I thought I'd never be warm again. Farrell loved me, but had to kill me. Mom, Infiniti, and Fleet were in danger too, just like Mom had said back at the cabin.

Farrell pulled away and studied my face, his fingers gently stroking my cheeks. Even after everything that had happened, and what we were still to face, he had my heart. "I love you, Farrell," I choked out.

"Forever," he said. He brought his mouth to mine and kissed me. I pressed up against him, desperate to feel as much of him as I could for as long as possible. Our kiss deepened until our bodies melded together. We clutched each other in wild desperation until a rumble of thunder sounded in the air. Slowly, we parted.

"Now what?" I panted.

He held my hands, his stormy eyes searching mine. "Don't let me find you." He released his hold and stepped away from me, as if taking on the role of enemy.

Every muscle in my body tensed and went on alert. "What?"

He squinted, as if in pain. "I have no control," he muttered. "But if you can get away, stay away, then maybe—" He moaned and pressed his fingers to his temple, as if fighting something from deep within him. Yet still I couldn't believe his words.

The guy I loved and who loved me back had to kill me. I knew I should get away or attack him, but I couldn't do either. My heart was dying and my mind raced while the needs to get away from him and go to him warred inside me.

"Farrell, what are you saying?"

He stepped back. "Run."

In the blink of an eye, I had transported back to the car. Infiniti still slept. Mom drove like normal. Strangely enough, Fleet glanced over his shoulder at me. "You okay?"

I opened my clenched palm and found it empty. "I'm fine," I muttered, my mind lost in what had just happened to me, questioning if I had really been at the beach at all. A suffocating anxiety set in, and I knew I had to get out of the car before I lost it. "I could use a bathroom break."

"Perfect timing," Mom chimed in. "I just saw a sign for a truck stop. We should be there in few minutes."

I shifted in my seat, paranoid and on edge. Grasping at the edge of the leather car seat, my fingers brushed up against a bristly object. The feather! I palmed it and angled my body away from Infiniti and toward the window, not wanting anyone to see the white feather. Slowly, I opened my fingers and found myself staring down at a black, dried out quill, its dark bristles clinging together in ugly desperation. I dropped the object as if it was poison, and it may as well have been.

My symbol of hope had turned to a sign of death.

And I had to run.

Mom slowed down and pulled into a truck stop. Rows and rows of eighteen wheelers lined the large and dimly lit parking lot. My exit strategy started forming in my head as I eyed the rigs moving in and out of parking spaces. Break away, jump into one of these trucks, and never look back.

After waking Infiniti, we made our way into the store and to the bathrooms. Luckily the men's and women's restrooms were on opposite sides of the building. This was it—my chance to escape.

After Fleet walked away, I ushered Mom and Infiniti forward. "Come on," I urged.

There were plenty of stalls in the restrooms. When we got in, I waited to hear Mom's and Infiniti's doors click. I counted to five in my head. "Crap," I announced. "I need my bag. Be right back."

"No!" Mom hollered. "Dominique, wait for—"

I sprinted out of there before Mom could finish her sentence, dashed out of the store, and raced to the parking lot. Truck drivers moved about, getting in and out of their rigs. I spotted one guy with a large brown bag just a few feet ahead of me. Short and squatty with a Santa Clause beard, he looked harmless enough. I rushed over to him.

"Excuse me, Mister," I said, catching my breath. "My stupid boyfriend got drunk and left me here. I could really use a ride." The ease of the lie spilling from my mouth surprised me. The man scratched his head, considering my request. I twisted a strand of hair around my finger, panic and a sense of urgency prodding me on. "Actually, Mister, he's not very nice to me. I'm afraid he might come back."

"Well, why didn't you say so? Come on then," he said. "I could use the company."

His short legs moved unexpectedly fast toward a dull yellow and black truck in the middle of the lot. He opened the door for me, and then climbed in on the other side. He fired up the engine and started pulling out of the parking lot. "Where you headed?"

To death, I thought, Farrell's threat to kill me ringing through my head, not to mention Colleen somewhere out there plotting my end as well. I wondered if there was any way I could change my destiny, but I knew I wished for the impossible.

I wrapped my arms around my waist, as if they could protect me. "As far away as possible."

THE END

Note from the Author:

Thank you so much for taking the time to read *Final Stand!* If you enjoyed the story, I would appreciate it if you would help others enjoy this book, too.

Lend it. This e-book is lending enabled, so please share it with a friend.

Recommend it. Please tell other readers why you liked this book! Word-of-mouth goes a long way! You can also recommend it at your favorite e-retailer and/or review site.

Review it. Long or short and sweet, every review counts! Please tell other readers why you liked this book by reviewing it at your favorite e-retailer and/or review site.

If you do write a review, please email me at rose@rosegarciabooks.com. I'd like to personally thank you!

Once again, thanks for reading *Final Stand!* To stay in the know regarding my appearances and future releases, please subscribe to my newsletter at:
www.rosegarciabooks.com/newsletter.

You'll also be able to access some deleted scenes from *Final Stand* when you sign up! And for those active on social media, you can find all my social media links at the bottom of each page of my website:

www.rosegarciabooks.com.

I'd love to stay in touch!

ROSE GARCIA
FINAL DEATH
Lost Love. Lost Hope.

FINAL
DEATH

Book Three in The Final Life Series

By Rose Garcia

Chapter One

~ Trent ~

I always knew my life would end in tragedy. My parents were killed in a car crash. My grandfather died from cancer when I was little. My grandmother, who could "sense" things, had never mentioned anything negative about my fate, but something in her sad eyes always told me I was destined for doom.

And now, standing in my church in 1930's Houston, my great-grandmother's warning that I wouldn't make it back to my proper time ringing in my ears, I remembered something that happened to me when I was thirteen.

It was a hot Houston summer day, one hundred degrees and climbing. My *abuela* had gone to church and I had promised to work on the yard. I had every intention of mowing the grass when a group of friends came by on their bikes and asked if I wanted to go with them to the nearby palm reader's house. For years my friends and I had wanted to ding-dong-ditch over there, but we had always chickened out. Surely a quick visit in the middle of a summer day wouldn't be scary.

Or so I thought at the time.

With enough excitement and energy to drown out

any logical thinking, we pedaled down the sidewalk of Fairland Drive, a busy road filled with cars, trucks, and eighteen-wheelers zooming up and down as if competing in the Grand Prix. Most businesses facing the street were gas stations and car mechanics, though every now and again you'd find a local *taqueria.* Amidst all the commercialism stood a one-story, bright yellow, wood-paneled house with a wide, circular concrete driveway. The home stuck out like a sore thumb, complete with a billboard in the front yard that read "Curandera" and a blinking red and black sign in the window of a deck of cards with the word "Advisor" at the top.

My friends and I dared each other the entire ten-minute ride over on who would ring the doorbell, only to find the house had two entrances—one to the right and one to the left. Closer inspection revealed mounted security cameras over each door frame, both aimed directly at us. Drenched in sweat and overcome with panic, I wondered if someone inside was watching us. I turned to my friends, ready to tell them we should leave, when a voice hollered, "Hey! *Chicos!* Get out of here!"

My friends hopped on their bikes and hauled out of there while I remained frozen, curious to see the infamous *curandera* who had scared me and my friends for years. I turned back around to face the house and there, at the door to the right, stood a tall, thin, dark-skinned woman, the age of most of my friends' moms. She wore a long, black skirt and a tight shirt with the letters MK in big, gold print—definitely not the crooked-nosed witch I had envisioned.

She narrowed her eyes at me. "Are you here for a reading?" A thick, Spanish accent laced her words. For a second there, I thought of answering in her native tongue, but quickly decided against it. I didn't want her to think I was mocking her.

Determined not to let on how scared out of my mind I was, I gave a quick nod. "Yes, ma'am."

"Do you have money?"

My grandmother had taught me to always have money in case of an emergency. I patted my jeans pocket, feeling for the crumpled ten dollar bill I had shoved in there before leaving my house. "Yes, ma'am."

She held the door open and waved me over. "Come on, then."

"Trent!" One of my friends yelled out over the whooshing of passing vehicles. "Run!"

The warning call fell short as I moved to the door and into a small room. The white-painted walls reminded me of a doctor's waiting room, complete with two chairs and a table in the middle. On the wall hung a black sign with white, plastic letters listing the services offered and their prices. Without making eye contact with me, the woman pointed at the sign and began reading out loud, but only a few words stayed with me—cards, crystals, palms—and none of it made any sense. When she waited for my response, I held out my folded up money.

"I only have ten dollars."

She snatched the paper out of my hand and then opened another door right behind her, which I hadn't noticed. "I can do a mini-reading for ten."

I followed her into another white-walled room that looked like an office. The odor of incense that smelled like Sunday mass flooded my nostrils and made my head swim. I even thought the floor tilted a little, like a creepy fun house you find at carnivals.

The woman made her way to the other side of a desk with a smooth, white top and sat in a big, black chair. I took a seat across from her and waited while I glanced over rocks, candles, and a framed picture of Jesus. My gaze settled on the bearded face. My mind imagined the Son of God telling me to get up and leave, but I couldn't. I didn't want to be a coward.

The *curandera* scooped up a cluster of crystals, some dull, others sparkly, and moved them from hand to hand. A thin, red chord was tied around her wrist. "For ten dollars, I can tell you a little of your past, your present, and your future." She talked loud and fast, keeping her eyes on her hands. "If you want to know more, you can come back, but you'll need more money. Understand?"

"Yes, ma'am."

"And you cannot tell anyone what I have said to you. If you do, it will bring you bad luck. Understand?"

"Okay," I said in a half-whisper, suddenly overcome with guilt for leaving my house without telling my *abuela*, and scared to death of the witch's warning.

"Take these stones and hold them," she said, holding her hand out to me but still not making eye contact.

I wiped my sweaty palms on my jeans, took the rocks, and held them tight. They were cold and smooth, like little eggs pulled right out of a refrigerator.

The woman opened her desk drawer and brought out a deck of cards. She shuffled them and laid out a single row. The cards were brown with pictures of men who looked like knights and ladies in long robes.

The woman eyed the cards with a frown, her hands hovering over them nervously. She grunted with annoyance, then scooped them back up into the deck. After another shuffle, she laid out a fresh row, and for the first time since I entered her presence, she stared directly at me. Her heavily lined eyes seemed like pools of dark knowledge—knowledge I suddenly knew should make me afraid. Chills swept across my skin.

"What is this?" she muttered to me before returning her gaze to the cards, as if accusing me of something.

My stomach dropped. The stones in my hand started to warm. I scooted to the edge of my chair and peered at the cards. "What?"

"You are everywhere," she whispered, "and nowhere."

My chest tightened and I knew I needed to get out of there. I pushed my seat back. The legs of the chair screeched over the marble floor. "I should—"

"No!" she commanded. "You cannot leave!"

She picked up the cards in front of me, set them aside, and laid out a third row. I eyed the images and immediately spotted a card in the middle with a knight on a horse holding a black flag with a skull on it. At the bottom of the card was the word "Death." She snapped up the card and held it to her chest. She stared me down as if I were some sort of devil.

"Get out! ¡*Vete de aqui*!" She jumped to her feet and threw the ten dollar bill at me. "Now!"

The burning rocks spilled out of my hands as I spun around, charging out of there as if my life depended on it.

***

"Hey, Trent. Back to the cabin," Farrell said, pulling me from my memory of the *curandera* and returning me to St. Joseph's church in 1930. The look of focus and determination on his face told me he believed I could take us back to the Boardman, the place from which we had time jumped, even if I didn't completely believe it myself.

Dominique, Infiniti, and Farrell moved into a circle. "Yeah, the cabin," I said, locking hands with Dominique on one side and Infiniti on the other. Fleet, who was really Dominique's traitor dad in disguise, took his place across from me and in between Infiniti and Farrell.

Dominique sneaked a quick glance my way. She tried to give me a reassuring smile, but her eyes revealed fear, as if she knew this time jump might kill me. And even though I felt the same way, I had to cast aside my doubt and do everything I could to get us back to our own time. I couldn't let premonition rule me. But the fortune teller's look of terror as she clutched the death card haunted me.

Get it together, man.

I blew out, tightened my grip around Dominique's and Infiniti's hands, and forced my mind to clear as I thought of the place we were before we time-traveled, the place we needed to get back to. I pictured the Boardman River in Michigan, the tall and naked trees, the snow underneath my feet, the attack by the Tainted. And then the death card. *No!* I screamed inside my head. *Not the card,* I pleaded to myself, struggling not to think of my encounter with the *curandera* on Fairland Drive, but suddenly unable to think of anything else.

I forced my mind to obey my commands. The Boardman, the cold, the snow, the attack, I repeated over and over in my head so fast I left no room to think of anything else. I kept my face down, willing myself to get us back home, when I felt a warm glow all around me, as if someone had turned on a giant heat lamp overhead.

The Boardman, the cold, the snow, the attack.

My fingers tingled. My skin prickled with electricity. I cracked open my eyelids and saw a glowing blue hue all around me. My aura! I had never been able to see it before!

"Hey," the fake Fleet said, "what's—?"

I clamped my eyes shut again and blocked him out, pushing all my thoughts to the Boardman, when I heard the church door fling open and bang against the wall.

"No one is allowed in the sanctuary at night!" the Mother Superior called out in her gruff voice.

"You devils!" shouted the young nun who sounded and looked like my old girlfriend Veronica.

I glanced over my shoulder, remembering how the Veronica look-alike had charged Dominique with a butcher knife the first time we were here, praying I could make us time jump before she got too close.

The Boardman, the cold, the snow, the attack. The death card.

"Shit," I said out loud, trying my hardest to push those cards out of my head when the young nun pulled out a pistol. Dominique shot a look of terror my way.

This was it.

The cards.

The premonition.

They were coming true.

But damn it if I wouldn't at least send my friends back to where they belonged. I was a special Transhuman, a Supreme, and even though I didn't know what that meant, I knew I could send them back home. *Really* knew.

The Boardman, the cold, the snow, the attack.

The nun aimed the long barrel at Dominique. With the cabin finally pictured perfectly in my head and my entire body so electrified I could star in my own superhero movie, I broke the circle and lunged in front of Dominique. A popping sound like a firecracker filled the air. A heavy blow crushed my chest, followed by a sensation like a red hot poker stabbing my back.

My body crashed to the floor and slammed against the cold surface.

"Trent!"

I craned my neck and saw multicolored swirling under Dominique and the others in a whirlpool of dust and light. Blood had splattered Dominique's face and white shirt, and I knew the crimson streaks were from me.

"Trent!" she called again, reaching out for me. Farrell held her back by her shoulders, and in a flash, they slipped from view, the ground opening and swallowing them whole.

Sirens howled in the distance. Mother Superior and the young nun rushed at the now-empty spot, circling around and looking for the four bodies that had stood there moments earlier.

"Where did they go?" Mother Superior asked out loud as if God himself could answer her somehow. Her voice echoed all around, bouncing off the concrete pillars and marble floor.

Hot, sticky wetness covered my chest. My breathing grew shallow. I had no idea where I was shot, but I knew it was bad. Real bad.

Mother Superior crouched at my side, her wrinkly face bearing down on me. Her stale, old-lady, smell thick in the air. "Where did they go?" she demanded. "Where!"

"H-h-h-ome." The second the word left my mouth, my body went numb. My vision tunneled until I couldn't see anymore.

ABOUT THE AUTHOR

Rose Garcia is a lawyer turned writer who's always bee fascinated by science fiction and fantasy. From a ver young age, she often had her nose buried in books abou other-worlds, fantastical creatures, and life and deat situations. More recently she's been intrigued by a blend science fiction and reality, and the idea that som supernatural events are, indeed, very real. Fueled by h imagination, she created The Final Life Series—a series books about people who can manipulate the energy in an around them. Rose's books feature gut-wrenchin emotional turmoil and heart-stopping action. Rose known for bringing richly diverse characters to life as sh draws on her own cultural experiences. Rose lives i Houston with her husband and two kids. You can vis Rose at: www.rosegarciabooks.com

Made in the USA
Columbia, SC
25 April 2018